LTHOUGH THIS BOOK is a work of fiction, it is solidly based on real history. The events of the 1837 Rebellion have been carefully researched and are presented as accurately as possible.

Captain and Mrs de Grassi and their daughters, and several other characters, were real people and, improbable as it may seem, the girls' work as spies and messengers during the rebellion days is fully authenticated. When it comes to presenting human beings, however, historical documents are usually uninformative. To bring the characters to life, I invented certain scenes and details, all of which I based carefully on what I learned about the de Grassi family, and on the life and circumstances of the time.

At the end of this book, there is a more detailed note about the sources for their story and the use which I have made of that material.

Rebellion

A Novel of Upper Canada
by Marianne Brandis

Suitably Embellished
with Scratchboard Illustrations by
Gerard Brender à Brandis

The Porcupine's Quill, Incorporated
Erin, Ontario

CANADIAN CATALOGUING IN PUBLICATION DATA

Brandis, Marianne, 1938-
    Rebellion

ISBN 0-88984-175-6

I. De Grassi family – Juvenile fiction. 2. Canada –
History – Rebellion, 1837-1838 – Juvenile fiction.
I. Title.

PS8553.R29R43 1996   jC813'.54   C96-930026-3
PZ7.B73Re 1996

Published by The Porcupine's Quill, Inc., 68 Main Street,
Erin, Ontario NOB 1TO with financial assistance from The
Canada Council and the Ontario Arts Council. The support
of the Department of Canadian Heritage through the Book
and Periodical Industry Development Programme and the
Periodical Distribution Assistance Programme is also gratefully acknowledged.

Represented in Canada by the Literary Press Group. Trade
orders are available from General Distribution Services.

Copy edited by Doris Cowan.

Acknowledgements

The author and illustrator gratefully acknowledge the help given by the following:

Carl Benn, curator at Fort York, and Doug Fyfe, a member of the education staff at Fort York.

Karen Evans, Librarian, and Mrs Dorothy Kealey, Archivist/Records Manager of the General Synod Archives for the Anglican Church of Canada.

Susan Hughes, Curator/Administrator, and the staff at Todmorden Mills Heritage Museum & Arts Centre.

Mima Kapches, Associate Curator in New World Archaeology at the Royal Ontario Museum, and Ian McGregor, Educator at the McLaughlin Planetarium.

Elizabeth Macnaughton, Librarian at Doon Heritage Crossroads.

Ken McEachern, General Manager of Fantasy Farm.

Lorraine O'Byrne, Curator of Collections; Gwynneth Cunningham, Head, Livestock Department; and Shirley Homer, Costume Designer, at Black Creek Pioneer Village.

John Ridout, President of the East York Historical Society.

Dr Ronald J. Stagg, Chair of the History Department at Ryerson Polytechnical University.

Vicky Von Schilling, Acting Curator at Toronto's First Post Office.

Ann Guthrie, Chris Raible, and Charles Sauriol.

They also wish to thank the staff at the Baldwin Room of the Metropolitan Toronto Reference Library and of the Ontario Archives, and to express their appreciation for the financial support received from the Ontario Arts Council and the Canada Council.

The map is based principally on the *Plan of the Town and Harbour of York, Upper Canada* of 1833 (which, though useful for the town itself, does not include the area outside the town limits) and the maps in the *Illustrated Historical Atlas of the County of York*, printed by Miles & Company in 1878. These Miles & Company maps depict the county as it was at a time later than 1837, but they are the earliest ones to provide the information I needed for the area beyond the city limits. In order to prevent anachronism, my map shows only the features which are mentioned in *Rebellion* and for which I found no earlier source. I also referred to the *Topographical Plan of the City and Liberties of Toronto ... Surveyed Drawn & Published by James Cane* in 1842, and other maps which gave information about some specific aspect of the area. I used the verbal descriptions given in Henry Scadding's *Toronto of Old* (the edition by Frederick H. Armstrong) and other books. The curve which my map shows in Yonge Street north of Gallows Hill does not appear on the maps I used but is derived from Scadding's description of Yonge Street.

The route of Mill Road is conjectural; it is based on the description in Scadding's book and on a reference in Captain de Grassi's unpublished 'Narrative'. Because it lay beyond the city limits, it was not included in town and city maps of the appropriate dates; the earliest maps I found of the area east of the Don River show the road's course after it was straightened.

Approximate Scale:

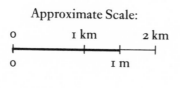

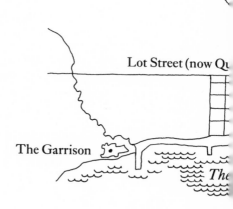

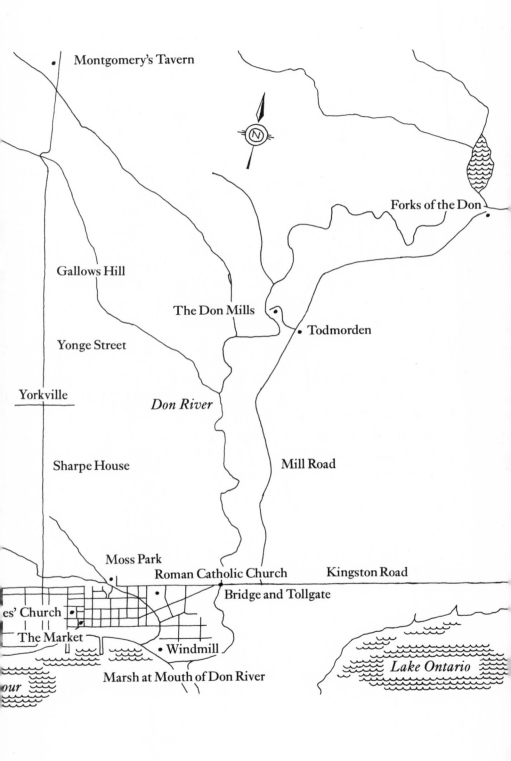

Upper Canada

Autumn

1837

Chapter One

OST OF THE ADULT immigrants were crowded along the railing at the starboard bow of the ship, watching as the fortress of Quebec became visible through the late-September haze. The small children, uninterested, were playing in clusters here and there on the deck. Only two boys were alone – Harry Wheeler, who had seen all there was to see of Quebec and was idly kicking the stove on which the immigrants cooked their meals, and his cousin Adam Wheeler who was staring at the broad expanse of the St. Lawrence River behind them and thinking of England.

Harry wandered over to join him.

'Ain't never seen a river this big before,' he muttered, grumbling, not wanting to show that he was impressed and a bit scared.

'No,' Adam said. He'd been thinking the same thing but the other way around, remembering the little stream that wandered through the countryside near the labourer's cottage where he'd lived in England – a shallow brook with reedy banks, cows drinking from it, and dragon-flies hovering above it.

'More like a ... like a ....'

Like an ocean, Adam thought. It was even more overwhelming than the Atlantic itself had been, because you expected oceans to be huge. Even if you'd never seen one before, you knew that much. Adam thought he knew about rivers, but this one ....

A sailor carrying an empty bucket paused near them.

'You lads're looking down in the dumps. Changed your minds? Wanna go home?'

He waved upstream, towards the stretch of river that lay under the brow of the fortress-topped north shore. In it were anchored several ships much like their own.

When the boys did not answer, he chattered on. 'Catch a lift with one o' those, likely. Most o' them'll be heading back to England one o' these days. Only you'll have to pretend you're a piece o' timber 'cause that's all they carry on this trip.'

Adam and Harry knew what he was talking about. One day in July, while idling about Portsmouth harbour waiting for their own ship to leave, they had been puzzled by the sound of hammering coming from one of the moored vessels. Exchanging quick, secret glances – because they had already learned that boys were not welcome on board ships being loaded or unloaded – they had darted up the gang-plank and dropped down a ladder into the hold.

The pounding of hammers in the hollow space made an almost unbearable racket. Four or five lanterns, and a couple of open hatches, barely lit a big, empty cavity still littered here and there with bark from the timber it had contained. The boys knew that many vessels brought timber from America to England because they had watched one being unloaded. Now, standing in the hold of this ship, they thought at first that unloading was still going on, because there were piles of rough lumber lying around. But then they realized that the lumber was being used to construct frameworks of some kind.

The nearest workman was a boy their own age. When he finished driving in one nail and reached into the pocket of his leather apron for another, he spotted Adam and Harry. Adam wondered whether he would tell them to leave, but he only nodded a greeting.

'What're you building?' Harry asked.

'Berths.'

'Berths?'

'Bunks. For sleeping on.'

'For who to sleep on?'

'Emigrants. Folks going to ....' He jerked his head towards what was probably meant to be the west.

Adam and Harry exchanged glances. They themselves were emigrants about to set off on a voyage westwards.

'How many berths?' Adam asked. 'I mean, for how many people?'

The carpenter shrugged. 'A few hundred.'

'A few *hundred*? Living in *this* space? For weeks and *weeks*?' The cavernous space suddenly looked very small.

'You mean to say,' Harry demanded, 'that the same ship carries people one way and timber back? And they build these things for emigrants to sleep on and take them apart again after every trip?'

The kid with the hammer laughed at the look on Harry's face. 'That's right. Timber or people – it's all the same to the ship-owners.'

At that moment an older workman bawled at the young carpenter to get busy and at Adam and Harry to get the hell off the ship.

The carpenter was right about the number of passengers. Two days later, when the Wheelers boarded the ship that was to take them to Canada, they found that the hold accommodated 310 people.

They had already been told earlier that they would have to supply most of their own food – the ship-owner provided only water and some oatmeal and ship's biscuit. Now they learned what that meant in practice. The food they brought had to be stowed in the same bunks where they slept, and it had to be cooked on a stove on deck, each family doing its own cooking in turn. The water provided for them, even though it was filthy-looking and nasty-tasting stuff, was only for drinking; there was not enough for washing. In bad weather the passengers were shut into the hold, with the overhead hatches closed so that they had no fresh air and only a lantern or two for light – shut into the violently heaving box that was their dwelling and might at any moment become their coffin. One storm lasted for three days and nights.

The Atlantic crossing had taken more than six weeks. The first land they sighted was what the sailors called Newfoundland, a strip of darkness along the horizon. They had not put ashore there. Since then they had been travelling for two weeks up this huge river, big as another ocean in the beginning and only recently become narrow enough so that you could even believe it *was* a river. Adam agreed with Harry that there was nothing like it in England, at least not in the small part of Sussex and Hampshire that they knew.

The sailor with the empty bucket was still hanging around. He was a bit simple-minded, Adam had decided earlier in the voyage, and now he seemed to be waiting for someone to tell him what to do next. He looked alternately at the anchored ships and at the two boys.

'Hey?' he urged, prying, needling, eagerly searching for signs of homesickness. 'Wanna go home? One o' them ships'll take you.'

'O'course not,' Harry said, brushing him off. 'We just got here. We're gonna make our fortunes.' He shoved his hands into his pockets and swaggered a few steps away, staring aggressively at the shore.

Adam said nothing, and the sailor left off needling. There was something about Adam – dark-haired and quiet, small for his fourteen years – that did not encourage it. Harry was several months younger but bigger, and blond. He looked like a bluff, cheerful, sociable person; Adam, who had lived two doors away from him, knew that he was lazy and selfish, and occasionally cruel. Harry never gave a thought to anything uncomfortable; it did not matter to him whether he lived in England or Upper Canada because he was convinced that wherever he was, and whatever he did or did not do, things would turn out all right for him.

Adam, by contrast, suspected that, for himself, things were not likely to turn out well. They never had, he thought. He was emigrating with his Uncle Ted and Aunt Lenore and their three children, of whom Harry was the oldest, because his dad and his new stepmother had not wanted him. Adam wasn't sorry to leave them, but he was angry at how it had been done.

Not that he blamed his father entirely. James Wheeler was a farm worker who, unable to find a permanent job, had travelled about the countryside taking temporary work where he could get it. His wife and Adam had lived with Adam's grandfather, old Mr Wheeler, in a dirt-floored cottage that was part of the same row of labourers' dwellings as the one occupied by Ted and Lenore Wheeler and their children. They were all landless labourers, but Ted at least had full-time work in the dairy on a big farm. Old Mr Wheeler had worked on the same farm; he had been a shepherd until rheumatism forced him to stop, though he still helped out at busy times like lambing.

It had been a happy enough household. Adam and his mother worked in the fields, and Adam helped his grandfather and the shepherd with the lambing. He'd liked that – the quiet nights out on the hillside in the lambing season, cold nights in late winter and early spring with the great sky arching over them, the low voices of his grandpa and the shepherd, their lantern making one of the two spots of light on the whole enormous hillside, like a star dropped down from among the flock overhead. The other light came from the shepherd's hut where, on a cold night, the shepherd would take a newborn lamb to get warm.

Adam loved watching his grandpa and the shepherd moving among the flock, the dim light of the lantern making their pale-coloured smocks almost luminous.

The two older men would talk about the hard times, the poverty, and how things used to be when they were young.

Between bursts of activity, Adam would drowse, half listening, half dozing. He had enjoyed being with the men, being accepted and, almost unawares, learning about their lives and work. He'd liked the newborn lambs, delicate-looking and yet eager, most of them, to live – and the ewes so protective.

The main shadow over his life was that he was always tired and often hungry. Wages were terribly low. Though all of them earned a bit, they had to ask for poor relief – but the amount of relief money was so tiny that even with it they had barely enough to survive.

They'd had one small extravagance. When he was still working full time, Grandpa Wheeler had insisted on Adam learning to read and write and count. He had paid for him to go to a dame school run by Mrs Wright, the widow of a clergyman. It was not very expensive; for a couple of pennies a week, Adam had spent an hour each morning in Mrs Wright's parlour, reading from the Bible and a few battered books of sermons and travels, and learning to write on a slate passed around among the four or five children.

Adam had been sorry when it ended. After grandpa stopped earning, they simply couldn't afford it any more. Adam, instead of costing them money, had to work full time to contribute what he could.

The real troubles had begun this past spring, when Adam's mother died. It had happened suddenly. Adam, tiptoeing out of the cottage early one morning to fetch the water that he'd been too exhausted to carry up from the river on the previous evening, had noticed something odd when he passed her where she always slept, on a pallet on the floor of the downstairs room. He'd kneeled down to look and listen. Then, holding the unbearable knowledge away from himself – he knew about death because he'd seen sheep die – he had continued tiptoeing out so as not to wake his grandfather in the big bed, and gone to the wood where the bluebells were. The intense colour of the flowers, the rust-and-green haze of new leaves on the trees, the exultant birdsong, were half soothing and half agonizing. He leaned his forehead against a tree-trunk.

It couldn't be true. Not his mother. Not *dead*.

But it was. When he went home, he found his grandpa looking for him.

For nearly two months, the two of them managed on their own, with some help from Aunt Lenore and other neighbour women. Then, in June, Grandpa Wheeler had suffered an attack. Again Adam learned about it one morning when he woke up. The old man's right arm was completely limp and useless. Adam had gone to Aunt Lenore, and together they'd helped him dress and eat something. Then Adam, feeling that it would be best not to show his real feelings to his grandfather, had gone down to the river. He sat on the bank, his head in his hands, trying not to cry, trying to think. What was going to happen now? Was this attack – a palsy, Aunt Lenore had called it – his fault for not looking after his grandpa properly? What else could he have done? He knew they didn't always have enough to eat, but he'd managed as well as he could.

Because of the palsy, Grandpa Wheeler needed more care than Adam could give him, so he moved in with his daughter Kate, married to a cobbler and living six miles away in Petersfield.

By then, Adam's father had remarried. His new wife was called Abigail, and she was also a wandering farm labourer. Adam had not met her until a day or two before his grandfather's attack, when she and James Wheeler had been hired for the haying by Mr Higham, the owner of the farm on which the other Wheelers lived and worked.

Though Adam had not met her until then, some of the neighbours apparently knew about her. He overheard one of them saying that James Wheeler and Abigail had already been 'together' for a while.

Adam hadn't liked Abigail. She made him uncomfortable. She was a loud-voiced, loud-laughing woman with fly-away red hair and a long-legged stride – easy, when you saw her walk, to picture her life, to imagine her walking across the countryside from farm to farm searching for work.

He still shivered when he remembered their meeting. She had looked down on him with scornful green eyes, and then turned away to Adam's father.

'I thought you said he was fourteen, James. He's awful small.'

'You're fourteen, ain't you, Adam?' his father had asked.

'Yes.'

Abigail had shrugged.

So it was that Adam's dad and Abigail were on the spot when, a day or two later, Grandpa Wheeler suffered his attack and went to live with Aunt Kate in Petersfield. Aunt Kate could not, however, take Adam. She and her husband had four children of their own, as well as an apprentice, and the old man's presence crowded the cottage to bursting point.

A couple of days after the carrier's cart had taken his grandpa to Petersfield, Adam overheard his father, Abigail, and Uncle Ted discussing what was to be done with him. He was in bed, lying on his straw pallet in the attic. The grown-ups, on that fine June evening, were sitting on the doorstep of the cottage, the door open so that Adam, who was only a few yards away, indoors and up the ladder, could hear every word.

'Take him to Canada, will you please, Ted?' Abigail had demanded impatiently. 'We can't be doing with a boy, not the way we live. Bad enough for us, finding work. If he travels around with us, we'll end up having to feed him half the time. Or James'll have to try and find him a fixed job and lodging.'

Most kids of Adam's age worked full time; the problem was not that he was too young but that in their part of England there were so few jobs.

'Or else,' Abigail added, 'he'll go on the parish, and they'll

[18]

grumble because he ain't really an orphan. But in Canada he'd be an extra pair of hands.'

'And an extra mouth to feed.'

'It's different there, they say. No shortage of food, not like here. Everyone buys some o' that cheap land and grows their own food. For God's sake, Ted, take him along. You've got kids already. He's small – you won't hardly notice him.' There was a moment's silence, during which Adam heard a thrush sing far away. Then Abigail spoke again, in a different voice, wheedling and persuasive. 'We could let you have a penny or two, couldn't we, James?'

'You got money to spare?' Uncle Ted demanded.

Adam's dad had muttered something about Abigail picking up a bit extra now and then, but didn't say how.

Several coins clinked together.

''Tain't enough,' Uncle Ted grumbled. 'For a puny kid like that.'

'Come on, Ted. He'll earn his keep, once you get there. This is just to help pay his passage.'

Adam, listening tensely, wondered how much money had changed hands. 'A penny or two' was just Abigail's way of talking. How much had she paid to be rid of him? It was almost like being sold. It *was* being sold. He hunched his shoulders in misery.

'Well ...,' Uncle Ted had said, dragging out the word.

So the whole summer had been one shock after another. Adam had loved his mother and was desolate at losing her. He had carefully looked after his grandpa, whom he also loved and respected and who had always treated him well.

Finally, to be handed over to his aunt and uncle like that ... *sold* ... and to be brought to Canada like a parcel, or an animal, something with no will of its own, something that another person would *pay* to be rid of! No one had asked him whether he wanted to live with Uncle Ted's family, or whether he wanted to leave England.

Whenever his thoughts reached this point, a small voice in him said, 'Why should they bother asking? Even if they had asked, what could you have said?'

All the same, stubbornly, he wished they'd asked – and wished desperately that there had not been that exchange of clinking coins.

Before again going off with Abigail to look for another temporary job, Adam's dad had a word with him.

'Great chance for you, boy!' he had said. 'New country, lots o' land – I wouldn't be surprised if you was to own your own farm by the time you're twenty.'

His father and Uncle Ted had talked a good deal about the 'land of opportunity'. Adam was not impressed. It was all just talk. He knew where they got it – from a promoter who went from town to town encouraging people to emigrate.

The promoter had addressed a market-day crowd in Petersfield. Among the listeners was a man who had actually been to Upper Canada. After the promoter had said his piece, this man talked to some people standing near him. Adam was one of them.

'Went out in '32,' he said. 'The country out there ain't nothin' but trees. You never saw such a lot o' trees, an' all o' them huge. You'd got to cut them down, one after another, just tree after tree ....' The weariness sounded in his voice. 'And *then* you ain't got a farm, just a ... well, you can't hardly see no soil. Only stumps, broken–off branches, brush. You clear away what you can, pull out some o' the stumps or leave 'em to rot in God's good time, plant a bit o' somethin' between them. That ain't *farmin'!*'

Adam, listening to him, thought of the smooth rolling land in this part of England.

'No ploughing?' he asked. Maybe the man had left out a bit. How could you plant without ploughing?

'Not the first or even maybe the second year. You couldn't, not with all them stumps and roots, an' ....' The man shrugged. 'Went out in '32, like I said. Cholera year. The cholera killed my wife and son. No point stoppin' on there so I come back. No sense doin' all that God-awful work, cuttin' down all them damned trees, once the boy died.'

This man was not the only one to talk like that. One or two people from Petersfield, who had emigrated, occasionally wrote letters to their relatives at home, and the news was passed around. They too mentioned hardships, though they said that with a lot of hard work and some luck you could do better for yourself in Canada than in England.

Adam had told Uncle Ted about the man who had been to Canada and returned, defeated, to England. This was what the promoters didn't tell you, and Adam felt that Uncle Ted ought to know.

But Uncle Ted had made up his mind.

'Nonsense, boy. The fellow was just belly-aching because he couldn't handle it. It takes a man with a bit of gumption, a man of vision, to make his way in a country like that.' He puffed out his chest and preened, imagining himself such a person.

'But the work ...!' Adam protested. Uncle Ted always did as little work as he could.

'In a year or two we'll all be landowners and gentlemen. Land aplenty for everyone, not like here!'

He spread out his arms, indicating the land that surrounded the dirt-floored cottage where they were talking – land that would never in a million years belong to farm labourers such as Ted Wheeler. And since every landowner they knew was a gentleman or on the way to becoming one, it went without saying that the possession of land brought you to the top of the heap. A landowner, a gentleman, hunting to hounds, dining lavishly, always in company with other men of like tastes, and of course never doing any work – that was how Uncle Ted saw himself living in Upper Canada in the near future.

It was magic he wanted, and magic wasn't real.

Nothing had changed. There he stood, further along the deck of the ship, a big, blond, good-looking man, lounging against the railing, smoking his pipe and talking to two other fellows, amusing them. Most people liked him, with his easy ways, the sense he gave of not being burdened by worries and responsibilities. The more perceptive, even those who took to him at first, soon discovered that he was also lazy and unreliable.

Adam could not forget the man who had returned from Canada. He had thought about him often during the long voyage.

Now, on the St. Lawrence River near Quebec, he watched as nimble figures swarmed up the rigging of one of the anchored ships, setting the sails for departure. Should Adam follow the half-witted sailor's taunting suggestion and go home on one of those ships? He could probably work his passage back, and then ....

And then, what? There was nothing there for him, with his mother dead, his grandpa living with Aunt Kate in the crowded cottage in Petersfield, his dad and Abigail relieved to see the back of him. If he returned, he'd have to make a new place for himself, find lodging and work. No point going back to the area of Sussex where he'd come from; people like Uncle Ted were leaving because there was too much unemployment and too much poverty and too little hope for improving one's life. He'd have to go to a city and try to find something in a mill. If he succeeded, he'd work twelve hours a day, sixty-nine hours a week. That was what *success* would be like; failure would be even worse – the workhouse, or begging, or starvation.

Not much to go back to. He might as well see what Canada was like. He turned around and looked at Quebec, the fortress on the cliff up ahead.

Chapter Two

HEY WENT ASHORE BRIEFLY in Quebec, and from there a steamship towed their brig upriver to Montreal. They spent one night in a crowded boardinghouse, then travelled by coach to Lachine, by steamer to Cornwall, by coach to Prescott, and then by steamer again to Toronto. All this took eight more days.

They saw hundreds of miles of Canada, mostly forest but with small towns and villages, and isolated farms, carved out from among the trees. It was the end of September, and the leaves on some of the trees had turned red and gold, brilliant against the dark green of pine and spruce.

They also saw something of Canada at closer hand. When they changed from coach to ship and back again, they usually stayed overnight at a boardinghouse or an inn. Then Adam went out to explore. The towns looked raw and rough to someone who came bearing with him the images of stone-built English villages. But Adam also brought memories of earth-floored cottages, some of them outwardly picturesque but all of them dirty and squalid inside – dirty even when the housewife made an effort, as his mother and Aunt Lenore had done, to keep them clean. Earthen floors were impossible to clean.

From out on the water, and in the places where they put ashore, Adam saw some small, hut-like dwellings. He was thinking about them during dinner at an inn one evening, wondering if the New World would prove to be just like the old country with its divisions between rich and poor, land-owners and labourers, when he overheard the innkeeper laughing at Aunt Lenore's calling these huts 'cottages'.

'Shanties is what we call 'em, mostly. The shanty is only

[23]

for the first year or two. Then folks build themselves a proper house.'

Several times, Adam realized now, he had seen the signs of this: a farm with both a shanty and a larger house on it. The houses were not big – most of them were not even what in England would have been normal-sized farmhouses – but they had several rooms, proper chimneys, and glass in the windows.

Back home, if you'd been born in a dirt-floored cottage you probably lived in one for the rest of your life. The only hope of change was to move from poverty in the countryside to poverty in a city. There was something to be said for a place where you *did* have a chance.

*

By the time they were on a steamer carrying them along the north shore of Lake Ontario from Kingston to Toronto, Adam felt as though travelling had become a way of life, as though they would never stop, as though they would forever be picking up their luggage – a small wooden crate for Uncle Ted and Harry, and cloth bundles for everyone else – and carrying them to wherever someone told them to go next.

He was talking about this to Aunt Lenore on a Friday morning at the end of September. That afternoon they would reach Toronto.

'It's two months and two weeks and one day since we left Three Corners Farm,' he remarked. 'Today is the twenty-ninth of September.'

'How do you know?' Aunt Lenore asked, giving him a curious but friendly look.

Out of his jacket pocket he pulled a stick and a small stone with one sharp corner. He showed her the rows of scratch marks on the stick, one for each day. 'Here's the day we started. July the fourteenth. And every morning, I ....' He made a cutting gesture with the stone.

'What a boy you are!'

They were sitting on a bench on the north side of the ship, watching the shore creep by: forest, bare rock outcrops, islands now and then, occasionally a village or an isolated farm. At some of the villages the ship docked briefly at a jetty to take on a load of the wood which was its fuel, perhaps to set down or pick up a few passengers and some freight, and then it resumed paddle-wheeling its noisy and smoke-belching way past more forest and islands and rock.

For the moment, Adam and Aunt Lenore had the bench to themselves. It was a bright but chilly day and most of the passengers were on the other side of the ship enjoying the sunshine. Aunt Lenore had been mending Harry's spare shirt but now her hands lay limp on the fabric in her lap – hard-worked hands, thin and muscular, the knuckles too large, the tendons showing.

'D'you think we'll be better off here, Adam?' she asked. When he was silent, she went on. 'Your Uncle Ted is so sure we will, but I wonder ....'

'I think we *could* be,' Adam said cautiously. 'Lots of people seem to be, though you can't always tell what their life was like back home. Or how much they brought with them – money, and letters to important people here who can help them.'

At the inn in Prescott they had heard a boastful young man, the son of rich people in England, brag about having letters of introduction to the lieutenant governor of Upper Canada, Sir Francis Bond Head, and to other important men.

'It's easier if you have money or friends,' Aunt Lenore said quietly. 'We don't have much money, and no friends, not where we come from nor where we're going.'

'There's other things people bring. A trade, or ... like Uncle Ted having worked in a dairy. That's worth something.'

But where Uncle Ted was concerned, he wasn't hopeful.

Any skills Uncle Ted had weren't of much use when combined with his laziness and his silly expectations of how he'd live in the New World.

'You'll do all right,' Aunt Lenore said abruptly. 'You're ... I don't know. The way you handled all the changes in your life this summer. You'll manage.'

He gave her a quick glance of wonder and thanks. All during that difficult summer, no one told him he was doing well. Aunt Lenore and the other neighbour women had said how sorry they were when his mother died, and had helped now and then in caring for his grandpa – with mending and such – but no one had praised him.

Now he realized that Aunt Lenore had been watching him, perhaps even watching over him.

He looked at her again, feeling a new kind of contact – looked at her as a human being rather than just someone who was always there.

As a girl, she had been a beauty, Adam remembered his mother saying, and her dark hair, though partly grey now, still curled out from under the edges of her cap. Her eyes were dark too, with something mysterious as though behind them lay a secret life or perhaps a lot of thinking.

But she was thin and looked old. Her parents had died when she was a child, and from the age of eight she had worked as indoor servant at Three Corners Farm. Then, married to Uncle Ted, she had led a hard life housekeeping and raising a family while also doing field-work when she could get it. She had given birth to seven children, of whom three were still alive.

A big, hearty laugh rang out. It was Uncle Ted doing what he enjoyed most, being with other men, laughing and joking and telling stories.

Adam wondered, as he had often done in the past couple of months, how Uncle Ted would *really* manage in Canada – how they would all manage with their lives in his keeping.

[27]

Uncle Ted's laughter was still ringing in the air when a small girl came around a corner and trailed slowly towards them.

'There's Ella,' Aunt Lenore said.

Ella was six years old and Ruth nine. Earlier, Adam had seen them playing with other children. It was typical of Ella to be the first to leave off playing and come to her mother. She was a pale, thin, sickly child, and she had been ill during the Atlantic crossing. No one knew what ailed her, although the women in the steerage had talked about it endlessly – it was one way of passing the time. They had decided that it was just a worse form of what they all suffered from – bad and insufficient food, and being crowded together in that horrible ship. Different people reacted in different ways. You saw it most clearly during storms, when being shut in the hold made some passengers hysterical, some desperate, some quarrelsome, all of them gloomy and anxious. When they reached Quebec they had been filthy, half-starved, ill, weak from lack of exercise.

Since then, the Wheelers had recovered a little, though they still looked pale and underfed.

Ella sat down beside her mother and snuggled into a sheltering arm.

'Where's Ruth, darling?'

'Playing.'

'How are you feeling?'

'Tired.'

'You have a rest, then, lovey. Right here, beside me.'

When she had tucked her shawl around Ella, Aunt Lenore spoke to Adam again. 'I've heard about people going home for a visit, and then coming back here again. Can you imagine doing that? Making that trip two more times?'

'I can *imagine* doing it – but not in the steerage, not until I can afford to travel in a cabin.'

The cabin passengers were the aristocrats among travellers. Their own sailing ship had offered no cabins, but in Portsmouth Adam had caught a glimpse of one and of the people who would occupy it – not the very rich, because such people rarely went to the New World, but gentlefolk like former army officers who travelled with a great many trunks and special luggage like writing cases and boxes to hold bottles of wine.

'Cabin passengers probably get just as seasick as we did,' Aunt Lenore remarked.

'But in more comfort.'

Yes, that's how he would travel if he ever crossed the ocean again. He wouldn't go until he could afford to. When he was his own person, not a parcel to be sold and carted about.

Chapter Three

THEY REACHED TORONTO THAT afternoon. Once again almost all the adults were at the ship's rail to catch their first sight of the place which had been their destination for so long.

This time Adam was with them.

Toronto was hidden until the ship rounded a flat, wooded peninsula. They passed a lighthouse and there it was, spread along the shore. At the end nearest them was a fort, in the distance a windmill. It was the kind of town they had learned to expect in Upper Canada, a sprinkling of buildings with open space between, and here and there a tree. Behind it, far back, was a ridge of low hills. There were ships anchored in the harbour and moored at the two or three wharves. The wind made flags snap and lifted spray off the tops of the waves.

For almost the first time since leaving England, Adam felt a stirring of pleasure and hope. He could not have said what brought it on but the bracing, brisk weather was part of it, encouragement for getting on with one's life after the interruption of the voyage. He liked the scattered arrangement of Toronto: nothing crowded, lots of room, no sense that newcomers like himself would be kept out. An open kind of place. This town was being created still, unlike English ones, which looked as though they had been finished long before Adam was born. He had no idea how or where he would fit in, but suddenly he felt he might.

*

It was a good thing that he had such a cheering thought, because as soon as they left the ship the problems began.

The main one was finding a place to stay. Every immigrant

on board the ship, except those who had relatives or friends to go to, needed a lodging for at least the first night or two, and when the ship docked they all set off to find one.

Uncle Ted asked the name of the best hotel in town. The Wheelers went there, but it was full. So they tried other hotels, and then boardinghouses. They learned that there were even sheds for immigrants too poor to afford anything else.

'Sheds! Not for us!' Uncle Ted said indignantly when they were told about them at the fifth full boardinghouse. The jauntiness with which he had begun the search had disappeared.

The crowding made Adam realize that they – their little group of six – were part of a great horde of people migrating across the ocean to the New World. Nearly every day a ship like theirs arrived in Toronto, each one bringing dozens, perhaps even several hundreds, of immigrants. If you really thought about it, you were not surprised that the hotels and boardinghouses were full.

At each place where they were turned away, Aunt Lenore asked for advice about where to try next. This led them eventually to an area close to a church – an area that was poorer than anything they had seen yet. Small houses and shacks huddled together with only narrow lanes between. In the beginning, probably, it had been a neighbourhood of labourers' cottages, each with a yard, but by now these houses had acquired a barnacle growth of lean-tos until there was almost no open space except the lanes and alleys.

The woman at the last place had directed them here. 'Try Stuart's Block,' she had said, pointing. 'It's right by St. James' Church. Ask for Mrs Perkins – she's one o' the best.'

When they finally found Mrs Perkins' house, they stood in front of it for a few moments, looking around.

The area was crammed with people. Children played everywhere, mingling with dogs, hens, and pigs. Adults stood, talked, smoked, pushed barrows or carried buckets. People lay huddled on the ground against walls. All of them were dirty and ragged. Here and there were signs of useful activity: in a lane, a woman was washing clothes in a pail of water, and a man cooked something in a pot supported by stones over a small fire. But it was a depressing sight. Was this what became of folk who did not succeed in the New World?

'We're not stopping here,' Uncle Ted said angrily.

'Everywhere else is full, Ted. You saw that yourself. We can try one of the sheds they mentioned. It might be ....'

'I'm not sleeping in any damn shed!'

'Well, then ....'

'All right. But it's only till I get me some land of my own.'

As it turned out, Mrs Perkins had room for them. She led the way up a steep, narrow, twisting little staircase to an attic so low-ceilinged that Uncle Ted could not stand upright. It had three beds in it, each of them a wooden platform with a straw pallet for mattress and a single blanket as cover. On the floor were pallets for children and the even poorer lodgers. The Wheelers, she said, pointing, could have one bed and two pallets, one for the girls and one for the boys.

'Or pack yerselves all into the bed. Do what you like, only don't take more'n one bed. Dinner's in a coupla minutes.'

When she had gone downstairs, Uncle Ted exploded.

'What the hell! I didn't come to this country to lodge in a place like this!'

'Now, Ted,' Lenore said. 'It's not so bad. It's better than the cottage at Three Corners Farm.'

'Sharing with all these others ....' He gestured at the litter of pallets, at the beds with moth-eaten blankets in huddled piles just as their occupants had left them. There were no personal belongings; either all the guests had gone for good or they carried their possessions with them every day to prevent theft. And it was dirty. The floor, where it was visible among the litter of pallets and ragged blankets, was filthy and there were masses of cobwebs among the rafters. A mouse ran along a window sill to fetch a crumb. Adam, watching, could picture someone standing near the window eating a meat pie or a chunk of bread, putting it down on the sill for a moment and, when he picked it up again, leaving crumbs for the mice.

Indeed, after the glowing promises of the promoters, it was not what any of them had expected. Even the letters from earlier emigrants had not mentioned conditions like this.

Adam had a moment's sympathy with Uncle Ted. He had been misled and had a right to be angry, but at the same time he had been much too ready to ignore what even Adam had recognized as more reliable information.

'Sooner I take up land of my own, the better,' Uncle Ted growled. 'We'll build ourselves a decent house. We're respectable people. We'll be gentlefolks ....'

After several years of living in an earth-floored shanty, Adam added silently. *After* cutting down hundreds of trees and clearing away the underbrush and pulling the stumps, maybe half starving after a bad harvest, half freezing in a cold winter.

His spirits, which had lifted at the distant view of Toronto, had dropped like a stone now that he'd seen what it was really like. A raw clearing in the woods – or, worse, something that was not yet a clearing – was even less appealing.

He had no idea how much money Uncle Ted had brought with him, but it couldn't be a great deal. Not enough, for instance, to buy a farm already partly cleared and with a house on it. Such things existed, as they had learned, but they cost much more than uncleared land. Nor could Uncle Ted afford to hire men to help with the work. It would be Uncle Ted and Harry and Adam himself against the forest, with Aunt Lenore and the girls doing what they could.

But neither Uncle Ted nor Harry was a hard worker. Once or twice, to avoid working, Harry had deliberately hurt himself.

The system in England, until recently, had allowed Uncle Ted to get away with doing as little as possible. His employer – Mr Higham, the farmer who rented Three Corners Farm from a large landowner – paid his labourers less than a living wage, and gave the merest pittance to the women and children who worked in the fields. The difference between those earnings and the amount needed for a family to survive was made up by the parish, out of the taxes paid by property owners. If you were lazy and the employer reduced your wages or dismissed you, you'd still receive enough to live on – *barely* enough. Whether or not you worked hard, you were half starved most of the time.

Uncle Ted had done as little work as he could. 'The parish'll look after us,' he said.

Maybe that was part of the trouble with him. Because he was only a labourer, someone had always looked after him as though he were a child. He did what he was told. Because the life he led offered him almost no choices, he'd seldom had to make important decisions until he got the idea about emigrating.

Would a miracle happen how? Would Uncle Ted learn to be more sensible? Would he turn into a hard worker if that earned him more money or helped him clear land faster?

No way of knowing. They'd have to wait and see.

*

Everyone in the boardinghouse ate at a single table in the kitchen, crowded on benches along the sides and a couple of stools at each end. Mrs Perkins and two husky, bare-armed girls enough like her to be her daughters served the meal, which consisted of stew, bread, and cheese. A whisky jug stood in the middle of the table, for the guests to help themselves, and there was also tea. The kitchen was hot and smelled of cooking and human bodies.

The Perkins family – Mrs Perkins, the two girls, a boy of

about twelve called Josh, and a skinny, stooped man who appeared to be Mr Perkins – sat at one end of the table. Four single men sat in a cluster at the other end speaking what Mrs Perkins said was Welsh. Between those groups were the Wheelers on one side of the table and, across from them, three respectable, middle-aged people whom Mrs Perkins casually identified as 'the Carpenters' – two brothers and the wife of the elder. The younger brother, slender and not robust, said that he was looking for work as a clerk or teacher. His older brother had been, in England, a maker of stained-glass windows.

'Not much demand for that here, I shouldn't think!' Uncle Ted said, in what was meant to be a joke but sounded like criticism.

'There are and will be churches built here,' Mr Carpenter replied calmly. He was partly bald but fit-looking, and very sure of himself. 'Besides, I can turn my hand to other kinds of glazing, and anything connected with lead. Plumbing, lead roofs ....'

'I haven't seen any lead roofs here – no more o' *them* than there's stained-glass windows.'

Mr Carpenter gave Ted a sharp look. 'And what is *your* occupation?' he asked.

'Dairyman. Pretty big dairy – part of a large farm.'

Adam kept his head down. He didn't want to reveal, by so much as a look, how misleading this was. The way Uncle Ted put it suggested that he had been manager of the dairy – 'dairyman' could mean that – while actually he'd been just one of the men milking cows and doing chores.

'From where?'

'Near Petersfield. That's in Hampshire, but we lived over the border, in Sussex. And you?'

'Kent, near Canterbury.'

'A bad area for farm workers. Lots of rioting thereabouts in '30, wasn't there?'

He was referring to the so-called 'Captain Swing' riots seven years earlier. 'Captain Swing' was an imaginary person whose name had been used to sign threatening letters sent by landless farm workers to landowners and employers. The letters demanded higher wages and warned that, if this demand were not met, the workers would burn haystacks and destroy the threshing machines which deprived them of their work. Adam remembered the uprisings near Petersfield; he knew that his father and Uncle Ted had been involved but had not been caught or punished. Those less lucky – hundreds of them – had been transported to Australia.

'Yes, a fair amount of unrest, a fair amount of distress. In your area, too, I heard. Is that why you came here?'

Uncle Ted wasn't listening. 'Not that *you'd* be affected by the miseries of the country folk, you being a tradesman. Had a shop of your own, did you?'

'We suffered, right enough,' Mr Carpenter said with an edge in his voice. 'We were the ones who paid the rates so that you people could receive poor relief.'

'Poor relief!' Uncle Ted said angrily. 'Just a way of letting our employers pay us less than a living wage because the parish made up the difference. And even *then* we hadn't enough to live decently. Look at us!'

He gestured at the family. The Wheelers were not actually in rags, but buttons were missing from their clothes and everything was patched and mended until the original cloth was scarcely visible. All the family's belongings except a table and benches had come with them in a small wooden crate and a few cloth bundles. Aunt Lenore seldom got enough to eat because she gave some of her share to the others, and even they were thinner and less energetic than they might have been on good food. The way they gobbled Mrs Perkins' stew showed how hungry they were.

'So you're a bit of a radical,' the younger Carpenter brother said.

'I don't know about that,' Uncle Ted said evasively. During the Swing riots, it was unsafe to be labelled 'radical'.

'Don't think I'm criticizing. Even though I'm a school teacher and not a labourer, I was sympathetic to your cause. So were a lot of us. A friend of mine went with the local farm workers, on one of their so-called riots, to show his support.'

Mrs Carpenter had been brooding while her men folk talked.

'You're so sorry for the poor,' she said abruptly and tensely to her brother-in-law. 'But what about us? *We* were squeezed between lower earnings and the higher rates we had to pay for supporting the poor. 'Tain't possible to live like that. That's why we was forced to come here.' Her face tightened with anger and resentment.

'Times have been bad in England, as we all know,' her husband said in his more moderate manner. 'We'd been thinking for a couple of years about moving to the colonies, and this year ....' He shrugged.

''Tis on account of all the poor what *won't* work!' his wife said. 'Them as is fit and able ...!' She glared at Uncle Ted.

'I worked!' he protested. 'All I wanted was a living wage, a chance to feed my family.'

'We know that you folk didn't have enough to do. All them threshing machines, and you standing back and watching ....'

'We didn't just stand back! Me and my like broke up the threshing machines because they took our jobs.'

It was true. Uncle Ted had gone out on several hay-burning expeditions, and one time he'd come home limping with an injured leg. In the following days, he had to conceal the fact that he'd been hurt; the injury would, rightly, have been taken as a sign that he was one of those who had burned Mr Higham's hay-stacks.

'There, now,' Mrs Perkins said, 'you're just like all the other newcomers, bringing your quarrels with you. It makes me real mad! Get off to a new start, that's what I say, and live at peace with your neighbours.'

'In hard times it's not easy to be at peace with your neighbours,' the younger Mr Carpenter said. 'And I'm told that you've been having troubles yourselves. Bad harvests, poverty and hardship, agitation to make changes in the government or even to break away from Britain and join the American states....'

'Oh, well, as to that, there's quarrels right enough. Things ain't run the way they should be. Folks is angry at the governor and the big men who do what they like and don't pay no attention to what the people want. There's that Mr Mackenzie what writes the newspaper....'

'He talks about nothin' but reform now,' Mr Perkins mumbled. 'Makes a lot o' sense sometimes, I hafta say.'

Mrs Perkins interrupted. 'It'll be all right,' she said, giving her husband a disapproving look and then turning to Uncle Ted. 'You plannin' to take up land?'

'That's the idea. Look into it tomorrow or next week. Soon's I can.' Uncle Ted spoke in an offhand way, as though buying land was a very casual and unimportant matter.

The elder Mr Carpenter regarded him gravely. 'Might be a good idea to work for someone else this winter and buy land in the spring. Shouldn't be too hard to find work. Dairyman, did you say you were? If you can turn your hand to other farm chores as well....'

'I didn't come here to work for someone else! I had enough o' that. I mean to take up land, be my own master.'

'So do we all, of course, but unless you have a fair amount of money....' He looked questioningly at Uncle Ted.

Adam was also interested in the answer. Uncle Ted never revealed where he'd got the money to come to Canada, but Adam had heard Aunt Lenore tell someone on the ship that a charitable organization had donated it. He knew there were people in England whose purpose was to give the poor a chance to make a new life for themselves in the colonies – and to relieve the burden on English taxpayers, who considered that a one-time contribution was cheaper than supplementing low wages year after year.

Some landowners, too, Adam had heard, paid to help their tenants emigrate. Adam couldn't picture Mr Higham – a plump, rosy-faced man with a fist of iron – doing such a thing, but maybe he had.

Uncle Ted did not like having to ask for charity. When he did, it was always with an air of grievance against whoever or whatever forced him to do so. But he'd always taken money from the parish, and no doubt he had accepted what he needed to emigrate.

And there was that 'penny or two' from Abigail to take Adam off her hands. Adam winced again at the memory.

This time, as always, Uncle Ted dodged the question. He gave a shrug and a grin.

'Well, then,' Mr Carpenter went on, 'there's a government plan by which a really poor man can get fifty acres of land free.'

Aunt Lenore looked up alertly, but Uncle Ted snorted. 'Fifty acres, hell! I'm aiming for a lot more'n that.'

'Ted …,' Aunt Lenore ventured, 'that would be free land, something to give us a start.'

'And everyone would think of us as paupers, having had to *ask* for land!' He glared at his wife and Mr Carpenter. 'We'd never be rid of the mark.'

Mr Carpenter went calmly on. 'I suppose, then, that you wouldn't want to know about an organization that helps needy immigrants.' He took a sip of his much-diluted whisky. 'Taking up land's the only thing you're interested in. Well, one way or another you'll have to keep yourselves all winter and right through the spring and summer until harvest. That's fine if you've got enough money. Otherwise – well, of course you can go ahead and buy land now, and still work for wages until spring. If you can't find anything in the dairy or farming line, the government often hires men to work on the roads.'

It seemed sensible advice, but it was given in a patronizing way, as though Mr Carpenter, after only a week in Toronto, already knew best about everything.

Uncle Ted scowled. 'I didn't come here to do slave labour on the roads! I'll spend a month or two working for wages on a farm or estate, if I have to, but ....'

'Ted, please,' Aunt Lenore murmured.

' ... but I'll take up land of my own right away so that no man can treat me like dirt. I didn't come here ....'

Adam had heard it over and over again, on the ship, in the inns and boardinghouses on the journey from Quebec, Uncle Ted declaring that he was going to be a landowner and a gentleman. Sometimes he admitted that he might have to work for someone else for a month or two but more often he rejected even that. He saw himself instantly transformed from his present state into a gentleman in a fine suit of clothes riding a handsome horse and having the peasants touch their hats to him. Some such vision might have led to his taking part in the Swing riots in England, and when they had achieved little he had looked to the New World.

Adam wondered what it would take to make Uncle Ted more realistic.

Chapter Four

HEAP BOARDINGHOUSE IT might be, but it was better accommodation than the Wheelers had occupied for the last several months. The snores and tossings of the eighteen or twenty other people in the attic were not as bad as those of the three hundred in the hold of the ship, and sharing a pallet with only one other person was better than sharing a six-foot-wide berth with three or four. Vermin there were in both places but Adam was used to scratching.

He woke early and lay thinking, suppressing his restless desire to be out exploring the town. From where he lay he could see the night sky turn pale and hear the gradual increase of the noises of cattle lowing, horses' hooves, men shouting.

The market, he said to himself. Mrs Perkins had mentioned yesterday evening that the next day, Saturday, was market day. 'It's just down here,' she'd said, pointing. 'No more'n along the alley a step, past the church, and across the street.'

Adam liked markets. Back home, he'd lived out in the country with nothing close by except an alehouse called the King's Head. The nearest village, a mile away, contained only a small church, another alehouse, and a shop. 'Town' was Petersfield, across the county border in Hampshire, where he sometimes went on market day, and those were special and wonderful outings. He loved the excitement of a market, the smells of cheese, fresh bread, onions, leather, and all the other merchandise, and the farm smells of animals and manure and hay. Even the sickish smell of freshly slaughtered carcasses was part of it.

Most of all, he loved the bustle and uproar, the atmosphere of work and holiday combined.

Over breakfast, the elder Mr Carpenter said to Uncle Ted, 'I suppose the first thing you'll do today is go to the Emigrant Office.'

'Emigrant Office? What for?'

'Information about buying land, other things you need to know. Sometimes they hear of people looking for servants or hired hands. Useful. The Canada Company also sells land.'

Clearly Uncle Ted had not thought about the practical steps to be taken now that he was here. He pursed his lips as though weighing Mr Carpenter's suggestions against half a dozen other important alternatives, and then nodded.

'Yes, I'd say that was the first thing. I also mean to buy a newspaper, see what's going on in this town. I suppose there *is* a newspaper?'

'Six or seven of them,' said the younger Mr Carpenter.

'What! Six or seven newspapers?'

'No shortage.'

For a ha'p'ny, Mrs Perkins' son Josh was engaged to show Uncle Ted the way to the Emigrant Office, and Adam and Harry went along. Aunt Lenore and the girls stayed behind and borrowed Mrs Perkins' washtub to launder the family's few spare clothes.

*

The Emigrant Office, Josh said, was in the Parliament Buildings, and the route there would take them through the main part of Toronto.

Shortly after leaving the house, they passed the market, which was in full swing. Livestock, meat, vegetables, all the products of the autumn harvest were being sold and bought. They had heard yesterday from Mr Perkins that, because of a lot of wet weather, the crops this year were worse than normal. However, the market seemed busy enough.

'Bad harvests?' Uncle Ted had asked.

While Mr Perkins gave details, Adam shivered. Back home the crops had been poor lately, making food scarce and expensive. The riots of a few years earlier had been brought on partly by bad harvests and high food prices. Many farm labourers' families had barely survived.

For Adam, it had meant Dick dying because, they said, he didn't have enough to eat. Dick was the son of the people who had the King's Head alehouse. He and Adam went to Mrs Wright's school together.

Then Dick stopped coming out of doors. They said he was sick, that he needed better food. Last year he died. Adam had walked to the churchyard to see the funeral.

So now the comment about bad harvests worried Adam. Back in England he'd never heard Uncle Ted or anyone else saying that in Canada there might also be bad harvests – and poverty, hunger, overcrowding, the very things which were driving people away from the Old World.

On this bustling Saturday morning, however, Adam's gloomy thoughts did not return. There was so much to look at, so much to make him happy to be in Toronto, with the awful journey over and a new life beginning.

The streets were busy and full. There were gentry in carriages and on handsome riding horses, and a few soldiers in red uniform coats, but most of the people on the street were working folk in home-made clothes or the dark coats of clerks and shop assistants. Josh pointed out Indians, dressed in a mixture of native and European garb, and Adam caught sight of a black man going into a shop.

Their route led westwards along King Street which, Josh explained, was the main street of the city. To their left was the market building, a red-brick structure with an archway into the courtyard where most of the selling and buying were being carried on. To their right was St. James' – Josh called it 'the English church', to distinguish it from the

Scots church, which he also pointed out – and the court house and jail. After that there were shops on both sides, and then another poor district. Every time they crossed a north-south street, they could clearly see the harbour to their left, with a ship or two out on the water and the low-lying peninsula beyond.

After about three blocks, they came to what Josh called Yonge Street. 'It's an important street,' he said. 'It goes way up north. But we go along here.'

He led them down to the shore and turned right, and abruptly they were in a different kind of neighbourhood. The lake was immediately on their left now, sparkling in the morning sun. On the landward side were handsome houses surrounded by grounds and gardens. Driveways led to stables and outbuildings at the back.

'This is where the big men live,' Josh said. 'Folk call them the Family Compact, 'cause most of them's related to each other. They run everything.'

The houses, though smaller than the manors and mansions Adam had seen in England, were impressive. 'Forty-five years ago,' Josh was saying, 'there weren't nothing here at all. Just bush 'n' Indians 'n' mosquitoes. Well, we still gets the mosquitoes 'n' black flies in summer. But the bush – you have to go *miles* now to see real bush.'

Forty-five years, Adam thought. His father was forty-five years old. To think of all this having been created in such a short time!

Beyond several blocks of the handsome houses was a row of three public buildings facing the lake.

'These're the Parliament Buildings,' Josh said. 'Behind them, over there, that's Government House where the lieutenant governor lives. Sir Francis Bond Head. Represents the Queen.' Gesturing more widely, he added, '*That's* the college, and that's the hospital. There's the Garrison, up there along the shore.'

Around and between the buildings there was open space, including a shallow ravine with a stream in it.

Josh pointed to some simple structures close by, between the Parliament Buildings and the lake. 'Those are sheds for emigrants. If you wasn't staying with us, you might be staying there.'

He was being cheeky, and Adam wondered whether Uncle Ted would get annoyed. But he seemed not to notice it. He was looking around in a bewildered way.

'The Emigrant Office is in there, in the Parliament Buildings,' Josh said. 'Okay now? Want me to wait for you?'

'No, no, this is fine. Just fine.'

Josh touched his cap and went back the way they had come.

Uncle Ted surveyed the buildings, then looked around as though admiring the scenery. He's putting it off, Adam thought. Afraid to go in?

Adam remembered the first day he went to Mrs Wright's little school. He had hung around outside, just like this. Maybe it wasn't so surprising that Uncle Ted should be bewildered by the strangeness of this new country.

While they were still standing there, two men who had been on the ship with them approached.

'Goin' to the Emigrant Office, Wheeler?' one of them asked.

'Just on my way in,' Uncle Ted said, evidently relieved. He turned to Adam and Harry. 'You boys go and look around,' he said, swaggering again. 'Find your own way home.'

Adam was glad to be no longer trailing after Uncle Ted on adults' business but he would have preferred also to be free of Harry. However, Harry showed no sign of wanting to go off on his own.

'What'll we do?' he asked. 'I know, let's go to that fort.'

*

They walked westwards. On their left, close to the road, was a small house with a verandah on which stood a red-coated soldier who stared at the boys as they passed. Beyond it, down on the beach, were warehouses and a wharf.

To the right of the road was a big building identified by a sign as the Greenland Fishery Tavern, several private houses, a cemetery, and a building at which firewood was being unloaded from a cart. For the rest, the area was empty except for weeds and scrubby bushes.

All this time, as they walked, the fort lay ahead of them, an earthwork wall with some roofs showing above it. As they drew closer, they saw that it was bordered on this side by a ravine and a stream. The road dipped down, crossed the stream by means of a simple bridge, then rose steeply to reach the gate in the wall.

'That's a drawbridge,' Harry said as they approached the stream.

Adam looked at it doubtfully. 'You sure?'

'All castles have drawbridges.'

So far as Adam knew, Harry had never seen a castle, any more than Adam himself had. Harry had not even been to the dame school to hear Mrs Wright describe them. But they had both listened to the stories of an old soldier, Sergeant Phillips, who had been on the ship crossing the Atlantic. He had never tired of talking about the wars against Napoleon, in which he had taken part. He loved gathering boys around him and telling about some battle or other, using handy objects like bits of wood to create a model on the deck. 'This is the wall of the castle,' he'd say, 'and this is us here, coming up to it. The moat's here, and the gate *here*.' A short, fierce forefinger with a deformed nail sketched and stabbed.

'I don't know about *all* castles,' Adam said. 'I don't even know whether this is a real castle. It doesn't look much like one. Sergeant Phillips said that drawbridges are called that because they can be pulled up by chains or something. To

[48]

prevent the enemy crossing the moat. I don't see any chains.'

'Well, *I* think it's a drawbridge.'

Adam kept silent.

The gate stood open and there was no one nearby except a groom leading two fine saddle horses. He glanced at the boys but said nothing about their not being allowed in.

There were other signs of life. A couple of men chopped wood, a woman took washing off a line, children played, men sat on benches and doorsteps smoking pipes. Three officers in red coats crossed from one of the scattered buildings to another, and two more, mounted, came cantering towards Adam and Harry and out through the gate. They glanced at the boys but did not challenge them. Perhaps everyone assumed that Adam and Harry belonged to one of the soldiers' families who evidently lived in the fort.

'Hey, look!' Harry said. 'A cannon!'

Adam was about to comment that cannon were not unusual things to find in forts, but then he saw what Harry had spotted – not the guns mounted on the walls but one that stood near a building inside the gate.

Harry went to have a closer look, but Adam was more interested in the blockhouses. He crossed to the nearest one and stared up at the horizontal slits high in the walls, just below the overhanging upper storey. The slits were closed now, but it was easy to see how they'd look open and with musket barrels pointing out.

He was picturing himself inside the building defending it, and then outside it attacking, when he heard a shout behind him.

'You! Kid! Stop that!'

He spun round, dodging the imagined enemy, but the shout had been directed at Harry, who was poking a stick into the cannon's barrel. A furious man in a red uniform coat charged out of the nearby building and clouted Harry over the ear.

'Hey!' Harry protested, apparently taken by surprise.

'Stop that, kid! Don't you know that guns can go off and kill people? And you're tampering with Army property. You could damage that gun.'

'Damage that big gun with this little stick?' Harry demanded with a sarcastic laugh.

But the soldier was big and angry, and was again raising one huge hand. Harry changed his tactics.

'Sorry, sir,' he said, giving the disarming grin which he used as a way to get himself out of trouble. 'I've just arrived and was looking around. Grand place this is.' He gestured at the fort.

'You get away from that gun, kid.'

Harry grinned again. 'I really wasn't doing any harm, sir. And it wouldn't be loaded, would it? A gun standing here in the middle of the fort? What kind of gun is it? I'm interested in becoming a soldier ....'

It was the first Adam had heard of *that*. Harry was just charming his way out of a tight spot.

'Your pa connected with the garrison?' the man asked, cooling down noticeably. Adam could almost hear what he was thinking: suppose this brat is the son of someone important!

'No – I'm just looking around.'

'Well, you've seen all you're going to see. Get the hell out.' And he pointed to the gate.

'Aw, I barely got here. I'd really like to look around a bit more.'

'Out!'

By now Harry had spotted Adam, still standing near the blockhouse. He gave a shrug and twitched his head towards the gate.

The soldier glared suspiciously at Adam but said nothing to him. He did, however, watch until the boys were outside the gate. Adam, glancing over his shoulder, saw him dust his hands against each other and then turn away.

'One o' those fellers what hates kids,' Harry grumbled.

Adam thought the man was right to dislike boys who poked sticks into the barrels of guns, but he kept silent. It was never any use arguing with Harry – and even less use now, because after charming himself out of trouble he always became surly and, if he had lost, took it out on whoever happened to be near.

Chapter Five

NCLE TED RETURNED GLOOMY and silent from the Emigrant Office. He had clearly been to a tavern on the way home, though he was not drunk. He had also bought two newspapers. He went to the kitchen, evidently intending to sit where it was warm and spread the papers out on the table – just as though it were his own kitchen – but he was chased out by Mrs Perkins. Grumpily he went upstairs and sat on the edge of the Wheeler family's bed to read them and smoke his pipe. At dinner he had little to say; the Carpenters were not there and Uncle Ted chose not to talk to a family called Davis, nor to a single man with a glum face, nor to the four Welshmen or the Perkins family.

The next day, at Aunt Lenore's insistence, they attended church.

On Monday Uncle Ted went out, not telling anyone where, and Aunt Lenore sent Adam and Harry to explore the town. Adam wondered what she and the girls would do. Occupy themselves with sewing and mending? Walk around town themselves? What did women do when they didn't have a home to keep them busy?

But he soon forgot to think about that. This time he and Harry wandered inland, finding more poor districts, more commercial areas, and more handsome houses.

One of these houses, north of town, was built on the far side of a ravine with a swollen stream in it. The house was square, handsome, confident but quiet in style. Adam could imagine the sober-suited gentleman and dignified lady who might live there – people like the gentry he'd seen on King Street. The house reminded him of manor houses back home except that it was surrounded not by tamed and tidy parkland but by the rough ravine in front and, behind it, a clearing with a few stumps remaining at the far edges and then the raw fringe of the Canadian forest.

While he was standing there looking at it – Harry was down by the stream trying to catch a muskrat – a boy of about five came along leading a scrawny cow.

'Who lives there?' Adam asked on impulse.

'That's Mr Allan's place,' the boy said. 'Moss Park, they call it.'

'Mr ...?' Adam asked, thinking that 'Allan' was a first name.

'Mr William Allan. You new here or something?'

'Nice house.'

'Mr Allan's *rich*,' the little boy said.

'I can see that.'

The boy and the cow walked on and Adam stared again at the house.

Moss Park.

He liked Moss Park. It grabbed his imagination more than the other big houses did. Who was Mr William Allan? An immigrant who had made good? One of the gentry who were already several steps up the ladder when they arrived? Was it possible that Adam himself might reach this point some day?

His thoughts were interrupted by Harry scrambling up the bank towards him.

'Catch it?' Adam asked, hoping that he hadn't.

'No. Got wet for nothin'.' His boots and trousers were soaked halfway up to the knee.

They followed the ravine east. When it turned south, they clambered down the bank, crossed the stream on a makeshift footbridge, climbed the slope at the far side, and kept walking eastwards, past a big church, until they reached a valley with a bigger stream. This must be the Don River, mentioned by Mr Perkins the evening before.

Staying on the rim of the ravine, they followed the river towards where it emptied itself into the harbour. The land sloped down until there was no ravine left, only an area of swamp with patches of meadow and scrubby copses of willows and reeds. The Don River itself and a lot of little creeks meandered through it. On islands of solid ground, pathetic hovels had been built of a few boards and barrel staves, a broken cart, a piece of sailcloth, a rough thatch of branches and reeds. Because of the wet weather, the miserable little huts looked sodden – and in fact it was starting to rain again, causing Adam and Harry to turn up their coat collars.

A dog barked at them. Beside one of the streams, a girl in rags sat holding a fishing pole. An old woman carrying firewood came slowly into view, crossing a bridge made of a single plank.

This was even more wretched than the area near the Perkins' boardinghouse.

'Why build *here*?' Harry wondered out loud. 'When the river floods, wouldn't everything be washed away?'

'Land that nobody owns, I guess.'

'Nobody'd want it. Let's go home.'

A muddy road led back into town. On the way, they passed the windmill which they had seen from out on the water on the day they arrived. The light breeze moved its vanes very slowly, sighed through the weeds and bushes, and made small waves on the bay that whispered as they curled and died on the beach close beside the road. Ducks flew by overhead and landed skidding on the water. The air, though damp, was cool and fresh.

While walking, Adam mulled over what he had seen. Rich and poor, Moss Park and the hovels in the marshes. How, in a country like this, could anybody be so *very* poor? Some people had problems, of course – Mrs Perkins had lots of stories about that. To succeed in Canada, you couldn't trust to luck. You had to be sensible, to work and plan and figure out the best way to reach the kind of life you wanted.

The sight of the hovels, the realization that getting ahead was not something that happened automatically, just by coming to the New World, made Adam restless and impatient. He was irritated by Uncle Ted's delay in making decisions. He had expected that when they arrived in Toronto their active life, interrupted by the journey, would resume. But these days were as idle and aimless as those on board ship had been. He needed something better to do than wander around town with Harry.

All the same, he was coming to like much of what he saw of Toronto — not the slums or the muddy streets or the huts in the swamp, but the sense of space and openness. He liked the stores and the bustle of town, the sight of soldiers and officers from the garrison, farm folk from the countryside, handsome horses and well-dressed people. Toronto was a real city. What he'd heard in England, from the promoter and from the talk of people who got letters from Canada, was all about pioneer life on farms and in the backwoods. He hadn't expected a city like this, more interesting than the bush.

*

Back at the boardinghouse, as they were going up to the attic, Adam and Harry heard Uncle Ted and Aunt Lenore arguing.

'... didn't come here to be a hired hand!'

'For a few months, Ted. Only a few months. And I'd be working too! Mrs Carpenter says they need an indoor servant as well as a man for the farm work ....'

Adam expected Harry to turn back so that his parents could have it out by themselves. But Harry doggedly went on up the steep, twisting stairs.

'... land in the western part of the province,' Uncle Ted said. 'Good farming country, they say, being opened up right this very minute. We'll go there at once, start the clearing, run up a log house in no time, lots of fuel ....'

And what will you use to buy food? Adam asked silently. Uncle Ted's plan required enough money, or steady earnings from work off the farm, to keep the family fed during the first winter and spring and summer – nearly a year altogether – in which they had no harvest of their own to live on.

'But Ted, this job that Mrs Carpenter's heard about. There's a house for us to live in, and ....'

'And ten years from now we'll *still* be living there, working for someone else!'

'Only for the winter, Ted!'

Uncle Ted appeared at the top of the stairs, storming in rage. When he saw the boys, he said, 'Come on, Harry, let's go and look at horses. Adam can stay and talk to his aunt, if he likes.' He gave Adam a hostile look.

The words were an insult, as though talking to women was all Adam was fit for while Harry was the one to be taken along on male outings like looking at horses. It was not news to Adam that his uncle didn't like him; when Uncle Ted was in a good mood he ignored him, and when he was in a bad humour his dislike showed.

After Uncle Ted and Harry had pushed past him and clambered down the stairs, Adam looked up again. Aunt Lenore stood there, the everlasting mending in her hands.

Clearly she had heard her husband's words to Adam.

'Do you want me to stay, Aunt Lenore? Or would you rather be alone?'

'Come on up, Adam,' she said in a sad voice.

She led the way to their corner of the attic. Ella lay curled up on the far side of the bed against the wall, much as she had curled up on the berth in the ship, and Ruth sat on the floor playing with her home-made rag doll.

Aunt Lenore seated herself on the small wooden box that was their one solid piece of luggage, and Adam squatted cross-legged on the floor nearby.

'I don't know if you heard,' Aunt Lenore said, 'but Ted's

been offered a job.' When talking to Adam about her husband, she no longer called him 'your Uncle Ted' but simply 'Ted', as though Adam were an adult. 'There's a farmer who needs a hired man, and his wife wants help in the house. They usually hire a couple, and there's a shanty to live in.'

'Where is this?'

'Near a town called Dundas, not too far away, Mrs Carpenter says.' She smiled. 'I guess she means not too far as things are here.'

All of them were revising their ideas about distance.

'It sounds like such a good thing,' she went on. 'Roof over our heads, work for both of us, chance to earn a little and decide what next. All this time, living here in town, we're spending money that we're going to need later. Need real bad, I'm afraid.'

It might have been Adam's mother talking, careful, worried, perhaps too cautious but knowing from hard experience how important caution was.

'It seems like a good idea,' Adam said. He wanted to keep out of quarrels between his aunt and uncle, but he really did think Aunt Lenore was right.

'Ted won't see it,' she said mournfully. 'He listened to all those promoters talking big about becoming a landowner … well, about owning land. They said that over here anybody could become a landowner.'

'Not everyone here owns land, though,' he said, thinking of the hovels in the swamp. 'Besides, there must be lots of farmers who own land but are not gentry.'

'I guess owning land here isn't the same – isn't as *important* – as it was back home.'

'It certainly doesn't look as though it makes a person into a gentleman overnight – or even in a year or two.'

Aunt Lenore bent even farther over her sewing. 'We could starve, Adam. I see us in a tiny, drafty shack surrounded by snow and those awful stumps, with nothing to eat. Ted talks about there being plenty of game in the forest, but we can't afford to buy a gun. He could trap wild animals, but I think of him going out into the forest in the snow, getting lost .... And trapping is something you have to learn – the habits of the wild creatures, and how to make traps. All Ted knows is ... well, I guess it doesn't matter now if I tell you, but all he knows about trapping is from doing a little poaching back home. Only a little,' she pleaded, looking up at Adam. 'He never had much luck.' She bent her head again. 'But it's already October, and the thought of living for a whole winter in one of those shanties out in the woods, all by ourselves ...!'

He knew exactly what she was seeing in her mind. The two of them, while on the steamer carrying them along Lake Ontario, had got a close look at one of the clearings they passed, an area where the trees had been felled but stumps remained. The stumps were about three feet high and many of them as much as that or more in diameter, surrounded by a desolation of lopped branches and foliage, with a fire lit to burn the stuff. The fire had not even burned well, and the smoke hung over the stumps, penned in by the surrounding forest.

The dwelling was a small shanty, with a roof made of hollowed half-logs laid overlapping like tiles so that the ones with the hollow upwards carried off the rain. It had a chimney made of mud plastered on some sort of framework, and it also had the luxury of a pane of glass in its single window. But it was even smaller than the cottages they'd lived in back home.

Close to it was another shanty which, to judge by the manure pile next to it, served as a barn.

Looking at this, Aunt Lenore had said quietly, 'Picture it in the winter, Adam, with snow.'

Every emigrant knew that there was a lot of snow every winter in Canada. Would it be as high as the tops of those stumps? For a moment it was an attractive picture. If the snow were deep enough to cover the stumps, there would be a sheet of white around the two little buildings. The roofs would be laden with it. Smoke would curl out of the chimney into the blue sky.

And inside the shanty would be a whole family, already cramped for space but, in the winter weather, huddled even closer together to be near the fire. The floor would be damp and icy cold. Even by daylight, the room would be dim. There might not be enough food to eat, and water would have to be made by melting snow or found by hacking through the ice of a lake or stream. One crying baby, or one person with a bad cough, could drive the rest of the family crazy. And if there were worse illnesses, or other emergencies, someone would have to ride or tramp through the snowy bush for help.

'It's the loneliness, the distances,' Aunt Lenore had said broodingly. 'We're used to poverty, all of us. That shanty isn't really much worse than what we had back home, though I do miss the cleared fields and the hedges and the ... the feel of a country that's been lived in for centuries and centuries. But there, in England, we were only a step away from the neighbours. I know we could live close to a village here, but Ted wants a big piece of land and I guess that would have to be out in the forest somewhere. We'd be so alone.'

He wasn't the only one in the family, Adam thought, who was beginning to be uneasy about Uncle Ted's dream.

Chapter Six

N THE NEXT FEW DAYS, Uncle Ted changed
plans several times. He abandoned the idea of buying
land, then went back to it. He talked about working as
a dairyman. He was going to take the family further
west, or to the United States.

On the Wednesday evening, five days after the family's
arrival in Toronto, something happened which directly
affected Adam. It occurred at dinner in the boardinghouse.

By now the Carpenters had gone to a town called Richmond Hill, north of Toronto, where the elder brother
intended to set up a shop for making windows and the
younger brother to start a school. Their place had been taken
by a family called Keller, consisting of parents and three boys
a little older than Adam and Harry.

The talk turned to the work of clearing land and making a
farm, and Mr Keller proudly indicated his sturdy sons. 'With
boys like this, there ain't nothin' we can't do, workin'
together!'

The sons nodded – close-cropped round heads, pug-nosed
faces, all looking strong and determined.

Uncle Ted scowled sideways along the bench on which his
family sat.

'All I got's this – two wenches an' my own boy Harry. But
Harry 'n' me ...!' He pushed out his chest in a bragging way.
'And then Adam, my brother's boy, brought along as an extra
pair of hands. He'll be useful, I guess.'

The words were accompanied by a look which warned
Adam that he'd *better* be useful.

Adam was shocked into numbness that, a moment later,
turned to a pain so sharp that he didn't know how he could

bear it. The words were hurtful enough, but the dismissive tone and the threatening look made him wince in agony.

Aunt Lenore must have sensed how he felt. 'Adam's a very hard worker,' she said firmly. 'Back home he worked in the fields, and with his grandpa during the lambing, and he helped his mother by fetching water and firewood. And when his grandpa took sick ....'

Uncle Ted interrupted. 'He *nursed* his grandpa. All that, what you said, that's work for women or little kids. We're talking about man's work, cutting down trees, building a house and a stable for the horses, making a home for a gentleman and his family, future generations .... *Man's* work!'

Adam bent his head. He had always been shy about the fact that, though two months older than Harry, he was smaller and thinner. But *this!* To have it thrown in his face as an insult, a drawback, that he had cared for his grandpa and, except for the time spent at school, had always worked hard ... while Harry, who had never done anything at all if he could help it, was being praised!

Adam had known his uncle disliked him, but not that it was as bad as this.

He knew he should be grateful to Aunt Lenore for defending him, but somehow she made it worse.

After dinner he told her he was going out. It was dark and cold but he noticed neither that nor the evening life of the city. He wandered down to the lake and onto the wharf where they'd landed. Hands in trouser pockets, he stared out over the water, aching with hurt and with longing for home – for the home, completely and forever vanished, that he and his mother and grandfather had made.

Could he really live and work with someone who despised him so? Adam had already been unhappy at the prospect of clearing land and starting a farm but he had been prepared to do his share and more, if only to repay Uncle Ted for what Adam cost him.

True enough, Abigail's 'penny or two' would have paid for part of his passage. The rest ....

He wished he knew how much his passage had cost.

But it was not a matter of money alone. Ought he to feel grateful? From what Adam had overheard that night back home, and what Uncle Ted had said this evening, it was clear that Uncle Ted had brought him along reluctantly – brought him only because Abigail paid, and because Adam was an extra pair of hands.

Did a parcel have to feel grateful for being sent?

It was too complicated.

A wave of wretchedness and despair washed over him and he clenched his hands into tight fists. He didn't know what he was hanging onto, but he hung on. He needed help but he didn't know where to turn.

There was only himself in the dark night at the edge of the black water. Only himself.

*

The next day he went to the Emigrant Office.

'I'm Adam Wheeler,' he said, taking off his cap. 'The nephew of Ted Wheeler. Mr Edward Wheeler.' He thought the clerk would recognize the name; Uncle Ted had been here several times.

'What is it, son?' said the clerk at the desk, giving him an assessing look.

'I'd like to find a job. I've heard that you know about people who need servants or hired hands.'

'Aren't you with your uncle, lad?'

'I'd like to be on my own. I want to live away from my uncle and the family, but I need a job. Earn my living.' It sounded much too grand, but he wanted to make himself clear.

'There's always jobs for boys,' the clerk said. 'Work in inns and stables, or at big houses. Messenger work for business firms. Just about everyone has a boy to run errands and do chores.'

'I know. But I wondered about … learning a trade. I can't be an apprentice – don't have any money to pay a premium – but you don't have to be an apprentice to learn a trade. Carpentry or something like that.'

'How old are you, Adam?'

'Fourteen. I'll be fifteen in February.'

'Pity. If you were fifteen *now* … but you say you aren't looking to be apprenticed. All the same ….' The clerk thoughtfully tapped his pencil against his teeth.

Adam waited.

The clerk made up his mind and used the pencil to write something down on a tiny scrap of paper.

'Can you read, lad?' he asked as he handed it to Adam.

Adam read the note aloud to prove that he could. 'York Paper Mill, near Todmorden. Eastwood and Skinner.'

'They sometimes advertise for apprentices, aged fifteen or sixteen. Maybe they could use a lad around the place.'

'Where's Todmorden?'

'Just outside o' town. East to the Don River, across the bridge. The Mill Road's off to your left. Couple of other villages along the road, then Todmorden. When you get there, ask for the Don Mills – that's down on the flats by the river.'

'How far?'

'Three or four miles from here, about. Going to try it?'

Somehow Adam liked the idea of making paper, and the idea of living in a village but close to the city.

'Yes, sir. Thank you, sir.'

'Good luck, lad.'

*

He went first to the boardinghouse to tell Aunt Lenore that he would be away for the afternoon, then set off for Todmorden.

[65]

He and Harry had seen the bridge on Monday, though they had not crossed it. It was roofed over and closed along the sides except for open spaces high up under the eaves to let in some light.

Before entering the bridge, Adam looked upriver, towards Todmorden and the paper mill.

The valley was not very broad here but it began widening immediately. Across its floor, the river wound back and forth, its banks fringed with a tangled mass of trees and bushes. It was a substantial stream, wider than the others Adam had seen in this area though nothing like as large as the enormous St. Lawrence River. The valley walls were broken into outcrops and small hills; these were mostly wooded but on the far side someone had cut the trees and begun digging away the bank, apparently intending to use the soil to make a smooth slope down to the river. The project had been abandoned and the area was covered in weeds and scrubby bushes.

He entered the bridge and had walked about halfway across when a heavy wagon appeared at the other end, nearly filling the space between the floor and roof. It was a laden brewer's dray pulled by two big horses. Adam flattened himself against the wall. The driver, while nodding a greeting, gave him a curious look, and Adam touched his cap politely.

So there was a brewery out this way, as well as a paper mill.

At the far end of the bridge was a bar across the road. He was puzzled for a moment, then realized that it might be a tollgate, a place where you had to pay money to pass. There had been no tollgates near where he'd lived back home, but on the road from Petersfield to Portsmouth were several.

He had no money, not a farthing.

While he was hesitating, wondering what to do, a voice shouted something at him from the house right beside the tollgate. He went to the open window from which the shout had come; inside was a plump woman wiping a bowl with a cloth.

'Pardon, ma'am?' he said.

'Go on through. No toll for a person walking, only on horses and carts and livestock and that kind o' thing.'

As she came towards the window to put the bowl on a shelf near it, she added, 'You must be new here. Ain't seen you before. Where're you going?'

'The York Paper Mill.'

'Oh, Eastwood and Skinner's. You know the way?'

'Not exactly. The man said to take the Mill Road, which must be around here somewhere ....' Ahead, beyond the tollgate, were what looked like an inn and three or four houses, but he couldn't see a road.

She pointed in the direction in which he was looking. 'This here's the Kingston Road. The Mill Road turns off it, up there a short ways, beyond the last house. Not far. You can't miss it. Off to the left.' With a sweep of her hefty arm, bare to the elbow, she indicated the valley and forest to the north.

'Thank you, ma'am.'

The road to Todmorden and the Don Mills was a rough track, very muddy, bordered with bush and a few farms. He came to a tiny village and, seeing a family harvesting potatoes, asked his way. No, this was not Todmorden. Next one. Keep going, lad.

Todmorden consisted of little more than a tavern, a black-smith shop, and three or four houses with barns and farmland behind them. The paper mill? Down there, kid, follow that road. Ask your way when you get there, 'cause there's several mills.

The road curved along the side of the bank, another bad road scarred with heavy hooves and wheels, rutted and muddy. As Adam walked he could see, below him, a yard with mill-like buildings clustered around it. There were also orchards and gardens. A channel of water drawn from the river ran through the area and provided power to the mills. Beyond was the Don River itself in its broad valley. Several

women and children worked in the gardens, gathering produce into baskets. A cart stood beside one of the buildings,
the horse drinking from a bucket of water while two men
unloaded bales. At the back door of one of the houses, a maidservant let a dog in and shook a cloth. The rumble of turning
mill wheels and the smell of wood smoke reached Adam.

To the right of the curving road was a good-sized brick
house. Because of its position halfway up the slope, it looked
over the roofs of the lower buildings, and over the treetops, to
the valley beyond. Off to the left, a house was being built
which would have a similar view.

As Adam entered the yard, a man carrying a sheaf of
papers crossed from one building to another. The cravat and
black coat he wore showed that he was a clerk. He glanced
questioningly at Adam.

'I'm looking for the paper mill,' Adam said. 'Mr Eastwood
or Mr Skinner.'

'On what business, lad?'

'To ask about work.'

'Come along.'

Adam followed him to the building where the bales were
being unloaded.

Indoors, the rumbling and splashing of the mill wheel was
muted and blended with other noises. In a quick glance, while
following the clerk, Adam noticed vats of some whitish soup
and a machine that seemed to consist mainly of big rollers.
There were bales piled against one wall, near a couple of
women doing something at a counter, and stacks of paper
against another wall. Several men in hats and aprons supervised the equipment, and one was sorting sheets of paper into
different piles. The air was unexpectedly warm and damp.

'This way,' the clerk said, and he led Adam to a room
carved out of a corner of the open space – two rooms, as
Adam saw when he was inside, a small outer one for the clerk
and an inner one for the boss.

'Young feller to see you, Mr Skinner. About work.'

'Send him in.'

The man writing at the desk in the inner office did not raise his head. 'Well?'

'I'm ... my name is Adam Wheeler, sir.'

Mr Skinner, a small man with a North American accent, looked up. 'What did you say ... kid?' The last word came as an afterthought, when he'd had a good look at Adam.

'My name is Adam Wheeler. I'm new in Canada and I'm looking for work. The clerk at the Emigrant Office said I might try you. He said you sometimes advertised for apprentices.'

'How old're you?'

'Fourteen.'

'We only take lads of fifteen.'

'All I want is a job. I can't afford the premium for being an apprentice. The clerk said that you might be able to use a boy for ... for general chores.' When Mr Skinner looked him up and down, Adam hastily added, 'I'm stronger than I look, and I'm used to work. I'm ... they say I'm a pretty good worker.'

'Any experience, Adam?'

'Not with paper-making, or in mills, or anything like that. I know a bit about farming – about sheep and other livestock, haying, harvesting, hedging ....'

Nursing, he heard Uncle Ted say scornfully. He was not going to add that to the list.

'Not much call for hedging here, but lots of need for folks who'll do other jobs on farms.'

'I don't want to work on a farm. I'd rather ....'

He shrugged. How could he explain that the image he had formed of Canada scared him – the enormous distances, the millions of trees – and that so far the only place he liked was Toronto?

And the notion of making paper pleased him. Paper for books, newspapers – a civilized thing. 'Civilized' was one of the words used by Mrs Wright, his teacher back home.

Mr Skinner was silent for a moment, leaning back in his chair and looking thoughtfully at Adam.

'Got a bit of an education, have you, Adam? You're a well-spoken lad.'

'I can read and write and do simple figuring. I went to a dame school – Mrs Wright, whose husband had been a rector in the church. She taught us some history, and showed us maps in an atlas and talked about them. It was interesting. It was only a dame school,' he added quickly, having heard people make fun of such places, 'but ....'

'Dame schools are as good as the women who run them, and that can be quite good. Sounds like you were lucky. Most of the young fellers who come here looking for work ....' He made a disgusted face.

Adam waited, almost holding his breath. It had become very important – he was surprised to discover how important – to be hired by Mr Skinner.

'You here with your family, Adam? Just arrived, you say.'

'My uncle and aunt and cousins. My uncle is thinking of taking up land. I'd ... I think I'd rather stay near Toronto.'

'Don't get along with them too well?'

A lump came into Adam's throat. He shrugged again.

Mr Skinner spent another moment or two in thought.

'I guess you'd need a place to live?'

'Yes, if you please, sir. If you know of one.'

'Could sleep in our house. Run a few errands in your spare time for Mrs Skinner and Nelly – Nelly's the servant. That suit you? Six dollars a month and all your board. Tips for errands and such-like.'

'Six dollars? What's that in ...?' Adam stopped, afraid to show how ignorant he was about Canadian money.

'It's pretty well the going rate for lads like you. Give most of it to your folks, will you?'

'I don't know yet.' He swallowed. 'They don't actually know that I'm ....'

'That you're looking for work? Well, you'll have to tell 'em. I'm not going to hire you unless they approve.'

Mr Skinner began to turn back to his desk as though dismissing Adam, as though not wanting to spend any more time on him now that he knew he had not yet asked permission.

'Mr Skinner, please ... I'd like the job, and I don't see why they'd object. Please ... will you hire me?'

The man turned back to Adam, kindly again. Perhaps his turning away hadn't meant what Adam thought.

'Sure, lad. You've got the job, far's I'm concerned. Ask your uncle, though, and tell me what he says. Do that tomorrow, if you can. Move in Sunday, start Monday. Okay? Carver!'

'Yes, sir?' answered the clerk.

'This young lad here's coming to work for us. Adam Wheeler. Starts Monday – only got to check with his folks. Tell Morris to give him a quick tour.' To Adam he said, 'Come and bring me word tomorrow, then. If I'm out, tell Mr Carver here.'

The clerk took him into the main part of the mill and across to a man inspecting the white substance in one of the vats. Unlike the other mill hands, who wore the garb of ordinary workmen, this man was dressed in a neat shirt and waistcoat and cravat – nothing fancy, but enough to make it clear that he was a foreman or supervisor.

'Mr Morris!'

'Yes?'

'This is Adam Wheeler, who's starting here on Monday.'

Mr Morris turned and frowningly sized Adam up. 'Apprentice? I should've been consulted.'

'No,' Adam said. 'Just general work.'

'Oh, well, that's different.' Mr Morris lost his irritation, as well as his interest in Adam.

The clerk spoke again. 'Mr Skinner asks you to give him a quick tour.'

Mr Morris raised his eyebrows, as though this was unusual, but then he nodded. 'Very well.'

The clerk went back to his room, and Mr Morris led Adam over to the counter where the two women were working.

'The process starts here. This is the raw material for paper. Linen and cotton rags. We buy 'em from people in town, and Mrs McDonald and Mrs O'Neill are cutting them. They have to be cut into small pieces – sort of chewed up, really. They go into this vat here.' He walked to a vat of the white soup-like substance under the surface of which, out of sight, some sort of churning was taking place. 'This is the Hollander. It beats the rags into pulp – that's this soup, which is called "stuff". From here the stuff goes into this next vat, which is called the holding vat. It contains the pulp that's ready to go into the paper machine.'

He barely pointed to the holding vat as he walked to the big apparatus that filled the whole middle of the room.

'This, right here, is the paper machine. The stuff starts in this vat – that's the same stuff from the Hollander and the holding vat, which gets put in here when we're ready for it. Gets lifted out here, on this screen, and spread in a thin layer. See that?' he said, indicating a moving wire mesh covered with a coating of the white pulp. 'That'll be paper in a minute. Excess water drains out. Along here it gets moved from the wire screen to woollen felt. Pressed to remove more water. Rolled between these cylinders for drying. And *here* ....' As he talked and pointed, he had been walking along the apparatus. 'Here, out comes paper.'

From the far end of the machine rolled a continuous sheet of paper which, as it emerged, was chopped into pieces that piled themselves on a kind of tray. While Adam watched, one of the men in aprons picked up the tray, deftly slipped an empty one in its place, and carried the full one to a counter.

Adam stared, astounded at seeing the pulp turn into paper in just a few minutes.

'Any questions?' Mr Morris asked Adam in a discouraging tone.

He grabbed at the first of many questions he would have liked to ask. 'What makes it so warm in here?'

'The stuff in the paper machine is warm – the finished paper dries quicker that way – so there's a heater next to the vat. And these drying cylinders along here are heated too. Stoking the fires will be one of your jobs, I guess. You start on Monday?'

'Yes, sir. Thank you for the tour, sir.'

'See you then.' And Mr Morris turned back to the paper machine.

Adam was not sure whether, before leaving, he should check with the clerk. To be on the safe side, he knocked at the door of the office and, when bidden, went in. The clerk was writing in a large book.

'I've had the quick tour, Mr Carver. I'll be back tomorrow to tell you or Mr Skinner what my uncle says.'

'Right, lad. See you then.'

Chapter Seven

DAM, WALKING BACK TO Toronto, had no idea what Uncle Ted would say. Now that he was alone, and no longer trying with all his might to make a good impression, the bitter awareness of his uncle's contempt came flooding back. He was not looking forward to talking to him. They never *had* talked to each other about anything serious except the time when Adam wanted to pass on what he'd heard from the man who had been to Canada and returned to England. But he knew that during such conversations Uncle Ted quickly lost his temper.

As Adam approached the tollgate, there was a clatter of horses' hooves in the bridge. A moment later three riders appeared, a tall man on a handsome horse and two girls of about Adam's age on smaller ones. They were all dressed in English style, and the girls rode side-saddle. They could have come straight from one of the families Adam had seen from afar in England, gentry on their country estates.

In the first instant, the sight made him homesick, and then it made him slightly jealous. It *would* be nice to wear a navy-blue coat and glossy boots and to ride a fine horse.

But ... that sounded just like Uncle Ted!

Adam felt as though the breath had been thumped out of him.

Could it really be that he was *like Uncle Ted?*

This ... wanting a better life ... this was how Uncle Ted always thought. He too saw himself dressed as a gentleman and riding a fine horse.

If Adam himself had the same vision ....

Adam had been told over and over again by his mother and Mrs Wright that a person had to accept the place in the world into which he or she had been born. Adam was a labourer's son and that was where he belonged. Only a few working men, people with very unusual ability and opportunities, were able to move up out of their class. The rest had better be content with it.

In the light of this, Uncle Ted's ambition had seemed wrong.

Now Adam recognized that he was ambitious too. His wish of a moment ago might be a passing fancy, natural to any working man, but he'd had other and more serious thoughts like that. He remembered telling Aunt Lenore that if he crossed the ocean again it would be as a cabin passenger – and recalled that, on Monday, he'd wondered whether he would ever own a house like Moss Park. He *did* have a touch of Uncle Ted's ambition, and for a moment it horrified him. If it was wrong for Uncle Ted to have silly dreams, surely it was wrong for Adam too.

But it didn't *feel* so terribly wrong.

Meanwhile ... 'a cat may look at a king,' as grandpa used to say, so Adam looked at the three riders.

The girls sat their horses easily and gracefully. They seemed to be nearly the same age and had the same dark hair and eyes, but one was plumper, the trim riding habit revealing a shapely figure. The other was thin, more girlish, perhaps younger, and also livelier in her manner, talking and laughing. Both wore the feminine version of men's hats, with veils that fluttered in the wind but did not cover their faces. Both wore exquisite leather gloves and carried riding crops. They looked wonderful up there on their horses, female and yet powerful and commanding.

But they were more than just typical gentry; they were also human beings. The plump girl blew her nose into a sturdy handkerchief. Even the gentry could have colds.

For some reason, the gentleman paid no toll for himself and the young ladies. He merely called out to the tollgate keeper – the same woman Adam had talked to earlier – and asked her to open the gate. She did so, curtsying, and the three riders passed through. While the young lady with the cold was tucking her handkerchief back into her pocket, the slender girl said something which made all of them laugh. A family joke, Adam thought – well, maybe not a joke, exactly, but one of those little remarks that are part of the way relatives talk to each other. That made him homesick again.

All the same, he observed the riders carefully. Like the big houses, and the gentry on King Street, they were as much a part of Canada as the shanties and the stumps and the muddy roads.

When they noticed him, the girls gave him curious but not unfriendly looks. Adam took off his cap, and the gentleman nodded a civil greeting. Then they rode past him, eastwards along the Kingston Road.

As Adam crossed the bridge and walked back to Toronto, his mind went back to what he had been thinking about earlier.

Could ambition, wanting a better life, be wrong for one person but right for another? That didn't make sense.

Maybe what was important was *how* you tried to achieve a better life. Working for it was one thing – expecting magic was something else again. Uncle Ted seemed to expect magic.

*

Adam found the whole Wheeler family at the boardinghouse, huddled on and near their bed. They looked pathetic and miserable. Aunt Lenore was sewing. The two girls listlessly played cat's cradle with a piece of string. Harry was using a stick to draw idle patterns on the floor. Uncle Ted lounged on the bed reading aloud from a newspaper. Adam had never known him to do any reading before, but here he spent some time every day with the papers. In the evenings he went to a nearby tavern, one of the hundreds serving Toronto. He never came home drunk; to him, alehouses and taverns were places for meeting people. In any case, he had little enough money to spend on drink, though the whisky in this country was dirt cheap.

Uncle Ted was out of humour. In a sour, sarcastic voice he was reading something of which Adam caught only the words 'liberties' and 'Family Compact'. Obviously the newspaper was one of those that criticized the government and demanded reform. They had heard a lot about this from Mr and Mrs Perkins.

When Adam approached, Aunt Lenore looked up and smiled.

Unfortunately it was not Aunt Lenore he had to deal with. It was Uncle Ted, and he had to do it now, because it was nearly dinner time and after the meal Uncle Ted usually went straight to the tavern.

'Hello,' Adam said, mustering a smile for Aunt Lenore.

Uncle Ted stopped reading aloud. He gave a grunt and kept his eyes on the newspaper.

Adam perched on a corner of the bed. 'Uncle Ted ....'

'Hm ...?'

'I've got ... I've found a job.'

At the last word, Uncle Ted reared up and glared at Adam. '*Job!* Are you nagging me too? I don't like the sound of that job in Dundas, and I won't be pestered into taking it.'

'A job for myself. In a paper mill. I need your permission before I can take it.'

Uncle Ted frowned. 'You? A job? You don't need a job. There'll be plenty for you to do on my land. I need you.'

Adam had half expected something like this. Suddenly he was useful again, though yesterday Uncle Ted had talked as though he hardly mattered. How could anyone be so muddle-headed?

Aunt Lenore got up and took the others downstairs.

'I'm sorry, Uncle Ted. I ... I don't much like ....'

Uncle Ted's brows were gathered in a scowl, his eyes dark. Then his face became mournful. 'I took you on, back home, when your pa and Abigail asked me, 'cause I thought you'd fit in, that we'd all work together like one family. And now, when I'm planning a good life for us all ....' Abruptly he scowled again. 'Now, when I'm making these big plans, you turn rebel on me.'

Adam kept silent. No mention, he noticed, of the money Abigail had handed over.

While Adam watched tensely, Uncle Ted looked down at the newspaper, then up at Adam again. In the instant when their eyes met, Adam saw his uncle make some quick, sharp calculation. He wasn't really being muddleheaded. He was playing some kind of game.

'If I don't have you to help,' Uncle Ted said, 'I might as well give up the idea of buying uncleared land. If there's just Harry and me ....'

What was Uncle Ted saying – that Adam mattered so much that without him the whole plan would collapse? Could that possibly be true? Of course one person's labour would make a difference, but ....

Then Adam saw what Uncle Ted was up to. He was blaming Adam for his own disappointment – because it didn't take much to see that, in spite of this talk about planning a good life, he *was* disappointed by what he'd found in Upper Canada. He was not the sort of person to blame himself when things turned out badly, so he had to find someone else. It was childish – but then Uncle Ted was in some ways no more than a kid, with his silly expectations, his fits of sulking and anger.

'There's still you and Harry.' Adam heard himself talking as though to a child. 'And I'll be earning wages. I can send you some money every month.'

'It *certainly* means I'll have to take this damned job in Dundas.' He glared at Adam.

Adam said nothing, and Uncle Ted went on. 'You talk as

though you're grown up, able to make your own decisions.'

'I've made this decision, Uncle Ted. I'd like to work at the paper mill.'

Uncle Ted straightened up and leaned towards Adam. 'You're a goddamn *stinker*, kid, for all your namby-pamby airs! I bring you all this way, treat you like a member of the family, and now, when there's a man's work to be done, you duck out, you let me down. Bloody selfish little beast! Bloody *coward!*'

That sent a stabbing pain through Adam, like yesterday but even more agonizing. What a *mean, awful* thing to say!

Hurt, bewildered, stumbling, trying to find some safe ground and also trying not to make things worse, he said, 'I told you I'd give you part of what I earn ....'

Uncle Ted wasn't listening. 'Afraid of work, are you, Adam?' he taunted.

'No, of course not! I'll be working ....'

'Huh!' Uncle Ted grabbed his newspaper in a big, rough handful. With a final disgusted look at Adam, he stamped off down the stairs.

*

Adam, left alone in the attic, was miserable.

Then suddenly he was angry. Why shouldn't he go out and find work, decide what he wanted to do with his life? Uncle Ted's saying that his plans would fail without Adam – that was just bullying. And it was stupid to say that and then accuse Adam of being afraid of work.

And the worst was Uncle Ted's blaming Adam for his own disappointment.

Adam remembered that moment near the bridge, when he'd felt a sort of kinship with Uncle Ted. It was gone now. He hated Uncle Ted.

And now that they'd had this argument, it was even more necessary for Adam to get away. If that meant abandoning

Aunt Lenore ... well, she'd have to manage the best she could. She'd always managed before.

It was a good idea, to leave this man who did not really want him. He was old enough to be on his own. Most kids his age back home worked full time – worked long hours, in fact – living at home or with their employers, apprenticed or earning wages. It turned out all right most of the time. Why shouldn't it turn out all right now?

*

On Sunday evening after dinner, Adam went to the attic and rolled his spare shirt and underwear in a bundle. Then he went back to the Perkinses' kitchen to say goodbye. The family was still at table. Uncle Ted, though not doing anything except smoking his pipe and finishing his whisky, pointedly ignored Adam. Ruth gave him a shy little hug; Ella looked at him with dull eyes; Harry shrugged. It was only Aunt Lenore who really took notice of this important event in Adam's life; she told the girls to stay indoors and then walked with him for the first part of his trip to Todmorden.

'Ted's agreed to take the job in Dundas, Adam,' she said.

'Has he? That's why he's looking so glum, then.'

He himself was unhappy and scared. Now that the moment was here, he didn't want to leave the family – not even to leave the boardinghouse and the Perkinses. There had been too much moving and change in his life lately.

'Well, he half blames you for his having to take this job. I guess you know that.'

'He told me. He called me ... some nasty names. He said I was a rebel. Is this ... getting a job of my own ... rebelling? I thought I was just being sensible, deciding how I wanted to live. His blaming me ... it's not fair. It's not *my* fault that he has to take this job in Dundas, is it?'

'No, Adam, love, of course not. But ... he's got to blame someone. That's the way he is.'

[81]

'His ideas of how it would be here in Canada weren't –
aren't – very sensible.'

'No.'

They walked in silence for a few moments.

'I'm going to miss you, Adam.'

He swallowed. 'Me too. I mean, I'm going to miss you too
– *you*, Aunt Lenore.' He didn't like to say that he would not
miss the rest of the family.

'We'll write letters sometimes. You can always come to me
for help. I may not be able to do much, but I'll be there.'

'I'll help you too, if I can. And I told Uncle Ted I could
send him some of what I earn.'

'That was good of you, Adam. But we'll be earning, too,
for now. Why not keep your money? Save it for when you
need it. It's always handy to have something put by.'

'We'll see,' he said. Maybe it would help him feel less
guilty if he sent them some of his earnings, but there was no
need to decide until he had his first pay packet.

She gave him a very warm hug when they parted. He
looked back after a few yards and found her still watching
him. They waved. The next time he looked back, she was
walking away, her shawl pulled tightly around her so that her
thin shoulders poked the cloth into bumps.

Chapter Eight

WHEN ADAM HAD BEEN at the paper mill on Friday to say that his uncle consented to his taking the job – if 'Go to hell, I don't care what you do' counted as consent – the clerk had told him in which house Mr and Mrs Skinner lived. It was the brick one part-way along the road from the village down to the mills, the one with the view over the valley.

On this Sunday evening, therefore, Adam presented himself at the back door. He was scared at what he had undertaken, and sad to realize that his aunt would miss him. But it would have been far harder to go with them to Dundas and be with Uncle Ted and Harry all the time.

The door was opened by a maidservant, a thin, middle-aged woman with a squint, wearing a cap and a huge apron.

'I'm Adam Wheeler,' he said. 'I've ....'

'Oh, yes, I know about you,' she said briskly. 'Come along in, then. I'm Nelly. I'll show you your bed and then we'll have a cup o' tea and get to know each other.'

She led the way upstairs. At the head of the staircase was an open area like a large landing. Nelly pointed at two doors on the right. 'That's where the Skinners sleep. Mr and Mrs Skinner, and their boy Colin, who's ten. We're over here.'

'Over here' was beyond the open space. Next to a closed door which, Nelly said, was her room, there was an area with a partition but no door.

'This is where you'll sleep.'

Behind the partition was a simple bed with a shelf alongside it and three pegs to hang clothes on. The uncurtained window looked out on the wooded valley wall.

''Tain't luxury,' Nelly said.

'It's fine ... it's nice,' he mumbled, overwhelmed. To him, it *was* luxury. A room of his own, clean and warm and dry, with a real bed and a window! It had never occurred to him that he, as a mere hired hand, might live in such comfort. The boy who worked for his Aunt Kate's husband back home in Petersfield slept under the workbench in the cobbler's shop.

He put his bundle on the bed and then, noticing how untidy that looked, quickly took it up again and set it on the floor. Before going to bed, he'd hang his things on the pegs.

Once they were downstairs again, Nelly gestured to him to sit on the settle near the fire. The rocking chair across from it, which had a piece of knitting lying on the seat, was evidently hers.

The kitchen was a warm and fragrant place, with bunches of herbs and onions hanging from the rafters, a tabby cat washing itself on the hearth, and something simmering over a good fire. On the brick hearth next to Nelly's chair was a tea-pot on a trivet. Nelly poured tea for both of them: a bit of the black stuff from the pot that would have been steeping all day, diluted with water from a gently steaming kettle, and a generous helping of milk and sugar from containers on the table. The black tea and the hot water were just like home, but milk and sugar were rare treats for Adam.

Then she talked. Adam learned that she was a widow with a married daughter and a married son, both of whom urged her to live with one of them, but that she worked because she wanted to be independent.

He learned that, though the village at the top of the hill was generally called Todmorden, the area down here by the Don River, on 'the flats', was usually referred to as 'the Don Mills'. In addition to the paper mill there were a brewery and a distillery operated by the Helliwell family, and a small axe-grinding business owned by a man called Shepard. The Helliwells lived at the Don Mills; the Eastwoods, joint owners with the Skinners of the paper mill, lived in Todmorden village. At the Don Mills there were also some small houses for the Helliwell employees, and several unmarried brewery workers lived in the Helliwells' attic.

Besides that, there were barns for the horses and fodder, and sheds for the equipment and materials connected with the mills.

'So we're quite a village here too,' Nelly said, 'maybe even a bit bigger than Todmorden up at the top o' the hill.'

She told him that the Skinners were out that evening but would be home later.

'Oh, and about meals,' she said. 'In lots o' houses the servants eat with the family, but not here. You 'n' I eat in the kitchen, an' the mill hands, them that don't live nearby, have their dinner here. Bert, who's another hired hand, has his breakfast and dinner with us.'

She asked him about his family, and he told her, saying nothing about his quarrel with Uncle Ted.

'So you're on your own, Adam,' she commented. 'Well, so'm I, in a manner o' speaking. We'll be company for each other.'

After that, abruptly, she sent him to bed, saying that she hoped the chiming of the hall clock didn't wake him every quarter of an hour like it did her.

He wasn't sure he liked being told when to go to bed, just as if he were a little kid, but he obeyed this time. As he came to know her better, he'd figure out how he could go his own way without offending her.

*

The next morning he had breakfast in the kitchen – tea and a big bowl of porridge. He met Bert – if it could be called 'meeting' to be introduced by Nelly and exchange nods but not a single word. He also met Mrs Skinner, a small bustling woman with a preoccupied air, but the son Colin was only a voice shouting in one of the front rooms. The previous evening Adam had woken up when the Skinners came home but had fallen asleep again when the house was quiet. After three months of life on ships and in crowded boardinghouses, he thought, nothing except his own sad and fretful thoughts would keep him awake for very long.

Breakfast over, it was time to go to work. He was scared again. Everything was so strange, and he was more alone than he'd ever been in his life. His feet dragged as he went along the driveway and out to the road.

At that moment, the sun came out from among the clouds and struck the autumn-coloured trees at the far side of the valley into sudden flame. It was an amazing, unbelievable sight, all that gold and orange and crimson rising layer on layer against the far wall of the valley, and for a moment he stood still to soak it in. While he was doing so, a V-shaped flock of birds flew overhead, like an arrow aiming south. By their honking cry and long necks, he thought they might be geese. And when he turned his eyes down again to resume walking, he saw right in front of his feet a tiny animal like a brown-and-white-striped mouse sitting up to look at him, then dashing off high-tailed into the weeds alongside the driveway.

For some reason, Adam felt better. He took a deep breath of the cool, fresh air and walked on with a brisker step.

Once in the mill, he came under the direction of Mr Morris, the overseer and master paper-maker whom he had already met. Mr Morris introduced him to the other work-people – Mrs McDonald and Mrs O'Neill, who cut the rags; Sam, the apprentice; Steven, a nervous fellow of about twenty-five who supervised the Hollander, in which the rags were turned into the pulpy 'stuff'; Abe, a slightly older man who worked at the big paper machine; Steven's cousin Fred, who graded and counted the finished sheets; and Gavin McPhee, the porter and general labourer.

Adam's first task was to fetch wood for the fires that

warmed the stuff and the drying cylinders. Gavin showed him where the woodshed was – behind one of the barns.

'Bert 'n' I do the sawing and heavy splitting,' he said. 'You can help chop kindling.'

Mr Morris told Adam that Sam, the apprentice, as part of learning the trade, started the fires that heated the stuff and the drying cylinders. 'He gets up at three o'clock to start them. When he's done that for a spell longer, you'll take over. Meantime, you can do the stoking during the day. You'll have to learn how to keep everything at just the right temperature, not too hot and not too cool.'

Three o'clock! Adam groaned to himself. He hoped that Sam's 'spell' would last a good while yet.

Then he helped Gavin McPhee wrap stacks of paper to be delivered to the office of the *Constitution*, William Lyon Mackenzie's newspaper in Toronto. He recognized the names: the *Constitution* was one of the newspapers Uncle Ted had read, and Mr Mackenzie was its owner and editor, a man whom Mr Perkins described as a reformer.

'Mr Mackenzie's always bought his paper from us,' Gavin said. 'For the *Colonial Advocate* first an' now this one.' He dropped his voice to a low rumble. 'Good man, Mr Mackenzie. Got the right horse by the tail when he says there's big changes needed in this country. Only it don't do to talk too loud 'cause Mr Morris is a Tory.'

'Tory?'

'Tories is them that favour the government side, the lieutenant governor and the Family Compact. Mr Morris knows I'm Reform but he says as long 's I do my work and don't cause no trouble .... All the same, there's changes coming. Has to be.' Gavin reached for a knife and with a sharp slash cut short the ends of the string he had just tied around a parcel. The abrupt, savage movement was more about politics than packaging paper.

Adam also helped Gavin undo bales of rags – the rags that

[88]

the two women would cut up and that produced the stuff out of which the paper was made.

He asked how the rags were collected. 'Mr Morris told me that they're bought from people in town. How does that work?'

'We got a shop in town, in the Market Square, where they sell books, mainly schoolbooks and bibles and such. Almanacs. Paper hangings – you know, paper to stick on the wall. They also buy rags. Folks in town know they can sell their rags there.'

Adam found the rags disgusting, especially the old clothing – shirts and underwear and other garments too worn-out to repair and not even usable as cleaning cloths or for patching other garments or making rugs. There were also bits which had already been used as cleaning cloths, stained with things like stove black or boot polish.

'How does all this get clean enough to make white paper?' he asked.

'I dunno. That's Mr Morris's problem. But he wants us to throw away the worst of 'em. Like this.' He showed Adam a fragment of cloth that was one mass of axle-grease, then dropped it into a handy bucket.

To Adam's surprise, the morning passed quickly.

At mid-day he and Gavin and most of the workmen went to eat at the Skinner house, where they were joined by Bert. When they entered the kitchen, Nelly handed Adam a big pitcher but spoke to Gavin.

'Mr Skinner says Adam is to run errands for me, so he can fetch the beer from now on. Just show him this once where to go.'

'Sure.' As they went down to the mills again, Gavin said, 'Mr Helliwell, at the brewery, he sells beer to the folks here. 'Tain't a drinking place, not like a tavern, but just for buying an' taking home. You'll do this every dinner-time and supper-time and whenever Nelly asks.'

He led the way to a building which he said was the Helliwell brewery and distillery. Inside the door was a barrel on its side, on a rack, with a spigot inserted. Gavin filled the pitcher, then led the way out again and around to the back door of the Helliwells' house. Without knocking, he opened the door and revealed a kitchen much like Nelly's, with a long table at which workmen were seated, eating. A plump woman was putting wood on the fire.

'Morning, folks,' Gavin said to the men, then added, 'Jug o' beer for the Skinners, Meg.'

The woman nodded without looking up. Gavin came out again, pulling the door shut, and they went back up the hill.

'She keeps track, an' Mr Skinner an' Mr Helliwell settles between 'em.'

The dinner was a thick, tasty soup of meat and vegetables. In addition, the men ate bread and drank whisky, beer, and tea.

When they returned to the mill for the afternoon's work, Adam already felt more at home than he had done that morning.

*

The Don River, high because of the autumn rain but not actually flooding its banks, wound along towards Adam. Its valley lay east-west here, as Adam could tell by the angle of the afternoon sun, and the light shone on the ravine's wall and the choppy hills to his left as he walked upstream – shone on the autumn-coloured trees and lit them into a blaze of brilliant gold and red and bronze. Every time he saw this spectacle, he was amazed and stunned all over again. He'd never seen anything like it in England.

It was Sunday, his free day after the first week in the paper mill. It had been a good week. Mr Morris was reasonable though strict. Gavin McPhee, the person Adam spent most of his time with, had grumpy spells, but was mostly cheerful.

The others ignored Adam except when they had a chore for him to do.

From the talk during meals, Adam was learning a lot about Upper Canada. The main subject was politics. Adam heard all sides: Nelly was considered a moderate reformer – 'luke-warm water', Gavin called her scornfully – and Abe, being British-born, took the Tory side. Away from his superiors, Gavin expressed his radical views boldly. Adam did not understand it all but he gathered that the reformers were angry because ordinary people had no real voice in the government.

'If we had more power,' Gavin said one day, thumping the table with his fist, 'we could fix these things ourselves. *We* know what needs doing.'

'Who's "we"?' Adam asked. He'd learned that no one minded if he asked questions, and he wanted to know what was going on.

'The common people.'

'What sort of power?'

'Political power.'

Adam frowned. 'You mean in the government? Elections? Do you have a ... anything like the House of Commons in England?' He was proud of knowing this. Thank goodness, once more, for Mrs Wright and her little school back home.

'There's this Assembly that gets elected, all right, but anything it decides can be turned down by the Councils and the governor. So it don't have no power.'

'And right now,' Nelly put in, 'the Assembly is Tory anyway, and supports the governor. *You* folks – them that's got the vote – you elected it, so most of *you* must be Tories.'

'*I* didn't elect it,' Gavin fired back. '*I* ain't got the vote. But even when we had a Reform majority in the Assembly it weren't no use.'

'How can you change it?' Adam wondered out loud.

'Mr Mackenzie's got ideas about that.'

On another day, while working in the yard, Adam learned that Mr Eastwood and Mr Skinner were reformers, supporting Mr Mackenzie but, according to Gavin, in a half-hearted way. 'Well, they have to support him, don't they? Mr Mackenzie's *Constitution* is printed on our paper.' He gestured at the neatly wrapped parcels which he had just loaded on the wagon to be taken into the city. 'Mr Helliwell, though, he's Tory.'

'Does that cause trouble?' Adam asked. 'In a small village like this ....'

Gavin shrugged. 'Some. They got other things to fight over too – land boundaries an' such. I don't know nothin' about that. But there's hard words spoken sometimes.' He scowled, his square brown face a mass of wrinkles. 'There's a time comin', mark my words, when there'll be justice and liberty for the common people, for *us!*'

During the week Adam had been busy all day, and was so tired in the evenings that he'd gone to bed early. There'd been no time to brood. Now, wandering along the Don River, he felt lonely. Everyone else was doing whatever they usually did on Sunday. Some of them went to church or chapel, others visited friends or were busy at home.

Adam couldn't visit his family because they had gone to Dundas. On Wednesday, Harry had brought a note from Aunt Lenore to say that they were leaving the next day. Thinking of them was like a sore spot in Adam's mind that hurt every time he touched it. He could not get over his feeling that he'd let them down by going off on his own, and yet his anger at Uncle Ted was as strong as ever. To be called a rebel and blamed for what was Uncle Ted's own fault ...!

He tried not to think about it. To distract himself, he concentrated on exploring the valley.

He had come perhaps a couple of miles when, rounding a bend, he saw another mill, and a house or two. This was no surprise. He had learned that there were mills at what was called the Forks of the Don, where the east and west branches of the river met.

While looking around him, he was startled by the sound of thudding hooves. A pony came into sight, pounding along with reins and stirrups flying. A moment later there appeared, also running, one of the girls he had seen on horseback ten days earlier, near the bridge. It was the thinner one.

'Hey, there!' she shouted breathlessly when she saw Adam. 'Help me catch that horse!'

Adam knew better than to try to stop a galloping horse directly, but he stretched out his arms and drove it towards a bank of dense undergrowth fringing the path. The pony came to a halt, and Adam grabbed the bridle.

The young lady ran up, panting, took the bridle from Adam, and gentled the horse, which was tossing its head and stamping. This time she was dressed in a far-from-new riding habit. The skirt, longer on the left so that it would cover her feet when she was in the saddle, was hooked up to allow her to walk without tripping, and in her headlong run she had gathered it still higher to reveal scuffed boots. Her face was flushed and worried.

When she had made sure that the horse was not hurt and was calming down, she looked at Adam.

'It was a wasp, I think,' she said. 'There are always so many of them in the autumn, aren't there?' Then she added, 'Oh! You're the boy we saw ....'

'At the bridge last week. Yes, I am.'

'Well ... thank you for helping me to catch Nipper.' She smiled, poised and polite again in spite of her anxiety.

'I was glad to help,' Adam said. 'Handsome horse.'

'Father likes us to have good mounts. He says we mustn't let our standards slip any more than we have to. He won't let the servants eat with us, even though almost everyone else here does that.' Suddenly aware, she gave Adam another glance. 'I'm sorry! Are you ...?'

He drew himself up. 'I work in the paper mill.' That was better than being a domestic servant.

She gave him a quick, assessing glance that made her look older than she was. 'We all work at something, here.'

It was true: everyone *did* work, it seemed. As Adam had learned, in Upper Canada the British system of class distinctions mingled with more democratic American ways. Gentlemen settlers cleared land, milked cows, took their produce to market – things which no gentleman in England would ever do. On the other hand, almost any Upper Canadian farmer, whatever his background in the old country, could make his way into the ranks of the gentry – with hard work and a helping of luck. Servants did indeed, almost everywhere, eat at the same table as their employers. All this had not erased class differences, only complicated them.

There was not the slightest question of where this young lady fitted. Her accent was that of the gentry – in fact, of the gentry in the part of England where Adam came from. It was very different from the Yorkshire accent of Mr Eastwood and Mr Helliwell, the Yankee voices of Mr Morris and Mr Skinner, the Irish-American of Gavin McPhee.

Whatever the young lady's conclusions about Adam, she did not mount and ride away, and she made no objection as Adam walked along with her, back the way she had come.

When they had passed beyond a clump of dense brush, they saw a horseman cantering towards them. It was the gentleman whom Adam had seen with the two girls near the bridge.

'There you are, Cornelia,' he said, reining in. 'Dan saw you fall off and the pony bolting. I came to see ....'

Having just identified the young lady's accent as southern-English, Adam was extremely surprised to find that the gentleman, who he assumed was her father, spoke in an accent that did not sound at all English.

'It was probably a wasp,' Cornelia said, blushing. 'I'm sorry, father.'

What was she apologizing for? Falling off? Causing her father anxiety? Adam had no idea.

The gentleman looked at Adam. 'Hello, young man.'

'He helped catch Nipper,' Cornelia said.

'Oh! Thank you,' the gentleman said. His manner was dignified and distant – *he* had no doubt about where Adam fitted in – but he was the sort who would be polite to inferiors, especially when they caught runaway horses.

Something obstinate in Adam – or perhaps it was the loneliness – made him refuse to leave it at that.

'My name is Adam Wheeler, sir. I work at the paper mill and live with the Skinners.' He gestured downstream.

'How do you do, Adam,' the gentleman said with a nod. 'My name is de Grassi, Captain de Grassi, and this is my daughter Cornelia. Are you a newcomer?'

'Yes, sir. I arrived in Toronto only two weeks ago.'

'With your family, I presume.'

'An uncle and aunt, but they've gone to Dundas.'

'Where are you from? I detect an accent from somewhere in Sussex or Hampshire.'

'Near Petersfield, sir. Just east of there, in Sussex.'

Captain de Grassi smiled. 'Ah, yes. I have travelled through Petersfield. I lived in Chichester, in Sussex, for some years before coming here, but I am originally Italian, as you might be able to guess from the name.'

Adam knew nothing about Italian names, but he nodded politely.

These civilities over, Captain de Grassi looked at his daughter. 'We'd best be going home, Cornelia. Can you mount, or will you lead the pony?'

He gave a quick glance at Adam. If Adam had been their groom, it would have been his duty to help her mount, linking his hands stirrup-fashion for her to step on and lifting her into the saddle. For an instant Adam wondered whether he should, but he decided not to. So far as he could tell, in

Upper Canada there was nothing to be gained – except in the wrong way, with the wrong people – by putting yourself in the position of a servant. He did not expect to be treated as an equal by the de Grassi family, but he need not *make* himself inferior.

While her father talked to Adam, Cornelia had inspected the saddle. She made sure that the strap under the horse's belly was securely buckled and then led the animal to a log lying alongside the path. When her father asked whether she could mount, she stepped on the log, set her left foot in the stirrup, and swung her right leg with a swish of skirt over the saddle, then curved it back again so that the right knee was hooked around the leaping head and the right foot on the left side of the saddle. She wiggled herself into position, adjusted her skirt so that it covered her legs properly, and then looked at her father, presenting herself for his approval, though she also gave a tiny glance out of the corner of her eye at Adam.

Adam had never before observed a woman getting into a side-saddle by herself. He'd once, when passing an inn, seen a groom help a very elegant lady rider onto her horse, but watching Cornelia was different. He'd been interested to see how easily she moved under that bulky skirt – almost like a boy – but no boy mounting a horse would have given him that twitch in his insides, that stirring as she pulled herself up, stretching the short jacket tightly against her body, and then swung her leg over the saddle and curved it sideways in front of her.

Cornelia spoke to her father. 'The only thing I don't have is my hat. It fell off. Can we send Dan to look for it?'

'Certainly, my dear.'

With a nod at Adam, he half-turned his horse, waiting for Cornelia to precede him.

She gave Adam a friendly look. 'Goodbye, Adam. Thank you again.'

She wheeled and rode up the track.

The gentry on their horses, Adam thought, watching them. Just like back home. Ordinary folks like him walked, whether short distances or long, unless they had reason to travel by the carrier's cart. The gentry, on the other hand, always had horses – saddle-horses, hunters, ponies for the children, wonderful matched teams to pull their carriages. Outdoors they were hardly ever on foot. In that way, Canada was no different from England.

Yet Cornelia de Grassi had been on foot at first, and she'd been friendly. He'd had more contact with her in those few moments before her father arrived than he'd ever had with gentlefolks back home. It was something – but it made him feel even lonelier as he turned to go back the way he had come. He would have liked to continue walking up the valley, but it would look as though he were following the two riders, as though he wanted further attention or was nosy about where they lived. So, hands in pockets, brooding and yet absent-minded, kicking at stones and projecting roots, he went home.

Chapter Nine

EVERTHELESS, TO HIS PLEASURE, Adam did see the de Grassi family again. It appeared that Mrs Skinner knew them. One evening at the end of October, two weeks after his meeting Cornelia de Grassi and her father on that Sunday afternoon, she sent Adam to their house on an errand.

'Mrs de Grassi's servant is sick. Poor thing – I mean poor Mrs de Grassi, because she's not a very good manager, and her eyesight is failing. I want you to take this basket to her. Only soup and muffins, but it'll help. Tell her to keep the soup crock until next time. To get there, go up the hill and turn left in Todmorden village, the road that takes you *away* from Toronto. Keep going till the next settlement – that's the Forks of the Don – and then ask for the de Grassi house. You'd best take a lantern.'

He fetched a lantern from the shed, lit the candle in it, and set off.

He enjoyed the walk. The autumn night was crisp but not cold, and he liked the sense of being out in the immense spaces – the space of this enormous country where everything was so much larger than what he had been used to, and the space of the great starry night around him. For several days it had rained, but today had been clear and tonight the sky was full of stars.

After three weeks at the paper mill, he was beginning to have a sense of belonging. He stoked the fires that kept the stuff and the drying cylinders warm – only in the daytime, because Sam still started the fires at three o'clock in the morning – and he carried fuel. He helped the women to sort and cut rags, and Gavin McPhee to pack the finished paper.

He swept the floors and cleaned Mr Skinner's and Mr Carver's small rooms.

He was also picking up knowledge about paper-making. Steven showed him how the stuff ought to look when it was ready to move to the holding vat, and from Fred he learned about the blemishes and damage to be watched for when sorting the paper into grades.

Abe never talked about his work when he didn't have to – all he was interested in was girls.

And here Adam was on a Monday evening at the end of October walking along a track of frozen ruts, to deliver soup and muffins to the de Grassi family, just as though he had dwelt among these people all his life.

Once at the Forks of the Don, he asked further directions of a man on horseback just turning in at a gate. The man pointed to another house with a few windows lit.

Adam went to it and knocked. During the walk he had debated with himself whether to go to the back door or the front, and he had decided on the front.

It was opened by Cornelia, the girl whose runaway horse he had helped to catch. She was holding a candle.

'Hello,' he said.

'Good evening!' She recognized him but apparently couldn't recall where she had seen him before. Then she remembered. 'Oh! You're ....'

'Adam Wheeler. We met when ....'

'You caught Nipper for me.'

'I've brought some things from Mrs Skinner to your mother.' He moved the basket to where the candlelight caught it but not far enough forward to suggest that he wanted to hand it over.

'That's kind of her.'

'She heard that Mrs de Grassi's servant was ill.'

'Yes, she is. Come along. Mama is in the kitchen.' She led the way along the central passage to the back of the house.

'Mama, here's someone with a basket from Mrs Skinner.'

Mrs de Grassi was washing dishes. When Cornelia announced Adam's arrival, she dried her hands and peered at him through her spectacles. At the same time, from a pantry, came the other young lady whom Adam had seen on horseback at the bridge that day, the plumper one. All three wore big, sensible aprons, but the gowns underneath were those of the gentry, not of countrywomen.

The plump girl, after a quick smile at Adam, began removing freshly made candles from the sticks between two chairbacks on which they had been hanging to cool.

Cornelia took her mother's place at the dishpan.

'From Mrs Skinner?' Mrs de Grassi asked, in an English accent like Cornelia's. 'How very kind of her.' She glanced back and forth between Adam and the basket, as though not quite sure what to do about them.

Just then the back door burst open, admitting Captain de Grassi and another gentleman.

'My dear,' Captain de Grassi said to his wife, 'Willis here brings us dreadful news. The governor has sent away all the troops from our garrison to help deal with the unrest in Lower Canada. That leaves the store of arms unprotected. I can't believe that he would be so foolish!'

'There will be a constable or two, I understand,' the other man murmured, embarrassed by Captain de Grassi's vehemence.

'A constable or two! We know what *that* means – no dependable guard whatsoever, not a real *military* guard. And at the very moment when there are signs of trouble in this part of the country too – that frightful Mackenzie fellow with his rabble-rousing newspaper, these so-called military trainings of men opposed to the government, these meetings and scuffles ....'

Adam listened with interest. By now he'd heard a lot about the discontent in the province, but most of it came from

Gavin, who favoured the Reform side and considered the discontent a good thing because it showed that the ordinary people were waking up.

Captain de Grassi, by contrast, was angry and worried, almost as if the protest were directed at him personally. Perhaps, Adam thought, that was how people in power felt when the lower classes demanded change. At the time of the riots back home he'd heard only the grievances of the labourers who were rising up against their employers. Now he saw how a member of the ruling classes viewed such things.

'The governor insists that there *is* no unrest here and that if any should develop it can be handled by the militia,' said Mr Willis.

Captain de Grassi scowled darkly. 'He is mistaken!' he said, his Italian accent suddenly even stronger. 'Who knows how many of the militia can be relied upon? If the reformers actually begin mustering men, how many of the militia will join *their* ranks rather than ours, the side loyal to the Crown?' Suddenly he turned to Adam. 'You, lad, you work for Eastwood and Skinner, I seem to recall. They are known to favour Reform. What do you hear about this matter? Do they boast about the number of militia who would rally to their cause?'

'I've never heard them *boast*, sir. I hardly see Mr Eastwood, and ....'

'I don't know whether Eastwood and Skinner really count, Captain,' Mr Willis said. 'After all, they make the paper on which Mackenzie prints that filthy rag of his. They *have* to pay him lip service at least.'

Captain de Grassi took no notice. He was still staring at Adam, demanding an answer. 'But you must hear something. It's well known that some of the mill folk in town are as radical as the farmers in York County who elected Mackenzie to the Assembly over and over again. There are radicals – reformers is too mild a word – right in the city. It wasn't the *farmers* who elected Mackenzie mayor of Toronto three years ago – it was the people of Toronto. The hands in Armstrong's axe-grinding factory and in Dutcher's foundry are reputed to be ....' He threw up his hands as though words failed him to describe how radical the mill workers were. Then he looked at Adam, still expecting an answer to his question.

'One of our people says he's radical, sir, but I've never heard him speak of numbers.'

'Does he talk about rebellion, about the use of force against the government?'

'Philip, my dear,' Mrs de Grassi interrupted, 'is it quite fair to make the boy speak about his employers and fellow-workers behind their backs? Only think – if he should lose his position on account of it ....' She turned to Adam. 'I'm sorry, boy, I don't even know your name.'

'It's Adam Wheeler, ma'am.'

Captain de Grassi gave a sigh. 'You're right, my dear. My concern for the situation led me too far. But I'm so worried about this foolish action of the governor's – foolhardy, even. I know that Colonel FitzGibbon of the militia takes all this training and the formation of political unions very seriously. He's a military man, as I am, and His Excellency is *not!* It takes a military man to sense when trouble is brewing. The unrest in the lower province ...! These things *spread.* And political unions ...! We know about them from England. They claim to press for peaceful reform but in England, as we saw, they led to mass protests, to the Reform Bill. And the same will happen here, I warrant you. *Any* gatherings of the restless and rebellious among the common people must be viewed with the greatest alarm. Only Colonel FitzGibbon, he alone among the men close to the governor, seems to see it.'

'William Allan is, I understand, also of your mind,' said Mr Willis.

'*Is* he? *Is* he, now? I'm relieved to hear it. Very relieved to hear it.' Captain de Grassi, not looking at all relieved, stared broodingly ahead of him for a few moments, then roused himself.

'Thank you for bringing this news, Willis, distressing as it is. I will fetch the newspaper which you came to borrow.' And he went off towards the front of the house.

While he was gone, Mrs de Grassi unpacked the basket, then looked at her daughters with a bewildered expression. 'I always like to put something in a basket so as not to return it empty,' she said, 'but what *can* I put in it? Charlotte? Cornelia?'

So the plump daughter was named Charlotte. The two girls were very close in age – Charlotte was probably the older – and both had their father's dark colouring. Cornelia appeared to be livelier, and Charlotte was quieter but not at all shy. While putting the candles into their metal container, she had listened intently to the conversation.

It was Cornelia who answered her mother's question about what to put in the basket. 'All I can think of is one of the kittens,' she suggested with a laugh, 'but I hardly think it's fair to give someone a kitten without asking first.'

'Of course we can't give Mrs Skinner a kitten,' Charlotte said firmly.

'A few new-laid eggs?' Mrs de Grassi wondered aloud. 'But we haven't overly many for ourselves, with the number declining again.' She had the air of someone burdened by problems piling endlessly on top of each other.

Captain de Grassi returned with a newspaper, which he handed to his friend. 'This is the latest from Chichester. My London papers are at present in the hands of another friend but I will pass them on to you when I can.'

'Thank you, Captain. As always, I take this as a great kindness.'

'Not at all, not at all.'

Meanwhile, the de Grassi women had agreed among

themselves that the only thing available to send to Mrs Skinner was a few apples. 'She probably has plenty of apples herself,' Charlotte objected, but her mother insisted that the basket must *not* go back empty. So Cornelia fetched half a dozen apples from another room, laid them carefully in the basket, and tucked the cloth covering around them.

'We'll see you again, I hope,' Cornelia said when she showed him out.

As he walked home, he wondered what he could possibly have done – what impression he could have given – that would make them wish to see him again. It seemed to him that he had been very silent and stupid, standing there in the kitchen, unable to answer Captain de Grassi's questions – just a boy with a basket.

But he also hoped to see them again.

*

After a few dry days, the wet weather returned. It made a nearly impassable swamp of the Mill Road, the road that led from near the east end of the Don Bridge to the village of Todmorden and the Forks of the Don. Mr Helliwell, driving the brewery wagon to Toronto to deliver beer, got stuck and returned on foot to fetch a team of oxen to help pull the wagon out of the mud.

Mr Eastwood, coming home on horseback, had to make a detour through the woods to avoid the worst stretch, and after leaving the horse in his own stable he came down to the paper mill to have a word with Mr Skinner. Then he summoned Adam.

'We're going to have to put brush on that road again,' he said. Seeing Adam's look of puzzlement, he explained. 'When the road is very bad, some of us bring our teams and haul brush out of the woods to spread on the mud. It's best if we have several men with teams working together. We want you to go up the road tonight and ask Sinclair if he's free tomorrow.'

That evening Adam delivered the message. On his way home, as he was passing through Todmorden, the door of the alehouse crashed open, releasing an explosion of noise from inside. Two men stumbled out into the darkness, fighting as they came, and continued their fight on the ground outside so that Adam had to dart briskly out of the way.

'It's that Gavin McPhee again,' said a woman behind Adam, and the light from her lantern showed that indeed one of the men was Gavin.

'I'm not surprised. He was talkin' rough at dinner.'

That was Nelly's voice. Adam looked up, thinking that she was addressing him, but she was talking to the woman with the lantern, who was a sturdy older person – a country-woman, to judge by her dress. Beyond her, also pausing on their way to somewhere else, was a younger couple who appeared to be gentry.

As Adam looked up, Nelly recognized him. 'Hello there, Adam.'

'Hello,' he said, shy at being addressed in this adult company. 'What ... what d'you suppose they're fighting about?'

'The usual, I guess. Politics. You heard Gavin at dinner, goin' on and on about it and drinkin' more than's good for him. He gets like that in his moods.'

Gavin's 'moods', as Nelly called them, were not merely the daily ups and downs of his temper. They were spells of gloom and anger and too much drinking, and political talk that was even more hot-headed than usual. That evening he had helped himself generously to the whisky, and Nelly had given Adam a significant look.

Gavin had got onto the notion of Upper Canada separating from Britain and joining the United States. 'If they'll have us, the mess we're in,' he added bitterly. He himself had lived in the United States for a few years after leaving Ireland and regularly talked about going back there.

Now he was taking out his grievances in physical action.

His face was bloody and his clothes rumpled.

'Stupid to get hurt over politics,' Nelly scoffed.

'I'd rather have a man what *cares* about things,' said the other woman, 'than one o' them sissies .... Any road, I agree with him. Time someone spoke out and *did* something about that bunch what gets all the gravy and leaves us naught but dry potatoes ... if *that!*'

The male member of the young couple spoke up. 'If you hate Tories so much, Mrs Murphy,' he said sarcastically, in an English accent, 'I hope you don't put ground glass in the stew that you serve to your Tory guests!'

So the countrywoman with the lantern was Mrs Murphy. Adam had heard of her. She was a friend of Nelly's, a widow who owned a small farm in Todmorden and who, to help make ends meet, rented out a room or two in her house whenever she could. Being a widow and an owner of land, she had the vote. In the arguments that raged in Nelly's kitchen, Mrs Murphy was used as an example to show that the Assembly in Upper Canada was elected by a larger proportion of the population – 'some women, even!' – than the House of Commons in Britain.

'Are you a Tory, Mr Johnson?' Mrs Murphy asked in an unfriendly tone. 'You support that lot of ...?'

'Steady, now, Mrs Murphy,' Nelly said. 'Your guests can think whatever they like. No business of yours.'

Mrs Murphy snorted. 'Well, if they can't see how corrupt that crowd of spongers is, appointing their friends to everything, keeping all the power to theirselves ....'

'The Councils may be appointed, Mrs Murphy,' the young gentleman said patronizingly, 'but the people elect the Assembly. That's their voice in the government.'

'Mrs Murphy is one of the voters,' Nelly put in.

The young lady with Mr Johnson stared in disbelief at Mrs Murphy, as though wondering how such a person came to have the vote.

Mrs Murphy ignored both her and Nelly. 'Sure – we can elect a Reform Assembly all we like but it don't have no power. If the Council and the governor paid heed to the Assembly, like Mr Mackenzie thinks they should, it'd be different. An' the Family Compact holding most o' the land for theirselves, keeping other folk from settling near the towns ....'

Mr Johnson interrupted. 'That's all been changed, Mrs Murphy, as I'm sure you must be aware.'

'The Clergy Reserves ...,' she began.

'Yes, land was set aside for the clergy and the Crown at first. But ....'

'An' a terrible thing it was too, big blocks o' land with nobody living on them, nobody to help make roads an' ....'

'Mrs Murphy,' Mr Johnson said, overriding her, 'that's been *changed*. Those reserves have been put up for sale now and settlers are buying them.'

'I know some of them have been, and not before time neither. But there's still that big chunk near here.' She gestured eastwards. 'No talk of it being sold to settlers, so far's I've heard.'

Adam had lingered to listen to the talk. He was in no hurry to go home, especially if Nelly wasn't there.

'An' with all the important jobs like magistrate and sheriff all over the province goin' to the friends of the Family Compact ...,' Mrs Murphy muttered.

'They go to those qualified to do them,' Mr Johnson said. 'We can't have ignorant people holding positions like that.'

'They aren't all ignorant. An' how do you know they can't do the work if you don't give 'em a chance?'

'And make a hash of it while being "given a chance"!' he sneered. 'I call that "*taking* a chance" – a frightfully dangerous chance!'

'Are you one of those who actually favour armed rebellion, Mrs Murphy?' the young English lady asked in a voice pretending to be sweet but actually as sharp as broken bottles.

'If that's what it takes to get liberty and justice ....'

'Rebellion against the *Queen*?'

Adam had noticed before how reverently people spoke of the young Queen Victoria, only eighteen years old, who had come to the throne that spring. He wondered whether they had referred that way to old King William.

'We can have change without rebellion,' Nelly said. 'Rebellion means fighting, people getting killed ....'

They all looked at the fight in front of them, which was ending. Gavin, sitting on the ground, was wiping his bloody nose with a bloody handkerchief, and the other man was on his feet, leaning over him, his hands braced against his knees.

'Damn it, McPhee, if you hadn't made me so mad with your talk about us joining the American states ... I can't stand that sort o' nonsense.'

'Hell of a lot better than what we got.'

'Then go back there. We don't need the likes o' you here.'

Gavin McPhee merely shook his head, still silently arguing.

''Tain't such a bad place ...,' the other man began.

'It could be a great place if it was run better,' Gavin said.

'Oh, go to hell,' the man growled, walking away.

Adam said quietly to Nelly, 'Do you think Gavin's all right? Should we help him get home?' Gavin McPhee boarded with the family that occupied one of the workers' cottages near the mills.

'No need, lad. He'll be okay. He's been in fights worse'n this, and he always gets home. But you better run along. I'm goin' to have a cup o' tea and a visit with Mrs Murphy – that's what I come for.'

Chapter Ten

 WEEK LATER, ADAM was given a different assignment. By now it was the middle of November, and on a dark, drizzly morning, while Adam and Bert were still eating breakfast, Mr Skinner came into the kitchen.

'I want you to go into town and do a couple of errands, Adam. You can ride. Any sort of horseman, are you?'

'Not really, sir. I rode the farm horses back home a few times, when a boy was needed to guide them ....'

'Then it'll be Princess. She's old and quiet and won't get you into trouble.' Mr Skinner turned to Bert. 'You saddle Princess for Adam. Show him how, so he can do it himself from now on.'

Bert nodded.

Mr Skinner gave Adam his instructions. There was a letter to be taken to the post office and parcels to be delivered to the Eastwood and Skinner shop and to Mrs Thomas Helliwell. He handed them over, together with a leather satchel to keep them dry.

Adam knew about the Thomas Helliwells, the branch of the family that lived in town. Thomas Helliwell was a brother of William, and there were other brothers and sisters. It was William who lived here at the Don Mills and managed the brewery and distillery in partnership with their mother, Mrs Sarah Helliwell. Thomas, the brother living in Toronto, handled the administration of the firm and sold the finished products to the public; he was also a director of the Bank of Upper Canada.

The Helliwells and the Skinners were related, Mrs Skinner being the sister of Thomas and William Helliwell.

'When you're at the post office,' Mr Skinner said, 'ask if there are letters for anyone here at the Mills. Mr Howard will probably give them to you as a matter of course, but if he doesn't, be sure to ask. Here's money for postage, and for the tollgate.'

Mr Skinner also gave directions. Both the Helliwell house and the Eastwood and Skinner shop were on the Market Square, he said, and the post office was on Duke Street, just a block or two away.

With his cap pulled down and his coat collar turned up against the wet, Adam set off for Toronto.

The rain had again transformed the road into a swamp. It was nearly a week since the neighbours had gathered with their teams to haul brush out of the woods and spread it on the road. The brush had done some good at the time, but since then the heavy wagons and carts passing over it had shredded it and pressed the fragments down into the mud. Adam guided Princess to the side of the road where, close to the farm fences or the uncleared bush, there was the best chance of finding solid ground.

This was Adam's first trip to town since the Sunday evening, five weeks ago, when he had arrived at the Don Mills with his belongings in a bundle. He remembered how scared and lonely he'd been. Since starting to become a part of the village he felt better, though sometimes the loneliness returned.

Of all the new people he'd met, only Nelly seemed to have room and time for him. Most evenings, the two of them sat by the kitchen fire talking while she sewed or knitted. Often they merely went over the day's events, but once he had found himself telling her more about his mother and grandfather and Mrs Wright, and about how he had been handed over like a parcel to Uncle Ted and Aunt Lenore. Nelly, though quite a talker when she wanted to be, was also a good listener. Sometimes, in bed at night, Adam thought he must bore her terribly. But she didn't seem bored; she'd listen carefully, her mob–capped head bent over her work except when she looked up at him with her squinting eyes, and later she'd show that she remembered what he said. It was almost as though Nelly *was* family.

All the same, there were times when he felt very much alone.

And yet, would he be less lonely if he lived with Aunt Lenore and Uncle Ted? All during the journey from England, when he had been crowded together with them and with all those other people on the ship, he'd felt alone.

The people he really missed were his mother and grandpa, and nothing could bring them back. The next best was Aunt Lenore, who had moved away at the very moment when he was coming to love her.

Well, at least she was still alive and not too far off.

Meanwhile, he found himself a bit comforted by the quiet of the surroundings, the farms and forest and, today, the peaceful rain.

*

Toronto, when he reached it, looked oddly familiar, as though he had lived there for much longer than that one week at Mrs Perkins'.

He went first to the Helliwell house on the Market Square. Mrs Helliwell was not at home but he didn't need to see her personally. He handed the cloth–wrapped parcel to the maid-servant. Then, leading Princess, he walked to the Eastwood and Skinner shop, which was only a few doors away. He hitched Princess to a rail and went in.

The shop was small and, at that moment, empty. While waiting for someone to come, Adam looked around with interest at this branch of the firm he worked for.

A door in the middle of the back wall led to the rest of the house where, no doubt, the manager lived. Along one side of the shop ran a counter behind which were shelves of mer-chandise. The firm printed schoolbooks like spellers and readers, and also New Testaments, almanacs, and blank books. There was what looked like writing paper in neat bundles, each held together by a paper band. Several shelves bore rolls of what he guessed were the paper hangings Gavin had mentioned. Two lengths of wallpaper, partly unrolled to reveal the design, hung against the wall opposite the counter.

The door at the back opened and a thin little man in shirt-sleeves and a waistcoat hurried in, wiping his hands on his apron.

'Sorry, sorry, young sir, sorry to keep you waiting. I was busy baling rags to go to the mill. What can I help you with today? A spelling book? Or, no, you look like a chap with a mathematical bent. Here I have for you ....'

Adam interrupted. 'No, please, I'm not a customer. I work at the mill, and I've come to deliver this from Mr Skinner.' He laid the parcel on the counter.

'Oh! Oh! That's different!' The man looked from Adam to the package and back again. 'Work at the mill, do you? Apprentice?'

'General chores.'

'Well! Isn't that something!' Since there was no point in promoting the merchandise, the little man was at a loss for words.

Adam turned to the door. 'That's all I came for, to deliver the parcel. Good day to you.'

'Good day, good day. A wet one – but it can still be a good one. And it may clear up.'

He bobbed his head in farewell.

On the street again, Adam realized that he was unsure where the post office was – Mr Skinner's 'turn left' and 'turn right' had got muddled in his mind. So he asked a passerby, a woman carrying a basket and leading a child by the hand. She explained and pointed: up to King Street, turn right, go for two blocks, then left on George Street to Duke. Next to the bank, on the north side of Duke.

As Adam rode in that direction, his mind was on the books in the shop. Now that he was engaged in making paper, he felt a close connection with books. The only ones he'd seen so far in his life, other than his grandfather's and Uncle Ted's family Bibles, were the few belonging to Mrs Wright. Her late husband, being a rector, had owned a Bible and several volumes of sermons, but he had been interested in geography and possessed an atlas and three or four books of travellers' accounts. All were old and dilapidated, probably bought second-hand or passed on from family or friends, but Adam had loved them. He only wished that there had been something about North America in them but, except for a map or two in the atlas, they dealt only with Africa and India. Still, they had given Adam a sense of the larger world, of distance and history, of places where trees and houses looked different.

Civilized things, books, he had thought.

*

The post office was a new, handsome building with a flight of steps up to its door. Inside, there was a counter with pigeon-holes behind it. An elderly gentleman was doing business with the postmaster, and a woman stood to one side, reading a letter.

When Adam's turn came, he handed over the letter which Mr Skinner wanted to have mailed. As he did so, he thought briefly of Abigail, handing him over to Uncle Ted. Here's a parcel, here's money for the postage . . . .

He put it out of his mind.

'To Boston,' the postmaster said, reading the address. 'That means *you* have to pay the postage to Lewiston, at the U. S. border, and the folks in Boston pay the rest.'

'All right. And are there any letters for the Skinners – for anyone at the Don Mills?'

The postmaster pulled two letters out of a pigeon-hole. 'One for Mrs Eastwood,' he said, 'and one for "Adam Wheeler,

Todmorden".' Want to take that along too, kid? I don't recall seeing the name before, but someone there'll know.'

'That's me!' Adam said, surprised.

'Is it? Well, then ....' He looked at a list. 'From Dundas ... let's see ... that'll cost you fourpence ha'p'ny.'

On the counter, Adam laid the money Mr Skinner had given him and out of which he'd already paid the penny toll at the bridge.

'Fourpence ha'p'ny?' he asked, looking in puzzlement from the coins to the postmaster. 'That's *English* money, but here they also talk about dollars, which is American.'

The postmaster chuckled. 'Confusing, eh? No wonder. We use both here. It'll have to be sorted out some day.' He reached over to spread out the coins from Adam's pocket. 'That's fourpence, and here's a ha'p'ny.'

The ha'p'ny was literally half of a penny, a coin chopped in half. 'Is that how they make them here?' Adam asked.

'Not officially. It shows that someone somewhere once needed half a penny so he cut a penny piece in two. My wife grumbles because the rough edges wear holes in my pockets.'

Adam looked at the money that the postmaster had sorted out. Then something occurred to him and he shot out his hand to cover the coins before the postmaster could take them.

'Wait a minute! That's Mr Skinner's money! I can't use it for *my* letter! And there's still the letter to Boston to pay for, and the one that arrived for Mrs Eastwood. And I have to pay the toll at the bridge when I go home.' He looked at the postmaster again. It was all too complicated; he'd hardly ever in his life had any money to handle and, even without the confusion between English and American, he didn't know how to work it out. No one, not even Mrs Wright, had told him how to deal with money in Canada. It was embarrassing, but he couldn't help it.

The postmaster was obviously used to this. He did a quick

calculation in his head. 'You need three shillings sevenpence altogether.'

'I'll need a penny for the toll at the bridge.'

'Did you come through the tollgate this morning?' When Adam nodded, he said, 'Then you can return free today. You only pay once if you come into town and go back the same day.'

He reached over and counted the rest of Adam's money. 'You've got three shillings eightpence altogether, lad. That's enough to pay for the letters, and there's a penny over.'

'Does that include the one to me?' Adam asked anxiously. He couldn't bear to leave it behind.

'That one too.'

'Is it all right to use Mr Skinner's money for my letter?'

'You'll find it's okay. I know Colin Skinner. He'll let you pay him back.'

Adam put one penny in his pocket and slid the rest across the counter to the postmaster. In return he received the letters.

'Thank you, sir,' he said. He still didn't really understand about the two kinds of money but he'd ask Nelly.

'Glad to be of help.'

Adam put the letter to Mrs Eastwood in his satchel. The one to himself he held in his hand. He *had* to read it right away. During the talk about postage he had pushed aside his anxiety but now it flooded in. Dundas! It could only be from Aunt Lenore, and he was terribly afraid that it might bring bad news. Turning away from the counter, he opened the letter then and there.

Dear Adam,

This is to let you know that we are all fine, the house is small only one room but the roof keeps most of the rain out. Ted doesnt like the work much and is in with some men they call reformers who are all for changing the government or joining the american states or I dont know

*what all and Im worried about that but I dont think anything will
come of it. You know he doesnt like work and I think he thinks that
changing things will mean no more work but an easy life. Weve all had
colds but are better now except Ella who is poorly. I work in the house
its long hours but with our own shanty being only one room theres not
much to do in it so I guess I cant complain and I earn a bit. I like missis
Manley shes no lady but a good soul and sometimes gives me left overs
and an old coat for me to make over for Harry. Shes got three children
who are little devils. Dear Adam I just want to say I miss having you
with us Im sorry you stayed behind but I understand and Dundas isnt
so very far so maybe we can visit sometime and when you get a chance
you can write a letter. I have to stop now but Im thinking of you and
your poor mother and love from your aunt Lenore.*

It brought the tears stinging to Adam's eyes. Fancy Aunt
Lenore writing to him – and missing his company.

The actual news didn't matter. He was not surprised at his
uncle taking up with the reformers, after having been active
in the Swing riots back home. Ella was never well, and Aunt
Lenore seemed to be working as hard as always.

More important, the letter spoke of need and longing, of
his aunt's real life. He wondered suddenly: had she *wanted* to
come to Canada? It had never crossed his mind before. She'd
had a hard life back home, living in a dirt-floored labourer's
cottage and working in the fields or at whatever else would
earn a few pennies to add to Uncle Ted's low wages and the
money doled out to them by the parish. But she had friends
there. Was she lonely now? Who did she talk to? Could she
really talk to Uncle Ted?

He was bothered. He'd always assumed that of course hus-
bands and wives talked to each other. They did it all the time,
didn't they? But something in the letter made him wonder.
Naturally his aunt and uncle discussed ordinary things. But
what about their worries, their feelings, their dreams?

He himself was sometimes lonely because ... well, because

of his mother dying and now because he had no family at all near him. But did Aunt Lenore, with a husband and three children right there, also feel lonely? Did she ever cry in bed at night, as he sometimes did? If she cried, did she turn away from Uncle Ted or could she turn to him for a hug?

It was uncomfortable even to think such things about his aunt and uncle, but he wanted to try to understand.

Abruptly the door of the post office opened to admit more customers – who turned out to be Charlotte and Cornelia de Grassi, talking and laughing.

Adam was standing to one side, and in the dim room they didn't see him.

'Hello, Mr Howard,' Cornelia said. 'Any letters for us or anyone at the Forks?'

'Good morning, miss. No, nothing for anyone there. I hope you and your family are keeping well in spite of the wet weather.'

'Yes, thank you, Mr Howard. Good day.'

'Good day, miss.'

As she turned away from the counter, she saw Adam.

'Oh, hello, there!'

'Hello.'

'No post for us so we're going home. If you've finished your business in town, let's go together. Is that your horse outside?'

'Yes, I've finished.'

Outside, their ponies were being held by a groom, who had a horse of his own but was at this moment on foot. He helped them mount. When he too was in the saddle, Charlotte said, 'Thank you, Tom, we won't need you to come with us after all. We've met a friend who'll escort us.' She took a coin out of the pocket of her riding habit and reached across the gap between their two horses to hand it to him.

He looked doubtfully from her to Adam, now also mounted. 'I was told by Mrs Edwards to see you home, miss.'

'I know, and it was very kind of her. But we'll be perfectly all right with this young man.' Charlotte seemed to have forgotten his name, but her manner was friendly, and Adam was pleased that she trusted him to escort her and Cornelia.

The groom still looked uncertain.

'Really, Tom,' Cornelia said impatiently, 'we'll be quite all right. Adam lives near us and will see us home. Our parents know him. And there *are* two of us.'

Tom gave one more glance at Adam, then shrugged. 'Very well, miss. Thank you, miss.' He touched his hat to both of them, gave Adam a nod, and rode off. But when he turned the corner at the end of the block, he looked back at them as though still doubtful.

Charlotte checked whether a cloth bundle behind her saddle was firmly settled. Then they set off, heading east for the bridge.

*

For a few moments no one spoke. Adam searched for something to say; if he remained silent, the girls might think of him as nothing more than another groom. For the same reason, he rode determinedly alongside them, not behind as a groom would have done.

He was also afraid that the girls might begin talking between themselves – or, even worse, giggling – and leave him out. He hated girls when they giggled.

But what could he *possibly* say that would start a conversation? In spite of his determination not to act or be treated like a groom, he suddenly felt shy and inferior.

'How long have you been in Upper Canada?' he blurted out – a silly question but the best he could think of. Besides, he wanted to know.

'Six years,' Cornelia said. She was the one riding alongside him, with Charlotte on her other side. 'We arrived in 1831, the year before the cholera got here.'

'The *first* cholera,' Charlotte specified.

'There was cholera in England too,' Adam said.

'Yes, after we left. We heard about it. It was horrid.'

'We came over in a ship all by ourselves!' Cornelia said.

'In a ship all by yourselves?' Adam asked, startled, not understanding.

She made a funny face. 'Sorry – I mean that father chartered a whole ship just for us. It was going to Quebec with nothing but ballast, no freight. We were the only passengers.'

Adam didn't know what to say. Chartered a whole ship! He couldn't imagine how much that would cost. The de Grassis must be very rich – and that discovery made his heart sink because it reopened the gap between the girls and him, just when he thought it was being bridged.

'We brought cow-bells and sheep-bells,' Cornelia was saying.

' … because Father was expecting us to have an enormous estate …'

' … and ploughs – but they turned out to be the wrong sort. We don't understand about ploughs.'

'Then our house burned down the next year and we lost a great many of our belongings.'

'We lived in the stable for a while ….'

'Father sometimes says he's the unluckiest man alive.'

Unlucky, maybe, Adam thought, grasping a few bits of this jumble of information, but also rich – and foolish. It was bad enough for Uncle Ted to come to Canada with silly ideas, but Captain de Grassi, an educated man, should have been able to find out what kind of ploughs to bring with him to Canada.

'Why did he come here?'

It was a question worth asking. Though most people came to try to make better lives for themselves, Adam had heard some unusual and interesting reasons.

Cornelia answered. 'Back home in Chichester, father taught languages. French, Italian, Spanish, some German ….'

[121]

'*Taught languages? He was a teacher?*'

Adam heard the astonishment in his own voice and knew it was rude but he couldn't help it. How did a *teacher* earn enough to live that kind of life? The only teacher he knew was Mrs Wright, who could barely support herself, and he had assumed that all teachers were poor.

Maybe Captain de Grassi had come into money, so that he could afford to stop teaching and emigrate.

'Tutor to some of the best families round about,' Cornelia said. 'The Duke of Richmond's, and Lord March's, and Lord Paget's. Some of them gave him letters of introduction to people here, like Sir John Colborne, who was the lieutenant governor when we came.'

'Ours is a distinguished family,' Charlotte said proudly. 'Father's mother was the daughter of an Austrian baron.'

'That's why he's so keen on our preserving some of the old ways,' Cornelia added. 'But *we're* very democratic, we two.' She said it in a challenging way, then turned to Adam. 'Charlotte thinks we aren't *really* democratic. What do *you* think, Adam? Are we? Charlotte and I?'

Charlotte saved him from having to answer. 'Don't tease Adam, Cornelia. He scarcely knows us.'

Adam was glad to be rescued, but was embarrassed all the same. Had Charlotte rescued him because she knew that, if he were honest, he would have to say that she and her sister were *not* 'democratic'? That they took their position so much for granted that they were not even aware of it? They were friendly, but that was not the same thing. They still considered themselves superior – which they were, in rank. Charlotte, older and more thoughtful than Cornelia, realized it.

'Father wasn't always a teacher,' Charlotte said, changing the subject. 'Before that he was an army officer, first in the French army – Napoleon's army – and then in the English.'

Adam frowned, trying to remember what he had learned from Sergeant Phillips and Mrs Wright about the war.

'Weren't the French and the English fighting *against* each other? How could your father be an officer on both sides?'

'He first served with the French. Then he was taken prisoner by the Spanish, who were on the opposite side. The English were allies of the Spanish, and they released him. He arrived in England with only the clothes on his back and became an officer in the English army.'

Adam was confused. He'd try to figure it out later.

Then Charlotte asked him about his family. He told what he could without revealing how very poor they had been. When he mentioned Uncle Ted's plans to buy land, he realized again that he was just like Uncle Ted himself. But it was the only thing about his family that sounded hopeful and brought him close to these young ladies.

At the tollgate beyond the bridge, Charlotte paid toll for herself and her sister. As Adam now realized, that meant that they had not gone into Toronto that morning. Probably they had spent the night in town with the lady who had sent Tom, the groom, to escort them home. They didn't explain, and Adam didn't ask.

When they reached the turn-off to Todmorden, the girls had a choice of routes. They could take the Mill Road to Todmorden and then go on to the Forks of the Don, or they could go straight ahead along the Kingston Road and then north. By the way they slowed their horses, Adam knew that they intended to take their leave of him.

'We go this way,' Cornelia said, pointing straight ahead. 'We have to do an errand for mother.'

'I'll ride with you. You told that groom . . . .'

'Oh, no,' Charlotte said. 'That was only to set his mind at ease. We don't need an escort all the way home. We're often out by ourselves.'

'We'll be all right, honestly,' Cornelia said, smiling. She had sulked for a few moments after Charlotte scolded her about teasing Adam, but now she was in bubbly spirits again.

'It was nice to have your company this far. We'll see you again soon. Goodbye.'

'Goodbye.'

As his horse plodded up the Mill Road, Adam reflected on what he had heard. Back home in England, all he'd known about social classes was that there were poor labourers, big tenant farmers like Mr Higham who employed them, and the seldom-seen gentry and landowners. In the towns and villages you'd find the rector, a handful of tradesmen and craftsmen, and perhaps someone like Mrs Wright who taught a few children in her home and lived at a level which was more genteel but almost as poor as that of many farm labourers. Where in all this did Captain de Grassi fit? – a retired army officer, of good family but working as a teacher, even though his pupils were well-born? And how had he, after arriving in England with only the clothes on his back, become wealthy enough to emigrate in such an expensive fashion?

Had he come to the new world *because* he felt out of place in England? Had he seen himself as belonging to the upper class – grandson of an Austrian baron – and resented being treated as merely a teacher to the children of the English gentry? Adam didn't know what chance Captain de Grassi might have had of eventually owning land in England. Even if he had any chance at all, the same amount of money would probably buy a lot more land here than there, and make Captain de Grassi a larger landowner. So he had come here.

And he brought with him a dream that was the same as Uncle Ted's. Underneath all the differences, both of them saw the owning of land in Upper Canada as a way – perhaps the only way – to reach the position in the world which they felt they deserved.

Chapter Eleven

NE AFTERNOON IN THE FOLLOWING week, Adam was called from his work in the mill.

'Fella to talk to you, Adam,' Gavin said, coming in with a bale of rags on his shoulder.

Adam went out into the yard and was surprised to see Uncle Ted. Surprised, and wary. What was *he* doing here?

'Hello, Uncle Ted.'

'Hello, Adam.'

'Are Aunt Lenore and the children with you?'

'No – left them there for now.'

'There?'

'In Dundas. I came away by myself. Couldn't stick it out with that Manley. Slave-driver, the feller is. I knew I shouldn't have let myself be talked into taking that job. I'm going to find work here. Just for a short spell until I buy land of my own. Maybe not new land. Buy a farm that's already started, from one of these fellers that couldn't make it.'

Adam said nothing. Such farms cost a great deal more than wild land. How could his uncle possibly afford it? He was still living in a dream.

'I've come to ask whether ... well, to say hello, of course, and ask if you know a place where I can sleep for a few nights while I'm looking around. Somewhere cheap. Even a loft .... Thought there might be somewhere around here.' He gestured at the mill buildings and houses.

Adam made an exasperated sound. *No!* he wanted to say. Don't pester me. I'm just getting settled here and you'll spoil everything. Go away!

He didn't say it, but neither did he make any sign of welcome.

'There's a woman up in the village who has a room or two for rent. Mrs Murphy. You could try her.'

Uncle Ted looked gloomy. 'Nothing right round here?'

'Not that I know of.' Adam was as discouraging as possible.

'Where're *you* living, then?'

Adam pretended not to hear. His uncle was quite capable of talking Nelly into giving him a place to sleep. To turn the conversation, he asked, 'How did you get here, Uncle Ted? Walk?'

'No, no, much too far. I got a ride with a man who has a wagon. Friend o' mine. Met some good people in Dundas, folk who've told me about the political situation. Got a head on their shoulders, some of 'em, though they're only farmers. I've been hearing about the terrible government they got here, and the Family Compact keeping all the power for themselves. An awful thing to find corruption in a new country like this.' He shook his head dolefully.

'I have to get back to work, Uncle Ted.'

'So anyway, I got a lift with one of these men. Had a good talk. Stopped the night with some folks he knows.' He took off his hat and ran his hand through his curly blond hair, then put the hat on again. 'Mrs Murphy, eh? Top o' the hill?'

Just then Mr Skinner emerged from the door of the mill and began walking in their direction.

Adam never learned what Mr Skinner's errand was because at that very moment a horse and rider came into view up near the Skinner house, trotting down the road from the village. Both horse and rider were small. Even sitting in the saddle, the man seemed to be in bustling or even feverish activity. Adam would have recognized him by that, even had he not seen the red wig under the hat.

'You were talking about reformers,' Adam said. 'That's Mr Mackenzie now, William Lyon Mackenzie, the man who writes the *Constitution* newspaper.'

'You know him?' Uncle Ted said, giving Adam a surprised

glance and then staring at the man on the horse. 'And he's coming *here?*'

'He buys his paper from us. He knows Mr Eastwood and Mr Skinner quite well.'

Mr Skinner, from where he was, had been unable to see the horse and rider, but he heard Adam's words. In a flash he disappeared back into the mill.

When, a few moments later, Mr Mackenzie rode up to Adam and his uncle, he dismounted in such a hurry that he nearly tumbled off the horse. 'G'day, g'day,' he said, thrusting the reins into Adam's hands. 'Mr Skinner and Mr Eastwood about?'

'Mr Eastwood's away for the day, I believe. Mr Skinner ....' Adam glanced at the door of the mill.

'In the office, is he? Good. Good. I'll step in and have a word with him. Things are happening in this province, and I know he's a reformer, one of us. Just want to make sure of his support.'

Before he finished talking, he was already trotting towards the door of the paper mill. As he approached it, he took off his hat, revealing the full glory of the red wig.

Adam, having other things to do than hold people's horses, tied the animal to a hitching post. When he turned back to his uncle to say goodbye, he found him staring after the little newspaperman.

'Mr Mackenzie! *Here!* That's something, now. So the folks you work for are reformers, are they, Adam?'

'They're reformers, but they're not radicals. They don't like the idea of armed rebellion. I don't think Mr Mackenzie will be able to talk them into supporting any kind of uprising.'

'If peaceful methods fail, we have to use other means. Show the Family Compact that the people won't be kept down any longer, that they'll have their say – with guns, if need be!'

Adam winced. Gavin, when he'd drunk too much whisky, talked like this. Many other people, however, wanted reform but drew the line at actual rebellion, and there was a big gap between them. It was scary to hear Uncle Ted sounding exactly like Gavin, and being so careless about who might hear him.

If he hung around the neighbourhood talking like that, he'd be a nuisance and maybe a danger to Adam.

'I have to go back to work,' Adam said again.

Uncle Ted spoke no more about seeking out Mrs Murphy. His eyes were fixed on the door of the mill – and his hopes were rewarded. Mr Mackenzie emerged with Mr Carver, the clerk.

'Didn't you say that Mr Skinner was here, lad?' Mr Mackenzie asked Adam. 'Can't seem to find him.'

The clerk caught Adam's eye and shook his head slightly.

So that's how it was! Mr Skinner was keeping out of sight. Adam, knowing that Mr Mackenzie was probably the paper mill's biggest customer, wondered at Mr Skinner's running away from him. Were politics really more important than business? But that was Mr Skinner's affair.

'I *thought* he was,' Adam said, putting on an innocent face. 'I saw him earlier, but ....' He shrugged, and was rewarded by an approving little nod from Mr Carver.

Mr Mackenzie paid no attention to the explanations. He fidgeted, snapped his fingers, looked around impatiently as though in search of more recruits.

'Annoying! Very annoying, damn it!' he said. 'I wanted to persuade him to take a firmer stand. We need determination, a dedication to principle.' He pulled himself up and looked over Adam's head. 'These are critical times and we need men of stature and substance on our side, men who'll take a bold stand against oppression, against the persecution by the powerful and the sins of .... We need men who'll join us in the fight for freedom!'

Obviously he had forgotten that he had only three listeners, standing out there in the cold wind. He talked as though there were hundreds.

A small tornado of dead leaves reminded him where he was.

'Well, I'm sorry I couldn't speak with your employers,' he said to Mr Carver. He put on his hat and looked about for his horse.

But before the newspaperman could begin walking in that direction, Uncle Ted stepped forward. 'Mr Mackenzie, sir, I hope you won't consider it a liberty but I'd like to introduce myself. Ted Wheeler. It's a great privilege and ... and inspiration to hear your words.'

Mackenzie looked at him, taking him in for the first time. 'Wheeler, did you say? Local man? One of our supporters?'

'I'm certainly a supporter. But I'm not settled yet. Arrived from England this autumn, planning to take up land. I've been working in Dundas and heard all about you. You have a lot of support in Dundas, sir.'

Mackenzie, flattered, put out his hand. 'I'm very pleased to meet you, Mr Wheeler. We can use men like you. Got any military experience? No, of course not. You'd have been too young for the war against Napoleon.'

While shaking hands, Uncle Ted said, 'Yes, sir, I'm afraid I was too young. No, I'm just a simple dairyman, but I think about things. I believe you're on the right road here, trying to make the governor and the Family Compact give up some of their power, make things fairer for *all* the people ....'

Adam watched. To his surprise, Mr Mackenzie was responding warmly, looking Uncle Ted square in the eye and nodding approvingly.

'We can use men like you,' the little newspaper editor said as he put on his hat. 'Where'd you say you were living?'

'Nowhere, right at this moment. I came back from Dundas to look for work around here.'

People took to Uncle Ted. He had a frank and open manner; he made them feel comfortable.

As for Mr Mackenzie ... well, whether or not you agreed

with his politics, he was a man of brains and experience. Besides being the writer and editor of his own newspaper, he'd been a member of the Assembly and mayor of Toronto. Moreover, he was good at firing people's imagination, attracting their friendship and support. It must show that his opinions of people were worth considering. If he took a liking to Uncle Ted, maybe there really was something there to like. And it suggested that getting along with people was a skill like any other, something important enough to build a career on.

By now he had mounted his horse. He touched his hat in a single salute to the three people watching him.

'Good day to you, then. Tell Mr Skinner I was looking for him and will be glad of his support.' He turned his horse.

Uncle Ted had ideas of his own. 'Going up the hill, Mr Mackenzie? So am I.'

'Glad of your company, Mr Wheeler.'

They set off, Uncle Ted walking beside Mr Mackenzie on his little horse.

When they were out of earshot, Mr Carver looked at Adam. 'Good for you, lad. Mr Skinner doesn't hold with all this rabble-rousing. But he couldn't just say so. Mr Mackenzie sounded him out once before, and this time Mr Skinner thought it best to .... But who's that man Wheeler?'

'My uncle.'

He knew his voice sounded flat and unenthusiastic. The clerk gave him a glance, then patted his shoulder. 'Right, lad. Get back to work, shall we?'

*

That afternoon, while helping the women to cut rags, Adam thought about Uncle Ted.

If Uncle Ted was good at dealing with people, maybe he could build a career on it.

Uncle Ted wanted to 'be somebody'. Was being good with people important enough to make you 'somebody'?

[131]

Back home, the only way was to own land or to have a land-owner as your patron and supporter. Uncle Ted obviously thought so too: that was why he was so determined to own land. The gentry had power and influence, and apparently did no work.

Here in Canada, however, it took an immense amount of labour to establish oneself as an owner of cleared and productive land, and even then you might be only a successful farmer, one of many, rather than a member of a small group of important and powerful gentlemen.

On the other hand, it might be possible to 'be somebody' without owning land or having a landowner to back you. Suppose Uncle Ted were to give up his silly dreams and try something completely different?

When he had a chance, Adam asked Gavin, 'Does Mr Mackenzie own land?'

'Own land? Not that I know of. Poor as a church mouse he is, always in debt. He may own his house and the newspaper office, but not *land*.'

'So you can be an important man without owning land,' he said, more to himself than to Gavin.

'Sure you can. Look at doctors. Look at some o' the big tavern-keepers – they might own the building they're in, though some o' them just rents it, but most o' them sure as hell ain't landowners. Look at some o' the merchants.'

'What could a man do who ... who wanted to get ahead but didn't have any money and didn't like work?'

Gavin stared at him and laughed. 'Guy who doesn't like *work* ...!'

'He's good with people.'

'If he can bring himself to pull handles in a tavern .... If that ain't too much like hard work ...!' He laughed again. 'If he ain't got no money, he's gotta do *some* work. But he don't need to own land to get ahead. I guess it depends on what the guy has *in* him.'

'So getting ahead doesn't mean being a landowner first.'

'Not here. And maybe it wasn't like that in the towns, back home, though it sure helped to have the gentry take an interest in you. Here, if you're good at something and want to get ahead, you've at least got a chance. And, yeah, you don't *need* to own land.'

It gave Adam something to think about, but he didn't know what he was going to do with the information. He couldn't just go to Uncle Ted and suggest ....

Never.

Maybe he'd talk it over with Aunt Lenore sometime.

Meanwhile Uncle Ted was in the neighbourhood, spouting dangerous talk and perhaps causing trouble.

*

To his relief, Adam saw nothing of his uncle during the next few days.

On the Friday of the following week, Mrs Skinner sent Adam to take a basket of provisions to a friend of hers who lived a little way north of Todmorden, on the road towards the Forks of the Don. After doing his errand, he nearly bumped into Uncle Ted in the village, near the alehouse.

'Hello, Adam!'

'Hello, Uncle Ted. How are you? Found work yet?'

Uncle Ted waved a dismissive hand. 'No hurry, no hurry. There's more important matters afoot. Mr Mackenzie's gone north. There are big changes coming!'

'Gone north?'

'It's starting, lad!' He stared past Adam's head, an intense and eager look on his face.

'What's starting?'

'Mackenzie is beginning to take action. There've been battles in Lower Canada and the reformers won. Mr Mackenzie gets all the news. And he's decided that the time has come. The date has been set!'

[133]

A chill ran up Adam's spine. It was not only Uncle Ted's news but the excitement he showed. He was thrilled by the prospect of action and upheaval and maybe fighting, just as he had been excited and even happy during the Captain Swing riots back home.

'Have you seen Mr Mackenzie again?' Adam asked. 'I mean, you say you know the date ....'

'It's a secret, of course. You don't go around telling everyone. A demonstration to show the Family Compact how we feel!'

'A demonstration? Nothing more than that? Not a ... an uprising?'

'A demonstration of strength.'

'But we've been hearing about all this military training, the drilling ....'

'A show of strength! Mr Mackenzie says ....'

'So you *have* seen him.'

'He's interested in what I told him about the Swing riots, when we demanded a living wage and destroyed the threshing machines that took away our jobs. The issues're different here but, like Mr Mackenzie says, reform is reform. The common people against the privileged.'

To do him justice, Uncle Ted had acted, had done something, at that time – acted in support of a cause which, from the landless labourers' point of view, was a just one, and taken action in the only way available to him. Maybe he'd taken action because burning haystacks was more exciting than milking cows, but all the same he'd endangered his life and risked arrest and punishment.

And of course risked losing his job.

An alarming question raised itself in Adam's mind. Had Uncle Ted been dismissed from the job in Dundas rather than leaving of his own will? Dismissed for his hot-headed talk, his radical ideas? If so, he would have left without a good character reference and that would make it harder to find other work. And it was still a bad time for taking up land. Adam shivered. December already. First of the month today. Winter coming on.

Exasperation made him blunt.

'Do you still have your job in Dundas to go back to?'

'I never got along with the bastard, not from the first day. For all his airs, he's no better than me. Back in England he was just somebody's hired hand. I soon found *that* out. And now he lords it over me.'

'Did you disagree about politics?'

'He's well fixed, with his big farm and his buildings and his cleared land, friendly with the magistrate and the sheriff. *He* doesn't want to change things.'

'And Aunt Lenore? Was she dismissed?'

'Oh, no, they kept her on. She doesn't mind kowtowing. It's easier for women. But a man's got his pride.'

Poor Aunt Lenore, Adam thought. 'Could she stay in that shanty? She and the kids?'

Uncle Ted shrugged. 'Sure. For now. Until the Manleys find someone to replace me. Another *hired hand ... !*' He spat the words out.

So Aunt Lenore might be without shelter any day now. With Uncle Ted away from home – looking for work, so he said, but actually getting excited about all this political business – she'd have to rely entirely on herself. The only hope was that Mrs Manley would keep her on as a servant even if the shanty were given to someone else.

Maybe, though, Aunt Lenore would do better with Uncle Ted away.

'You going back to Mrs Murphy's now?' Adam asked. Mrs Murphy's was on his way home and they could walk together.

'I'm not there any more. She wanted too much money. I'm staying with people on the Kingston Road, just east of the bridge.'

'Why are you here, then?' Adam asked, too worried by now to be tactful.

'Came to meet some fellers.' He cast a quick, sidelong look at the alehouse in front of which they were standing.

Meeting men at an alehouse was something Uncle Ted was always doing. Perfectly normal. But, taken together with his shifty glance and the news that he'd had further contact with Mr Mackenzie, it made Adam even more uneasy. He felt surrounded by invisible currents, and the scary thing was that he recognized the feeling. At the time of the riots back home he'd been only a little kid but he noticed that everyone always seemed to know when and where the next uprising would be, the next gathering of farm workers to burn a haystack or destroy a threshing machine. There would be a funny kind of tension in the air, sudden silences, then a lot of talk about nothing – and, worst of all, an occasional meaningful glance or a muttered message from one person to the next, making an invisible web.

Now, in Uncle Ted's talk and manner, he sensed it again.

It was frightening to think of Uncle Ted being part of it. These webs, though invisible, were powerful and dangerous.

A dim figure appeared for a moment around the corner of the alehouse. It signalled to Uncle Ted before vanishing again.

'Got to go, Adam,' Uncle Ted said abruptly and headed for the place where the shadowy figure had been.

Chapter Twelve

THE NEXT DAY, ADAM overheard a conversation between Mr Skinner and Thomas Helliwell, the brother who lived in Toronto and to whose wife Adam had delivered a parcel a few weeks earlier.

As Adam crossed the yard with an armload of firewood, Thomas Helliwell rode up to the brewery and dismounted. At the same moment, Mr Skinner emerged from the paper mill.

'Morning, Thomas,' Mr Skinner said. The two men, brothers–in–law, knew each other well.

'Morning, Colin.'

'Any news?'

'Meeting at Government House today. All the important men. Governor Head, of course, and Strachan and Allan and Robinson and Powell and all of them.'

'What about?'

'This talk of uprising.'

'Really? They're taking it seriously at last?'

'Looks like it. There's a chance of the militia mustering, or being told to be ready to muster, or something of that sort.'

The two men eyed each other. They were on opposite sides, Helliwell favouring the government and Skinner the reformers, but the rumblings of armed uprising brought them closer together. Both of them, as businessmen and land-owners, might lose more than they gained if there really was rioting or rebellion.

*

Adam learned from Nelly that evening about a sawmill further up the Don River that needed a hired man. The next

day, therefore, he went to find his uncle. All he knew was that he lodged with someone who lived near where the Mill Road turned off the Kingston Road. Besides a tavern, there were only a few houses; by asking, Adam had no trouble finding where his uncle was – or rather, where he had been, because he'd left.

'Gone north, somewhere up Yonge Street,' the woman told Adam.

'Had he heard of work?' Adam asked, trying to be hopeful although the phrase 'gone north' alarmed him. Those were the words Uncle Ted had used of Mr Mackenzie, and most of the military trainings and other unrest seemed to be taking place north of the city.

The woman's eyes evaded Adam's. 'Not that I know of. Well, maybe.'

'He came to Toronto to look for a job. Do you happen to know whether he was trying very hard?'

'Couldn't say. He was out all day and half the night with my son.'

'Your son?'

'David. They're great pals, even though David's only nineteen.'

So Uncle Ted was friends with the son, not the householder. Easy to understand; his charm and air of worldliness would appeal to young men. 'Is David here now? Perhaps I could ask him ....'

'He's gone north too.' Again her eyes shifted.

'You don't know where exactly?'

'No,' she said, but Adam knew she was lying.

*

Monday about noon, Captain de Grassi rode into the Mills area and went to see Mr Helliwell at the brewery. Later, when he had left, word spread from the brewery's clerk that the militia had been told to hold themselves in readiness for mustering and that there was talk of placing guards around the bank and the City Hall.

*

Adam was in bed that night but still awake – the hall clock had struck quarter past ten, and Mr and Mrs Skinner had come upstairs only a few minutes earlier – when he heard the sound of the church bell in Toronto ringing. That'll be a fire, he thought. The church bell was always rung to summon the fire brigade.

A minute later, Mr Skinner put his head into Adam's room.

'Adam! Are you awake?'

'Yes, sir.'

'We think that bell is the signal for the militia to muster. Mrs Skinner and I are afraid that Captain de Grassi won't have heard it because he's so much farther from town, but he should be told.'

Interesting, Adam thought, that Mr Skinner, though a reformer, now seemed to be on the side of the government – else why would he want to notify Captain de Grassi? He had supported Mr Mackenzie's desire for reform but had parted company with him on the subject of using force.

'Would you like me to go and tell him?'

'Yes. Take a horse. And a lantern.'

Adam dressed, shivering in the December night, and lit a lantern from the banked fire in the kitchen. He was still shivering as he saddled Princess. But by the time he was riding up the hill to Todmorden he was used to the cold. He was pleased to be entrusted with the errand, excited to be a part, however small, of what might turn out to be important events, and he rode as fast as it was safe to go over the frozen ruts and ice-covered puddles.

Upon reaching the de Grassi house, however, he found that he need not have come. When the church bell sounded,

Captain de Grassi had been outdoors checking around the place before going to bed. He had heard the bell and also taken it as a signal for the mustering of the militia. He was now dressed in uniform and about to set off for Toronto – and, to Adam's surprise, Charlotte and Cornelia intended to go with him. He and his wife had objected, but the girls had won.

'To Toronto? In the middle of the night?' Adam blurted out.

'Father will have to stay there with the militia,' Cornelia explained. 'We're going along so that we can bring the news back to mother, whatever news there is.'

It seemed absurd to Adam, but who was he to protest? So he mounted his horse again and set off to accompany them as far as Todmorden.

On the way, Captain de Grassi, his soldier's blood roused, told stories about the campaign in Spain during Napoleon's wars. He spoke about the number of prisoners he took on one occasion, and about pursuing enemy soldiers, thinking that his men were behind him, and being startled to find that he was alone against several dozen, and about being promised the Cross of the Legion of Honour but not receiving it because the general who intended to recommend it was killed.

Adam listened politely, but most of his mind was elsewhere, wondering if the ringing of the bell really had been a signal for the militia to muster, whether that meant there was a rebel army somewhere near, whether Uncle Ted was part of it. Somehow it was hard to make the images of 'Uncle Ted' and 'rebel army' fit together. Could a bunch of men like Uncle Ted really be called an army – an army like the ones that Captain de Grassi was talking about? Adam had heard over and over that the authorities were not alarmed by all the talk of drilling and training, that the rebels had very few guns. 'Country yokels armed with sticks,' Mr Helliwell had called them, according to Gavin McPhee. Yet here Captain de Grassi was, taking it all very seriously.

By now he was talking about the situation in Upper Canada. 'Colonel FitzGibbon has been warning everyone for weeks,' he said.

Colonel FitzGibbon had, like Captain de Grassi, been a professional soldier and was now connected with the militia.

'There were others who took it seriously, weren't there, sir?' Adam asked.

'One or two more. I myself felt that attention must be paid, and that Mr Mackenzie ought to be arrested for plotting treason against the Crown and the state. But he was not arrested, and now here we are, on the verge of a battle.' He sounded gloomy and excited at the same time.

At Todmorden, Adam took his leave of the de Grassis.

He pointed Princess towards home but had gone barely a few yards down the hill when there was a sudden burst of shouting behind him. Quickly he rode back to the main road and headed for the noise.

Charlotte de Grassi, still on horseback, was surrounded by men with lanterns. A few were armed with guns, the rest with pitchforks and sticks. One carried a scythe, which looked deadly dangerous as its blade caught the lanterns' flickering light.

Adam froze, instantly tense and alert. The scene reminded him of things he'd seen during the riots in England seven years ago – torches, and crowds armed with tools-turned-weapons – but the presence of a girl in the centre of it altered everything. On her horse, she was plainly visible above the unmounted men. The half moon, which had still given some light to Adam on his journey to the de Grassi house, had now set but there were enough lanterns to show her sitting erect and defiant.

There were thirty or forty men, farmers and labourers, all on foot. Rebels? Certainly they were men in arms – sticks and pitchforks were arms if meant to be used as such – and they were probably rebels since they had stopped Charlotte who, in her riding habit and sitting on her side-saddle, was unmistakably a young lady. The ordinary people against the gentry: it was such a common conflict, Mrs Wright used to say, that you didn't even need to ask what it was about.

Adam was one of the ordinary people, but his sympathies were with Charlotte rather than the armed men.

'A *girl?*' someone on the outer fringe of the crowd was saying as Adam ventured cautiously within earshot.

Charlotte's voice could be heard high and distinct. 'I have been summoned to the house of one of our acquaintances who is ill. Please let me through.'

'By yourself?'

'In the middle of the night?'

'An emergency,' Charlotte declared haughtily.

Adam was about to go to her aid when he had second thoughts. She was holding her own, and she might actually be safer by herself. Her father and Cornelia would not have gone far; her speaking so loudly meant that she expected them to be able to hear her. Had she deliberately put herself in the way of the group of rebels so that her father and sister could pass unnoticed?

He had to stay and watch – impossible to ride home and go to bed as though nothing was happening – but he hung back and tried to figure out how this encounter could have come about. The de Grassis had been heading towards Toronto – down the Mill Road towards the bridge – so the armed men had been coming up the road, away from Toronto. Where were they going? A group of men as large as this, out in the middle of the night, must be on its way somewhere – maybe to the mysterious 'north' that everyone talked about. That meant there was good reason for the militia to muster.

'Oh, hell, leave the girl be,' someone said. 'Let's go to Helliwell's and ....'

'Hey, yeah! Beer!'

'Who's for free beer?'

'Free?'

'Helliwell's a Tory, ain't he? Ya think we're gonna *pay* the enemy for beer? Hell, man, we're just gonna help ourselves.'

The thought of free beer distracted them from Charlotte. Adam, realizing that he was in the way of the stampede, pulled Princess to one side. When the rush was past, he rode towards Charlotte.

He spoke her name. Then, realizing that she might be frightened, added, 'It's me, Adam.'

'Oh!' she exclaimed. 'Did you see that?'

'Are you all right?'

'Yes,' she said, but her voice was shaky.

He drew up beside her. 'Where are your father and Cornelia?'

'Close by, I hope. Let's move on a bit.'

And in fact, when the noise of the charging crowd had faded away down the hill, leaving the village dark except for two or three candles lit by alarmed householders, there was a sound of horses approaching.

'Father?' Charlotte said softly.

'Yes, child. We heard you talking to Adam. You *are* all right, my dear?'

'Certainly, father,' she said in a firmer voice. 'Let's be on our way.'

Adam expected that, after this incident, Captain de Grassi would send his daughters home, perhaps ask Adam to escort them. But he did no such thing.

'Since it appears that our rebellious friends intend to regale themselves on Helliwell's beer, it is probably safe for us to continue. We will take our leave of you, Adam. Good night.'

'Good night, sir.'

Adam, more puzzled than ever at a father allowing his

daughters to come with him on such a mission, rode down the hill to the Skinners' house. He could see lights below him in the brewery, and hear the sound of voices. Mr Helliwell and his men seemed not to have come out to defend the merchandise – better lose a little beer than get hurt.

Quietly, Adam stabled Princess and went to bed. But it was a while before he fell asleep. He remembered that when he set off for the de Grassi house he'd been pleased at taking part in important events. That feeling was gone now. Charlotte's encounter with the rebels reminded him of how dangerous rioting and revolt could be. He couldn't put the picture of the gleaming, vicious scythe out of his mind.

He'd been wrong to feel pleased. War was a bad business, nothing good about it.

Another part of him worried about .... He tried to put his finger on what it was, and discovered that he was worrying about Mr Helliwell's beer. Not the loss to Mr Helliwell, not even the fact that soon there'd be several dozen drunken men rampaging around the neighbourhood. No, it was that these men felt they *could* help themselves to the beer. They were breaking the law by stealing, and they did not expect to be punished. Either they thought that before long there would be no law left at all, or they expected to win the fight that was looming and therefore be safe from punishment.

The men who had burned haystacks and destroyed threshing machines in England had known that if they were caught they would be punished. They were protesting against what their employers and the government were doing, but so far as Adam knew they had not intended to overthrow the whole system, the laws and everything. To judge by what Gavin McPhee said, Mr Mackenzie and his followers *did* want to overthrow the government, to form a new one themselves.

Adam did not want to take sides. He was too new here to understand what was really going on. But he was afraid of what might happen.

Chapter Thirteen

FTER A SHORT NIGHT'S SLEEP, Adam went grog-
gily downstairs for breakfast the next morning.

Before he even reached the kitchen, he heard
Nelly talking.

'Letting them two girls traipse around the
country! What kind of mother is that? And father! Of course
Italian folk may have their own way of doing things, but the
mother's English. What *can* the woman be thinking of! Only
thirteen and fourteen those girls are.'

Mrs Skinner, to whom she had been talking, came out of
the kitchen with a kettle as Adam arrived. They wished each
other good morning, and Adam went to the long table where
Bert was already seated, staring at nothing.

'The de Grassi girls?' Adam asked. 'Their father was with
them. I know it's strange for them to be out at night, on such
business as that, but with their father ....'

'They came back from town alone,' Nelly said. 'Half past
three Mrs Murphy saw them, just them two on their ponies
riding home as calm as you please. Half past three!'

'Did she speak to them?' he asked.

'They shouted that the militia was mustering and the
rebels gathering to attack the city. Their dad had stayed in
town and they were riding home. Alone, just the two of
them. And with that bunch of rebels still here drinking, or
maybe they'd just left.' She set bowls of porridge in front of
Adam and Bert, plunking them down with a bang in her
indignation. 'And if they *had* been caught by the Matthews
men ....'

'Matthews men?'

'That lot that was drinking here was led by a man called

Matthews. If the girls *had* been caught, what then? Eh? What then?'

There was no point answering.

'Maybe,' Adam said, 'their father sent them home, even in the middle of the night, because he thought it was too dangerous for them to stay in town. Is there any news this morning?'

'Mr Helliwell's going to Toronto to deliver beer. He'll be able to tell us when he gets back.'

'I'm surprised that he has any beer left to deliver, after last night.'

'Even that mob couldn't drink everything. Besides, these barrels was already loaded on the wagon. I guess Matthews didn't think of looking there.'

*

Mr Helliwell returned from the city as Adam and the other paper-mill workers finished their mid-day dinner. When they emerged from the back door, the brewery wagon, laden with empty casks, came bumping and rattling down the hill, and they walked behind it to the yard among the mills. Alerted by the rumble, Mr Helliwell's own workfolk came out, including the servant Meg, and women and children from the houses and cottages in the Don Mills. Adam had never before seen so many of them together; as Nelly had said on his first day here, they made quite a village.

They assembled so quickly that Mr Helliwell was still on the seat of the wagon when he was confronted with several dozen people eager for news. Adam watched him cast a glance around and consciously take on the role of messenger. He made no move to get down from the wagon, because up there he was in a perfect position to be seen and heard by everyone.

'What's goin' on in town?' one voice demanded, speaking for all the rest.

'The militia are gathering in the Market Square,' Mr Helliwell reported. 'They've got a gun – I mean a cannon. And muskets, of course. Plenty of muskets for everybody on the government side.'

'And the rebels?' someone asked.

'At Montgomery's Tavern, up Yonge Street. Lots of men heading there too. Only it seems they haven't got many weapons, only pikes and whatever they bring with them.'

'How many rebels are there?' someone asked Mr Helliwell.

'Nobody knows. Could be hundreds, could be thousands. A man was shot there last night, Colonel Moodie, riding down to Toronto from somewhere farther north to take the news to the governor. Another man got through to bring word of the rebels' rising and of Colonel Moodie's being shot. And a rebel was killed, they say.'

'So they'll be marching on Toronto ... when? Today or tomorrow?'

'No one knows.'

'And with all the troops gone from the fort.'

'It would none of it have happened but for that,' someone else said.

Mr Helliwell stood up in the wagon, reclaiming their attention. 'I know that most of you men are in the militia. The governor needs all the men he can get to fight for the Queen and protect the city, so I'm dismissing you for the rest of the day, and I guess tomorrow too. The shops and mills in town are closed. Go and report at the market house. That's where the governor's making his headquarters. I don't know when we get back to normal – we'll see how things go.'

'No beer for the troops, then, Mr Helliwell?' a man shouted.

'I'll keep things going as best I can with those of you who are too old or too young for the militia.' He looked over the crowd. 'Leonard and Phil, there,' he said, indicating two elderly men, 'and the McDonald boys.' Helliwell's employed the three young sons of Mrs McDonald, the woman who worked in the paper mill.

'We'll do what we can for a day or two,' Mr Helliwell said. 'Then we'll see. This is war, or it may come to be war, and we got to adjust. That's all, folks. Next time we're all together here, I hope it'll be in happier times.'

While he clambered down from the wagon, the crowd broke up into small groups, some agitated and some aimless.

'Where's Montgomery's Tavern?' Adam asked the man next to him.

''Bout four or five miles north of town, up Yonge Street.'

Montgomery's Tavern. At last the mysterious 'north' had a name. 'A tavern?' he wondered out loud. 'One? For a whole army?'

'I don't suppose they all sleep in the tavern. There'll be sheds, and neighbours' houses. An' I guess it's a good place to get to town from.'

'A long way to walk, and then fight, if there's a battle, and then walk back.' People often walked such distances, but did not usually fight a battle as well.

The man laughed. 'I don't know how many'll have to walk back.'

'You mean ... if they're killed?'

'Either way. If they win, I guess they'll stay in town, at least for a while.'

Uncle Ted, Adam thought, was probably at Montgomery's Tavern this very minute.

The man moved away.

Adam noticed that Mr Morris had buttonholed Mr Skinner. 'We'll have to close the paper mill too, sir,' Mr Morris was saying. 'All of us are in the militia. And McPhee's gone already – didn't show up this morning. Gone to join Mackenzie, I expect, knowing his politics.'

Mr Skinner looked gloomy.

Mr Morris went on, quietly insistent. 'We can't stay open,

sir. Can't run the mill with no hands to work it.'

'All right. We'll close for today and see what happens tomorrow. But keep in touch. We'll reopen as soon as possible.' He looked around at the rest of his employees, who were listening. 'You heard what I said to Mr Morris. You men can go and report, and the women have the afternoon free. You, Adam, you can split and carry firewood for Nelly.'

*

As Adam chopped wood and piled it in the shed outside the back door, he thought about Uncle Ted, now maybe part of Mr Mackenzie's army, and about Captain de Grassi serving with the loyalist militia. Again he thought about land – because, in spite of what Gavin had said last week, land *did* matter and he wanted to understand why it did.

Mr Mackenzie had promised his followers land – promised that the large estates belonging to the Family Compact and their friends would be broken up and shared out among those who joined the uprising. Yesterday evening, along with the talk about the war in Spain, Captain de Grassi had said indignantly that the scoundrel Mackenzie was after his land. Adam, unloading firewood from his arm onto the pile, sighed. He could understand why it mattered back home, where all the land was already owned by somebody, but why did it matter *here*, where there was plenty that belonged to no one?

Back home, if you owned land you were somebody. If you didn't, you hardly counted. If you rented land, like Mr Higham's renting Three Corners Farm, you sort of counted but you weren't nearly as important as the landowners were.

The fact that here, in Canada, there was plenty of land for everybody didn't seem to make any difference. People brought their ideas with them, and owning land still mattered – even though here it was the usual thing rather than the exception. Even though owning land meant hard work instead of a life of leisure. Things were different here, but the *ideas* seemed to be the same.

No doubt many of the men joining Mr Mackenzie already owned land, and they *still* weren't happy.

It was a puzzle, all right.

*

After Adam had been working for a couple of hours, Colin, the Skinners' ten-year-old son, rode into the yard. He attended the school in town and usually rode back and forth every day on his pony, though sometimes he stayed overnight with his aunt and uncle, Mr and Mrs Thomas Helliwell, in the Market Square. Adam didn't see much of him. Mostly he played with the Eastwood boys who lived in the village.

'You're back early,' Adam said as Colin dismounted.

'School's closed on account of the troubles.'

Colin unsaddled his pony and put it in the stable, then went indoors.

A few minutes later, Nelly came out to the shed where Adam was working. She stood, arms akimbo like a jug with two handles, and looked at the woodpile.

'All right, young Adam, I guess that'll do. Come in and have something to eat.'

Colin was at the kitchen table eating bread and jam. Adam sat down across from him, and Nelly gave him the same.

'What are things like in town?' Adam asked him.

'It's fun. I didn't want to come home. They were boarding up windows, and they put a cannon in front of the market.' He made his arm into an imaginary gun and pointed it at Nelly. 'Pow!'

'Stop that, now, Colin,' Nelly said calmly. 'It's not nice to pretend to shoot people.'

'Was there any fighting?' Adam asked.

'Only guys getting drunk in taverns. There was some shooting once, but that was only to try out the new muskets.

There's a lot of muskets, plenty for everyone on the government side, they say.'

A moment later, having finished his bread and jam, Colin went off on his own and Adam set out for town. Although by now it was mid-afternoon, it never occurred to him to do anything else with his unexpected free time.

The Mill Road was empty, but when he joined the Kingston Road he found that other people were also on their way into the city. A group of eight men strode along in a manner that was almost like marching. Once across the bridge, they headed straight for town, so they were probably militia loyal to the government. Looking down into the Don Valley from near the bridge, Adam saw two other men with pitchforks over their shoulders walking north along the trail on the flats, beside the river. Going to join Mackenzie at Montgomery's Tavern, likely, following a less travelled route and taking with them whatever they had that could serve as a weapon. Pitchforks against muskets ... but many of the men assembling at Montgomery's Tavern would have their own guns with them.

Just beyond the bridge, a wagon passed him, travelling away from Toronto, with two men on the driver's seat talking excitedly. Some distance behind came three women and a girl on foot, all carrying baskets.

The centre of Toronto was in a feverish bustle. As Colin had said, planks were being nailed over the windows of important buildings. Riders galloped back and forth, while other people stood in clusters talking and gesturing. Most shops might be closed, but the inns and taverns were doing lively business, with the customers spilling out onto the street, drinking and arguing.

The Market Square was the busiest of all. It was here that the militia were mustering, and the City Hall, which the governor was using as his temporary headquarters, was located upstairs in the market building. In front of the market stood a cannon surrounded by guards. Armed men were posted at the doors. Inside the building's courtyard was a crowd milling around and making a deafening noise.

Adam remembered Captain de Grassi's words a month ago when all the regular soldiers were withdrawn from the Garrison here and sent to Lower Canada – words about unrest. His prediction had come true. The government was unprepared, defended only by almost untrained militia, and with a rebel army gathering north of town.

Rebel army. Men like Uncle Ted.

Not just men *like* him, but Uncle Ted himself.

Men could be hurt in a battle, killed. If Uncle Ted were killed, what would happen to Aunt Lenore and the kids?

An uneasy feeling crept over Adam. Guilt, sort of. If he'd stayed with the family, gone to Dundas with them, he'd be able to help Aunt Lenore now that Uncle Ted was away, earn a bit, be company for her.

But he wasn't with her. There wasn't anything he could do for her. He'd cut himself off ....

It hurt to feel guilty. He had to do something to help Aunt Lenore.

Could he find Uncle Ted and persuade him to go back to his wife and family?

Nonsense! Uncle Ted wouldn't change his mind because of anything Adam might say – *especially* not Adam, whom he despised.

Adam felt a twitch of irritation at Uncle Ted for putting them all in this fix, for losing his job in Dundas, leaving his family, joining Mr Mackenzie ....

He clenched his fists. He saw no way of easing the guilt and hurt except to do something, anything, that might help Aunt Lenore. Damn it all – and damn Uncle Ted.

He turned away from the market building and headed west towards Yonge Street, which would lead him north to Mr Mackenzie's headquarters.

Chapter Fourteen

IS ROUTE TOOK HIM THROUGH THE open space in front of the court house and jail – twin buildings which, together with the fire hall, the Scots church, and the Methodist chapel, occupied a good-sized city block.

Here too were crowds milling around. Among the first people Adam saw were Charlotte and Cornelia, talking to a gentleman in a top hat and handsome coat and with a musket slung over his shoulder. The gentleman lifted his hat in farewell, and at the same time Cornelia saw Adam.

'Hello, there!'

He touched his cap and went up to them. 'Hello.' The movement brought him to a spot from which, through a gap between buildings, he could see a stretch of sky to the north. In it was a billowing cloud of smoke, distant but clearly visible.

'Smoke!' he exclaimed. 'A fire?'

'The rebels set fire to Dr Horne's house,' Cornelia said. 'It was Mr Mackenzie himself who did it, they say.'

'Who is Dr Horne? I mean, why burn *his* house?'

'He's an important man. Manager of the bank. One of the people the rebels hate.' This was Charlotte.

'I saw him this morning,' Cornelia told Adam. 'He was very worried because he lives up near the tollgate on Yonge Street and the rebels are gathering beyond there, at Montgomery's Tavern. "When they attack the city," he said, "my house will be right in their path." And he was angry that there was no picket – no guard – posted along Yonge Street to stop the rebel army or at least give warning of their coming. *And,*' she said, 'he was furious that no one from the government side had been sent to find out how many rebels

there were, or exactly where they were – because there was talk about them having left Montgomery's and being on the way to town. Well, when he saw me he asked me to ride up there and see. He said no one would suspect a girl of gathering information.'

'Spying, you mean,' Charlotte put in.

Cornelia ignored her. 'So I did. The rebels were at Gallows Hill....'

'Where's that?' Adam asked.

She waved northwards. 'Beyond Dr Horne's house but this side of Montgomery's Tavern.'

'Did you really go to the enemy's camp? In among the men?'

'It wasn't hard. They were just gathered on the road and in people's gardens.'

'Did they stop you?'

'No. If they had, I'd have said I was going to visit Mrs Howard, the postmaster's wife, who lives there.'

'What was it like? What was going on?'

'The rebel army was divided into two parts, I guess, because while I was there a rider galloped up saying something about the other column, and someone told the messenger to tell Mr Mackenzie something.'

'But if they were divided, how could you figure out how many men there were?'

'Dr Horne and I worked it out.'

'How could you even *guess?*' Adam demanded, thinking how hard it was to judge the number of people in a crowd.

'Well, the men I saw at Gallows Hill were on the road and in Mr Stanton's and Mr Howard's front gardens, pretty much in a group. Dr Horne asked me whether there would be enough to fill the church – that's our church, of course, St. James' – and I said not that many. So we worked out that there were maybe three or four hundred there, at Gallows Hill, and he guessed that there might be the same in the other column that was with Mr Mackenzie somewhere west of there. I knew they were to the west because that's where the messenger came from and went back to. And I could see that they didn't have many guns – some had nothing but sticks – and that most of them didn't look very keen to fight.'

'You told Dr Horne this?'

'Of course. He'd sent me to find out. I rode to his house to tell him where they were, and we worked out the number. He was home by then. He was shocked to learn that they were so near but relieved that there were probably less than a thousand. Here in town they'd been thinking that there were five thousand rebels. He told his wife and servants what to do if they came closer, and he sent me to tell Sir Francis, the governor, what I'd learned.'

'Did you see the governor?' Adam asked, awed.

'Oh, yes. I'd met him before – father knows him. He was worried – that's why he moved his headquarters from the Parliament Buildings to the City Hall, which he thinks is easier to defend. I guess he was one of the people who thought that there were five thousand rebels, and he had only a few hundred militia to defend the town.'

'He even tried to make peace with the rebels,' Charlotte added. 'Before Cornelia told him that Mr Mackenzie had far fewer men than everyone thought, the governor had sent three people with a flag of truce, offering to negotiate.'

'What did the governor say when you told him?' Adam asked Cornelia.

'He sort of laughed. I guess he was relieved. He said he needn't bother about a truce, then, but that he'd still be glad to have all the militia he could get.'

'Since then,' Charlotte added, 'we've heard that when the men with the flag of truce returned from the rebel camp, Sir Francis sent them off again, back to the rebels, to say that there'd be no negotiations. Meanwhile poor Dr Horne's house is burning.'

To Adam it seemed a very hit-and-miss way of doing things – not what you'd expect of important people such as the governor and the manager of the bank. Maybe even people like that didn't always act sensibly.

However, he had not forgotten his own plan.

'I'm going up there, to Gallows Hill or wherever they are now, to try to find my uncle,' he said. 'If you can pass safely, Cornelia, so can I.'

'Your uncle?'

'He's probably with the rebels. How far is it to Gallows Hill?'

The de Grassi sisters exchanged questioning looks.

'An hour's walking?' he asked, impatient to be on his way. He wished he had Princess.

'About that,' Cornelia said.

'I'll go, then.'

'It'll be dark soon,' Charlotte pointed out. 'Why do you have to find your uncle?'

'To ask him not to fight. If he's killed or wounded, what will happen to Aunt Lenore and the kids?'

Both of them looked at him curiously.

'Is that crazy?' he blurted out.

'No, it's ...,' Charlotte began, and then hesitated. 'It's kind of odd but nice of you to care what happens to them, to think of going to talk to your uncle. A lot of people wouldn't.'

'It *is* crazy,' he muttered.

'No,' Cornelia said firmly. 'I like you for it.'

That embarrassed them all.

'I'd better be going,' he said. 'Goodbye.'

''Bye, Adam.'

'Good luck,' Charlotte added.

*

The December afternoon was indeed darkening and the sense of danger stronger. Adam was not the only one who felt it. A mother scurried back and forth before her open door calling her children home. Another woman leading a horse was nearly running, forcing the horse into a trot. A rider cantered past, muffled to the eyes in his cloak.

Adam wished he had not left it so late. Had the idea of finding Uncle Ted occurred to him earlier, he could have gone from the Don Mills straight to Montgomery's Tavern or to Gallows Hill or wherever Mr Mackenzie's men were. It would have saved him miles of walking, and he would have had more daylight. Now he'd have to make most of the journey by dark, along unfamiliar roads, never knowing when he might encounter armed men like the ones who had stopped Charlotte de Grassi last night. As a working-class boy on foot he ought to be safe enough, but all the same ....

He remembered Josh Perkins pointing out Yonge Street, and when he reached it he headed north, keeping the still-glowing western sky to his left. He passed a tannery, recognizable by its foul smell.

Just up ahead there was a crowd, almost filling the street from side to side. By now it was dark enough for a few lanterns to be lit, and the people seemed to be gathered around an alehouse.

Could this be Montgomery's Tavern already? It was much too soon.

All the same, he thought he'd better find out.

'Is this Montgomery's?' he asked a man standing on the fringe of the crowd.

'No, it's Elliot's. The Sun Tavern. This here's called rebel corner, 'cause Elliot favours our side.' The man gave Adam a good look and then laughed. 'Bit young to be joining up, aintcha?' He turned to the man beside him. 'Look at this, Dave, a little kid gettin' ready to fight.'

Adam slipped away. He'd learned what he needed to know, but he was also annoyed. Little kid! Would he ever grow big enough to look his age?

[160]

Immediately north of Elliot's Tavern, still on the west side of the road, was a neighbourhood much like the one where Mrs Perkins' boardinghouse was, an unorganized and over-crowded huddle of small houses and shacks. Adam remembered having seen it on the day he and Harry wandered up this way. On the right, after a cluster of industrial buildings, was forest, very gloomy on this December evening.

But out here on the road it was not pitch dark. By the last glow of sunset, and the light of a half moon shining through the gaps between clouds, he could see well enough where he was going.

The poor neighbourhood to the left ended abruptly and was followed by white entrance gates looming in the dimness. Behind them was a big house with lights in several windows.

Two men shouted 'Good night!' to each other, and a door slammed. A horseman galloped past Adam towards the city. Adam kept walking north, now among fields and woods.

Maybe it was the man's calling him a little kid; whatever it was, Adam suddenly saw himself from the outside. It *was* a crazy errand. Stupid!

He had to do it, though. For Aunt Lenore, and to try to ease the guilt inside himself.

Suppose, however, that Uncle Ted really believed in what he was doing. People did do dangerous things when they believed in something, and other folk had to respect that. At the time of the Captain Swing riots back home, the landless farm workers had risked everything to protest against the poverty and injustice of their lives. They rioted because there was no other way. Certainly there would have been no point in being reasonable and cautious.

All the same, it was hard to think of Uncle Ted as a man with high principles. More likely he'd joined Mr Mackenzie because idling about with other men, and even fighting, was more fun than working and because, if his side won, there'd be easy pickings, a short cut to the life he wanted.

Perhaps that made Adam's errand even more useless. But somehow, obstinately, he felt he had to try. If he didn't, and something happened to Uncle Ted, he'd always feel guilty.

*

After passing another short stretch of emptiness, he came to more houses – one on the right and another almost directly opposite on the left, both with lights in the windows.

Somewhere up ahead a dog barked. At the same time, Adam made out sounds and movement, the tramp of many walking feet, a murmur of voices, a whiff of tobacco smoke on the breeze. Then he could see dimly what was happening – and what he saw was the road ahead filled with people coming towards him. Most were on foot but there were a few on horseback. Here and there was a bobbing, swaying lantern.

Such a crowd of men walking – marching – from the north towards Toronto could only be Mr Mackenzie and his followers. Something like eight hundred men, if Cornelia and Dr Horne were correct. To the governor, who had expected five thousand, that might be a small number, but to Adam it sounded like a lot.

An army.

And suddenly 'army' was the right word. In spite of the homely lantern light and tobacco smoke, the sound of those tramping feet meant battle.

And he was directly in their path.

He dashed to the right, and found himself beside a rail fence surrounding the yard of one of the houses he'd noticed earlier. As he hunkered down, someone on the other side of the fence sneezed. The sound was savagely muffled in a handkerchief or a coat sleeve, but it was definitely a sneeze.

There was no sign that the approaching men heard it. The mutter of talk, the tread of hundreds of boots on frozen ground, the clinking of metal heel plates on stones, were loud enough to cover the noise. But it alerted Adam. Cornelia had said that Dr Horne had urged the placing of a picket on Yonge Street to guard the city from the north. Maybe that's who was hiding behind the fence. He wondered how many men a picket consisted of. From what Cornelia said, it sounded as though it would be more a guard than a large fighting force.

Mr Mackenzie's army was coming nearer. Would Uncle Ted be with them? Would the men hiding behind the fence try to stop them? If it came to fighting, Adam was too late.

When the rebel force was within range, someone behind the fence shouted, 'Fire!' There was a blinding blaze and a stuttering roar of muskets going off, and a great deal of smoke. A moment later came flashes of musket fire from the army and, Adam thought, from behind a fence on the far side of the road. The noise resounded in his ears, and the air was full of a choking smell.

Blinded by the flashes, and with smoke added to darkness, Adam couldn't see much, but it looked as though the front line of Mackenzie's army had fallen. That meant there were men killed or wounded, and in horror at the thought he shrank closer to the fence.

There were a few more shots, and then everyone ran. The men who had been in hiding close to Adam vaulted the fence and headed for the city. If Adam had not been crouched low, right against the fence, he would have been struck by crashing boots.

At the same time, the rebel army turned tail and ran north, back up Yonge Street. There were a few shouts, but they were almost drowned out by the noise of pounding feet. If the shouting was intended to turn the men back to continue the fight, it didn't work.

But not everyone fled. As the sound of the two stampedes was fading away in the distance to the north and south, a couple of men bent over something dark lying on the ground. One of the dead or wounded men, Adam thought – but why was there only one? If that whole front line had fallen ....

Perhaps they had only been slightly wounded and were still able to flee. Or maybe they had ducked after firing their muskets so as to let the line behind them fire theirs.

The two men muttered something and half dragged, half carried the dead or wounded man to the side of the road, near where Adam was. Then they trudged off, heading north.

While Adam was wondering whether to go and see if he could help the victim, the front door of the house near him opened and a light appeared. A woman in apron and shawl, and carrying a lantern, came out. The lantern illuminated the area and she stooped over the heavy object dumped close to her fence.

'Oh, the poor man!' she exclaimed.

Adam was not sure whether to go to her. She might be frightened at the appearance of a stranger, but if she needed help ....

He cleared his throat. 'Excuse me, ma'am ....'

The lantern lurched. 'Who's that?'

'Adam Wheeler. I'm not one of the fighting men. I just happened to be here. Can I help?'

'There's a man here who seems hurt,' she said, her voice sounding tense. 'Or maybe he's dead. If you could hold the lantern ....'

He went forward. While handing him the lantern, the woman gave him a close look but was apparently not alarmed by what she saw. Then she knelt down, moving stiffly as though she suffered from rheumatism.

The man was lying on his side. It was not Uncle Ted, Adam was relieved to see, but he would be someone else's husband or father or son.

The kneeling woman moved the man's arm so that she could reach his wrist to feel the pulse. As she did so, the lantern light shone on his chest, which was a mass of blood.

Adam squeezed his eyes shut and cringed, ducking

sideways as though it was he who had been shot.

'Oh, dear lord!' the woman said under her breath. She felt for the man's pulse, then laid his arm where it had been. After a moment's silence, she got awkwardly to her feet.

'He's dead,' she said grimly. 'I'll fetch something to cover him. Will you wait here for a minute? Or are you afraid?'

'I'm not afraid, ma'am.'

Not afraid, maybe, but full of a turmoil of horror and grief. He couldn't bear to look at the dead man so he stared north, at the silence left by the retreating army.

But he knew the man was there. Husband, son, brother – a hole left in a family, a hole that for some loving, lonely person might never be filled. And such a stupid waste of a life, twenty-five or thirty years of living wiped out in an instant.

Adam remembered what had brought him here. Was there any point in *still* trying to reach Uncle Ted?

The dead man at his feet, a clear reminder that men were killed in war, made his errand even more important. But the thought of plodding up Yonge Street in the wake of that retreating stampede – plodding on to look for Uncle Ted in the darkness and confusion, searching among men who were frightened and angry and perhaps scattered all over the countryside . . . .

The woman returned with a bed-sheet, which she spread over the dead man. Then she took back her lantern.

'I'll send word to have someone fetch him in the morning. They'll find out who he is and tell his folks.' She spoke grimly. 'Ain't nothin' more we can do for now.'

Together she and Adam stood looking down at the shrouded form.

A dog barked, not far away, and the woman with the lantern gave a deep sigh. 'Hope the dogs don't get at him during the night.'

'I hope so too. Good night, ma'am.'

'I'm Mrs Sharpe. Good night, lad.' She nodded to him and

turned to plod up the path to the house, her lantern swaying slightly against her skirt.

Just ... good night? And what about this poor man? Was there really nothing more they could do? Suppose the dogs *did* get at him? Adam shuddered again at the thought. Mrs Sharpe could have taken the dead man into her house until his family came to get him. But it was not up to him to suggest it.

And what about Adam himself? Mrs Sharpe hadn't even asked where he lived, how far he had to walk home, hadn't offered him a cup of tea or the loan of the lantern.

Maybe it was silly of him to expect it. But he thought his mother, had she found herself with a dead man at the gate and a boy who had perhaps just had his first contact with violent death, might have been kinder, might have cared how he was going to get home.

Inside the Sharpe house, an invisible hand set a lighted candle on the sill of one of the front windows. It was something, perhaps, a token of respect for the dead man, but it did nothing for Adam himself.

He turned away and began walking home. After a few yards, he looked back. The white-shrouded mound was very small in the huge blackness of the night.

He sighed and again turned homewards, south along Yonge Street and then along the first road east. It was soon interrupted by some woods, but there was a well-worn trail through them. Beyond that, the road resumed, skirting along the south side of a ravine beyond which, to the north, was a big house with lights in several of its windows. Adam thought it was the one he'd seen during his exploration with Harry. What was it called? He remembered the little boy leading the cow. 'That's Mr Allan's place. Moss Park, they call it.'

On that day, Adam had been bored. He had overcome the boredom by making some decisions, finding a job, taking charge of his own life. And now this stupid war had come along, messing everything up.

But it was worse than messy. That dead man, alive one minute and dead the next ... the wastefulness of it. If a life could end so suddenly ... so *easily* ....

All of Mr Allan's money couldn't protect him. Adam's own attempts to build a life ... Aunt Lenore's endless sewing and mending .... They were all useless. There wasn't any point in anything.

If he stopped struggling now, just stopped right here and lay down beside the path ....

He plodded on, past the big Roman Catholic church, across the bridge, up the Mill Road.

When he opened the back door of the Skinners' house and stepped into the kitchen, the light blinded him.

'Where did *you* get to?' Nelly's voice demanded.

'What time is it?' he asked, numb.

'Gone half past seven.'

His eyes adjusted to the light, and he saw that she was washing the dishes. Now, frowning at him, she began drying her hands. 'I suppose you ain't had nothin' to eat.'

He didn't answer.

'What's the matter, lad? Here ....'

She came across, took the cap off his head, and had a good look at him. 'What's wrong, Adam?'

'I've seen a dead man ... there was a battle ... and ... I ... I tried to get to Uncle Ted but I failed ....'

He knew it didn't make any sense.

'Seen a *dead* man? Oh, Adam ....' She put her arms around him and held him tight for a moment, then led him to the settle by the fire. 'You sit here and get warm and eat some soup and tell me about it.'

He hadn't realized until then how cold he was – frozen cold inside and outside, his body clenched tight with it. It was the cold of horror and misery and emptiness as well as of the long walk in the December night. He held his hands up to the fire to warm them.

In response to Nelly's questions, he told a few more things. There'd been a battle on Yonge Street. Both sides had run away. A man had been killed. He couldn't find the desire or the energy to make a connected story of it.

'You were looking for your Uncle Ted?' she asked. 'Why?'

'To ... to ask him to think what would happen to the family if he were ....'

He couldn't say the word. The image of the dead man rose up like a bloody ghost, so that Adam had to squeeze his eyes closed.

Maybe it *hadn't* been such a silly idea to try to find Uncle Ted. But then on the other hand, maybe it had been even *sillier, more foolish*, to try to find him in that army and to get him to listen.

Anyway, he'd failed.

Chapter Fifteen

HEN ADAM WOKE THE next morning, it was slowly and reluctantly. Something in him didn't want to face this day, and he curled up tightly in the warm nest under the covers, trying to keep his mind blank.

But when he drew a deep breath, he realized that he didn't really feel so bad. The air he pulled into his lungs was cold and clean, and he felt like a slate wiped by sleep – and, he realized, also wiped by a dream which he couldn't remember but which somehow seemed to have left peace behind it.

He stayed very quiet, savouring the feeling. The sky outside the window was still dark, but he knew it was morning because he could hear Nelly busy downstairs – the clang of poker against kettle, the snapping of a wood fire freshly kindled from last night's carefully banked coals, a dish put down on the table with a clunk.

But in spite of feeling better, he sensed that last night's misery was hovering close by. Better get going, he thought, and slid out from under the covers into the cold.

After breakfast, he was put to work again on the firewood – for the mill this time, not for Nelly. 'Winter's coming on, lad,' Mr Skinner said when he gave Adam his instructions. 'Can't ever have too much firewood on hand. I want you to saw up those branches that Bert dragged out of the bush. And pile the stuff that McPhee split before he left. Stack it neatly, now – we don't want any toppling wood piles.'

'Yes, sir. I mean, no, sir.'

'But first take this note to Mr Helliwell at the brewery for me. You can leave it with Meg if he's not about.'

'Yes, sir.'

Mr Helliwell was still at breakfast but Meg, the servant, took the note. Coming back across the yard among the mills, Adam told himself that it felt like Sunday, with the paper mill and the axe-grinding shop closed and the brewery and distillery barely operating. A few crows cawed high up in a tall tree, and sparrows pecked the grain spilled near the Helliwells' storage shed. A dog lay asleep in a sheltered corner.

Come to think of it, though, on a Sunday there would be men around. It was quieter than any normal day, with something tense in the air. After all, there had been the fight yesterday near Mrs Sharpe's house – he didn't know whether it was important enough to be called a battle – and a man had been killed. That meant three men dead, including the two killed on Monday night, and Dr Horne's house burned down – and that was only what Adam knew about. Fighting ... men getting killed .... He crunched his eyes closed against the memory.

As he began work on the firewood, though, he once more started feeling better. It was a sunny day, crisp but not really cold, and after a while he took off his coat. Warm enough to be in shirt sleeves.

A little later, as he lifted another branch onto the sawhorse and slid it along to the right position for sawing off the first fireplace-length piece, he said to himself, 'A man's work!' He *could* do a man's work, in spite of what Uncle Ted had said. The teeth of the saw bit into the bark and down to the creamy wood beneath, spitting bright sawdust into the sunlight. Definitely man's work.

When he'd sawed far enough down, the piece broke off and fell by its own weight, landing on top of the three or four lying there already. Adam carried them to the pile under the shed roof – chunks too fat for kindling but not fat enough to need splitting.

Later still, when Adam was beginning to think he'd earned a short rest, Mr Skinner appeared, a piece of paper in his hand and a frown pulling his eyebrows together.

'Adam . . . .'

'Yes, sir?'

'Nelly says there was a fight on Yonge Street yesterday and that you saw it. What were you doing there? Dangerous place for a lad like you to be.'

At first Adam thought Mr Skinner was scolding him, but somehow he seemed more worried than angry.

'I'd . . . I'd rather not say, sir. It was personal – it had to do with my family.' He didn't want to tell the whole wretched story once more.

'Not joining the rebels, are you?'

Was this a joke? Adam couldn't make out what Mr Skinner was leading up to.

'No, sir.'

Mr Skinner sat down on the splitting block. 'Tell me about it – I mean, about the fight you saw.'

Something in his manner suggested that after all he was not going to scold Adam, that he was only looking for information. Adam stopped feeling quite so defensive, but he was not sure what Mr Skinner wanted to know.

'Well,' he began hesitantly, 'it was between a lot of people coming down Yonge Street – Mr Mackenzie's men, I suppose – and some others hiding behind fences, waiting for them.'

'Who won?'

'I guess . . . no one did. Both sides fired their guns and then ran away.'

'How many men?'

'It was dark. Maybe a couple of dozen on the government side, the ones in hiding. Not an army, just a guard. But there were more, a lot more, on the other side, the ones marching down Yonge Street. You could tell by the sound they made walking, and then running away. *They* were an army, all right.'

'Several hundred?'

'If this was the same group that was at Gallows Hill yesterday, it'd be about seven or eight hundred. Someone in town said that that's how many men Mr Mackenzie has – not five thousand, like they first thought.'

He hoped that Mr Skinner wouldn't ask where he'd got that information. For some reason, he didn't want to mention Cornelia's spying expedition.

Mr Skinner frowned as he listened.

'Eight hundred, eh?' He sighed. 'I'll tell you why I'm asking, lad. This note is from Mr Mackenzie, ordering paper. Seems he's got a press up there and wants to print something. We've been selling him paper for years, but now .... Well, it's politics, you see. We supported him when he was talking about reform, *only* reform. He's a good man, Mackenzie, really cares about the common people, about fairness. But he got ... kind of carried away, I guess. I didn't like his talk about taking up arms, and *now* ... I'd talk it over with Mr Eastwood but he's in town. That's why I was asking you about that fight on Yonge Street yesterday. If Mackenzie looks as though he's going to win, no harm in sending him the paper. If he loses .... Eight hundred men ....'

He brooded, staring at the ground that was littered with sawdust and wood chips.

He looked up. 'What do you think, Adam? I'm not asking you to decide anything, because you're only a lad after all. But you're a bright kid and you saw that fight yesterday. Did Mackenzie have enough men to ...? What do you think of his chances?'

Adam felt uncomfortable. How was he supposed to know? Mr Skinner said he didn't expect Adam to make the decision, but all the same he was hoping for something.

'I really can't say, sir. Maybe when Mr Eastwood gets back from town ....'

'That'll be too late. Mr Mackenzie wants his paper right away.' He brooded again.

Adam waited, half sitting on the sawhorse, picking at a bit of loose bark on the branch he'd been sawing up. It wasn't right for Mr Skinner to ask him to help decide anything as important as this.

'Eight hundred men ....' Mr Skinner muttered again. Then he rose heavily to his feet. 'Don't mind me, lad. I'm just talking to myself. I guess we'll send Mackenzie his paper. Two reams of foolscap. Come and help me pack it.'

As they walked across to the mill, Adam asked, 'How are you going to get it to him, sir?'

Mr Skinner was silent for what seemed like a long time. 'I'd send McPhee if he were here. I'd go myself, only I'm too well-known and don't much want to be seen in Mr Mackenzie's camp up there at Montgomery's.' He gave Adam a sidelong glance. 'So that leaves you. On horseback, of course. There'll be something in it for you, and I wouldn't be surprised if Mr Mackenzie was to give you a tip. And if he wins the battle ... well, you never can tell, can you?'

The last words were said in a hearty sort of voice that Adam recognized. His dad talked that way when he was embarrassed about something. Probably Mr Skinner was not too happy to be sending him to Mr Mackenzie's camp. If there was more fighting, and Adam got hurt ....

But any sensible person would notice when a fight was about to happen and would get out of the way in time, as he'd done last night.

In spite of the hearty voice, Mr Skinner looked worried. But he didn't say anything more until they reached the mill.

From one of the stacks of paper, he took the amount ordered. Two reams was about a thousand sheets; Mr Skinner put it on the work-counter and divided it into two piles.

'One for each saddle bag,' he said.

As they were wrapping the bundles in brown paper and tying string around them, Mr Skinner asked, 'Did you actually see Mr Mackenzie yesterday, Adam?'

'No, sir, not to recognize. Why?'

'That note ... there's something funny about it. The hand-writing is shakier than usual. And he left out a word – I had to figure out what he meant. I wondered whether you'd noticed anything odd in his manner, but if you didn't see him ....'

'He could have been in a hurry when he wrote the note.'

'No doubt he was. But he's a man who's always writing. You wouldn't expect him to make a mistake in what he does all the time. But never mind about that now. I've had another thought. While you're out on horseback, I'd like you to take a message to my brother-in-law, Mr Thomas Helliwell, in town.'

'You mean ... after I've been to Montgomery's Tavern?'

'Yes, deliver the paper first. Mr Mackenzie's in a hurry, so far as I can make out from this order of his.' He tied the final knot and handed the parcels to Adam while he turned towards his office. 'You go and saddle Princess while I write the note to Mr Helliwell.'

Adam felt very grown up as he put the saddle and saddle-bags on Princess. But he was not so happy about the errands he had to do. He had been uncomfortable when Mr Skinner talked about him carrying a message to Mr Thomas Hel-liwell. There was something wrong about that.

And then he realized what it was. He would be riding straight from one camp to the other, from Mr Mackenzie's side to the government side. Wasn't that dangerous? If there was a war on, you didn't just go back and forth between the two enemy camps as though everything was normal.

When Mr Skinner reappeared, Adam asked about it. 'Won't it look bad for me to ride from Mr Mackenzie's camp straight to town – to the government headquarters?'

'Oh, I don't think so,' Mr Skinner said casually. 'No one will know. The two camps are miles apart; no one can *watch* you go from one to the other.'

Adam hoped he was right.

Mr Skinner gave him two notes, one sealed and the other open. 'This one is to my brother-in-law,' he said, handing over the sealed one. 'And this is the note I received from Mr Mackenzie. If anyone – I mean a guard or anyone on Mr Mackenzie's side – tries to stop you from passing, show him this to make it clear that you're there for a good reason, to deliver the paper he ordered. But don't show it unless you have to.'

'Yes, sir.'

'Now, about how to get there. The shortest way is to cross the river and ride up one of the ravines. *Much* shorter than by the road, and safer. Keeps you away from places where you might be stopped and asked questions.'

Adam didn't like the sound of that last bit, but he pushed aside his uneasiness. He had to go through with this, so the safer the better.

'I cross the river here ...?'

From where they stood, in the Skinners' yard, they could see a good part of the valley. Mr Skinner pointed. 'Down to the flats and upstream to our dam. Just below there the river is pretty shallow and Princess'll wade across. On the far side is a ravine opening out into the main valley. Go up that – there's a trail – and it'll lead you to Yonge Street near Montgomery's Tavern.'

'How long will it take me?'

'No more'n an hour. Probably less. When you've delivered the paper to Mr Mackenzie, you can ride down Yonge Street and take the other note to my brother-in-law. See him in person if you can. If you get stopped by government pickets on your way into the city, don't tell them you've come from Montgomery's Tavern, and of course don't show *them* the note from Mr Mackenzie. Say you were delivering a message for me ....' He pondered for a moment. ' ... a message to Mr Bloor at the brewery, and you got lost. You're new in town and it's easy to lose your way.' He pointed again, this time towards the southwest. 'Bloor's brewery is in a different ravine from the one you'll be taking, and it's hilly and confusing country around there. Oh, and ....' Mr Skinner dug into his trouser pocket and brought out a few coins. He handed Adam two pennies. 'For the tollgates. You'll need one for the gate at Yorkville when you go into town and another for the gate at the bridge on your way home.'

As Adam used the mounting block to climb into the saddle, Mr Skinner said, 'Good luck, now, lad. Come and see me when you get back.' He patted Adam's knee and then Princess's rump.

As Adam rode away, what stayed in his mind was Mr Skinner's face, which somehow managed to be smiling and worried at the same time, serious but trying to pretend that this was nothing special.

*

When Princess discovered that she would have to wade across the river, she shook her head resentfully, with a jingle of the bridle, but on Adam's determined urging she obeyed. The water was perhaps two feet deep, down from where it had been a week ago when Gavin, coming back from doing some work at the dam, reported that it was nearly three feet deep below the dam and flowing fast.

Once he was riding up the ravine, Adam gave some more thought to Mr Skinner's smiling, worried face. What did it mean? Of course there was plenty for him to worry about. From the government's point of view, he was doing business with the enemy. Sergeant Phillips, on the ship, had called that a risky thing to do in wartime – only, as Mr Skinner had hinted, in order to know who 'the enemy' was you had to guess who was going to win the war. If you were trying not to take sides, 'the enemy' would be whoever lost.

If the government side won, Mr Skinner would be in trouble. So would Adam. He remembered Sergeant Phillips saying that it was no excuse for someone like him to protest that he was only following orders.

But going from Montgomery's Tavern straight into town?

Mr Skinner's reassurance that no one would *see* Adam riding out of one camp and into the other might be true but it was not comforting. By the time Adam reached town, he would be rid of the parcels of paper, but he'd still have Mr Mackenzie's note. He could understand why Mr Skinner had given him the note – to help him get past the guards and *into* Mr Mackenzie's camp. But if government soldiers stopped and searched him on his way to town, and *they* found the note on him ....

If that happened, there'd be no point in telling the lie about having been sent to Bloor's brewery. The note would show that he had been to the rebel camp.

Just as – he realized with a shock – the note to Mr Helliwell would show people on Mr Mackenzie's side, if they searched him, that after leaving Montgomery's Tavern he was supposed to go to town, to deliver a message to a man supporting the government.

The only thing to do was to hide the notes as carefully as possible – or rather, to hide each one in turn. At each stage of the journey, he would have to conceal the one that would get him into trouble *there*. He'd need Mr Mackenzie's note first, so he would put the other one ... where? Pockets were the first things they would search, but ....

All he could think of was to slide it up his sleeve. They'd find it if they *really* searched, but if that happened he'd be in trouble anyway.

So he took out the two notes, made sure he knew which was which, put the one from Mr Mackenzie back into his coat pocket, and slid the one to Mr Helliwell inside his shirt sleeve, where the snug fit of his clothes would keep it in place.

After he left Montgomery's Tavern, could he actually destroy Mr Mackenzie's note? That would make it safer for him if he were searched by guards on the government side.

But the note was an order for paper. It really ought to be put in the office for Mr Carver, the clerk, to file when he returned.

Surely, though, it would be all right for Adam to destroy it if it made things dangerous for him.

He wished he'd been able to say 'no' to this whole business. But he was only a hired hand and had to follow orders.

And after all he might be able to make use of it by seeing Uncle Ted and trying to persuade him to leave the rebel army while there was still time – the errand he'd failed to do yesterday.

*

The ravine he was following was deep and steep-sided at first but gradually became shallower. The trail continued, a clear path among the bare trees and tangled underbrush. In spite of his brooding, Adam kept his eyes and ears open. Once he was startled by a noise in the bush but it turned out to be only a deer. Another time a fox flashed across the path, and there were lots of squirrels and some crows. But he saw no human beings until he reached a point where the ravine had become little more than a slight dip and the trail emerged from the woods into an area being cleared. The trees had been cut but there were stumps and logs and lopped branches and crushed undergrowth everywhere. At the far right-hand edge of the clearing, quite a way off, two men were at work, one chopping at the base of a huge tree and the other removing branches from a felled one. As Adam watched them, he realized again how impossible it was to picture Uncle Ted doing such work. He'd never in his life done anything like it – anything which needed that much strength, both physical strength and the obstinate, dogged strength of mind needed to keep on and on at such a task. Adam couldn't imagine him lasting for even a day, let alone years.

In the ugly and chaotic wasteland of half-cleared bush, the

trail disappeared. Adam found it easier to stay inside the fringe of the forest; nature, though tangled enough, was tidier than the man-made mess out in the clearing.

The land to his right became neater as he went, with branches and undergrowth cleared away. In the next stretch, among the stumps, lay withered pumpkin vines. Beyond that was an area where even the stumps were gone and where, at a distance, stood a farmhouse and a low barn.

Adam, afraid of being questioned, stayed well away from the farmhouse. When he reached a north-south road, he guessed from Mr Skinner's directions that it might be Yonge Street. To his right was a smudge of smoke against the sky, and a little cluster of buildings. He headed for them.

*

As he approached the buildings, he saw half a dozen men lounging against a rail fence, smoking pipes and drinking from an earthenware jug which they passed around. Two came into the road to stop him. They were the only ones who carried guns; except for that, they looked like ordinary farmers in squashed felt hats and rough woollen coats and trousers.

'This is Mr Mackenzie's headquarters,' said one of them, taking hold of the bridle. 'What're you doing here, lad?'

Adam felt his muscles tighten but tried to speak calmly. 'Delivering some paper to Mr Mackenzie.'

'Paper?'

'For printing.'

'Who's this paper from?'

'Mr Skinner. The York Paper Mill. At the Don Mills, near Todmorden.'

With a twitch of his head, the leader summoned the other armed man – a gloomy-looking person chewing tobacco – to hold the bridle. Then, swinging his own gun over his shoulder by its strap so as to leave his hands free, he opened the saddle bags. He lifted out each package of paper, pinched and shook it, rummaged in the bag to see if it contained anything else, then put the paper in again.

'Looks okay to me,' he said, half to the other guards and half to Adam.

'Only Little Mac ain't here,' one of the lounging men said. 'He's . . . .'

The leader interrupted.

'That's right,' he told Adam. 'Mr Mackenzie ain't here just now.'

'Can I leave the paper with someone else . . . or with you?'

'Better take it up to the tavern. Give it to Mr Linfoot, the innkeeper.'

'I thought it was *Montgomery's* Tavern.'

'Mr Linfoot's running it now.'

They seemed about to let Adam go when another man came running towards them, this one wearing an eye-patch and carrying a spear-like thing that Adam thought was called a pike.

'What you got there? Another kid? Hang on to him.'

'Why?' the leader asked.

'You let a kid through earlier. 'Bout an hour ago.'

'Did we? Oh, yeah, a girl. What about it?'

'We're holding her for spying.'

'*Spying?* That little girl on the pony?' The man's face twitched into a grin but then became anxious.

'Well, we're holding her,' said the man with the eye-patch. 'She went to the wheelwright's, next door to the tavern, and asked how much a sleigh would cost.'

'Makes sense,' commented one of the men lounging against the fence. 'It's December. There'll be snow soon.'

'Yeah, but to come up here *now?* With all this going on? A girl *alone?* Anyhow, we're holding her for Little Mac to talk to. Besides, one of the fellas says there was a girl in our camp at Gallows Hill yesterday. Girl on a pony – could be the same one. If they're sending kids to spy on us . . . .'

Adam listened closely. It was probably Cornelia, and he was sure that the man was right in guessing that she was spying. Cocky about her success yesterday, she had tried the same thing again. But this time they were holding her – and because of her, Adam's own errand was riskier than it need have been.

At least he had the paper to prove that he was on a real errand, and he had Mr Mackenzie's note. But he could be delivering paper *and* spying. Certainly, now, it would be even more dangerous for him to ride straight down to Toronto.

Damn the girl!

'We checked his saddlebags,' said the leader. 'He really does have paper. For printing on, he says. You know Little Mac, always wanting to print things, and he's got a press up Yonge Street somewhere. Stands to reason he'd need paper.'

'Maybe so, but I don't like it. *Two* kids ....'

Adam pulled out the note from Mr Mackenzie to Mr Skinner and offered it to the leader, the one who had searched the saddle bags.

'Here's Mr Mackenzie's order,' he said.

'I believe you, kid.'

'That other man doesn't.'

The guard took the note, read it, and passed it on to the man with the eye-patch.

'If we don't let Little Mac have his paper ...,' the guard said. 'You know the state he's in. Half crazy. It'll be "off with his head" – *our* heads.'

'I'm not against him getting his paper. I just think we should hold the kid till Mac sees him.'

'All right, do it your way.'

'We'll send someone with him up to the tavern to make sure he doesn't escape. Can you spare one of your men?' His one good eye travelled along the row lounging against the fence.

'Joe here can do it,' the guard said, indicating the tobacco-chewing fellow holding Princess's bridle.

[182]

Chapter Sixteen

WHILE LISTENING uneasily to the argument, Adam had been sizing up the camp in front of him.

Montgomery's Tavern was a big, square building with a drive shed and other structures near it. From one came the clanging sound of a big hammer striking metal – a blacksmith, or possibly the wheelwright whom Cornelia had said she'd come to see.

In the open area around the buildings were dozens of men. One group was marching, no doubt being drilled by some enthusiastic militia officer who had transferred his loyalty – and his military training, such as it was – to the opposite side. Other men stood smoking, or sat on the platform in front of the tavern. Some were eating and drinking. A couple of bonfires had been lit; it was a fine day, but after all it was December.

Joe, Adam's escort, spoke not a word as they plodded to the tavern. He looked gloomy and discouraged. Adam wondered whether this was because events were not going as he'd hoped, or whether it was just his normal mood.

At the tavern's hitching rail, Adam dismounted. He wasn't sure what to do about Princess, and he looked at Joe.

'Do you stay here and hold her? Or do I hitch her up?'

'Eh?' Joe asked absent-mindedly.

'I have to take the paper into the tavern.' To show what he meant, he pulled the packages out of the saddlebags. 'Will you stay here holding my horse or do you come with me? If you come with me, we have to hitch her to the rail.'

Joe spat tobacco juice. 'I'll stay here.'

Adam went into the tavern, the door of which was standing

open to allow a constant stream of men to go in and out.

The rooms inside were crowded, noisy, full of pipe smoke and the smell of food and drink and bodies. When someone noticed him – a big man with a gun and, like almost everyone else, with several days' growth of beard – Adam asked for Mr Linfoot.

The man stared down at Adam in amazement, and laughed.

'Mr Linfoot, is it? Come on, lad.' He grasped Adam's shoulder and pulled him through the crowd, into one of the rooms and over to the bar, behind which four men were serving drinks as fast as their eight hands could move.

'Linfoot!' bellowed the man with the gun. 'C'm'ere a minute!'

One of the bartenders handed over the tankard he'd filled and came towards them.

'Lad here wants you.'

Adam lifted the parcels onto the bar. 'Paper from Eastwood and Skinner,' he said. 'Ordered by Mr Mackenzie.'

'He's not here.'

'I know. They said – the guards, I mean – that I could leave it with you.'

'Right, lad.' The innkeeper grabbed the paper and shoved it under the counter, then turned away to attend to a customer demanding whisky.

'Okay now, lad?' the man with the gun asked.

'Just one more thing – do you happen to know a man called Ted Wheeler?'

'Is he with us?'

'I think so. Big, blond man. Just out from England – he's been working in Dundas for the last little while. He's my uncle. I'd like to see him if I can.'

'I think I know the guy you mean.'

'Where can I find him?'

'Saw him not long ago. Try the other room, or just outside.'

The other room was slightly less crowded. It contained tables and chairs, all occupied, and among them some men standing. All of them seemed to be talking at the same time. As Adam looked around, he heard a laugh he recognized. He went across, heavy-footed now that he was actually near Uncle Ted.

His uncle was sitting at one of the tables, telling a story. Adam waited behind him until there was a convenient moment for interrupting.

As he waited, half listening to the story, he watched the scene. Uncle Ted was telling the story well, holding the attention of the three other men sitting at the table and two others standing behind them. Uncle Ted *did* have talents – if only he were more realistic, if only he were not so lazy.

When the story was finished and the listeners were laughing in a relaxed, appreciative way, Adam moved into view.

'Hello, Uncle Ted.'

As Uncle Ted turned towards him, his face for a moment showed fear, the same uncertainty and defensiveness that Adam had seen when they were standing outside the Parliament Buildings. Then immediately he scowled.

'What're *you* doing here?' he demanded, almost snarling.

'Came to deliver some paper to Mr Mackenzie. Can I talk to you for a minute – outside?' He was uncomfortable under the curious eyes of the other men at the table, and was convinced now that talking to his uncle was a bad idea. But the thought of Aunt Lenore working hard in Dundas to support herself and the kids while Uncle Ted sat here talking and laughing, drinking beer and smoking his pipe, risking his life in a way that could affect them all, made him stubborn.

Uncle Ted was clearly about to refuse when one of the other men at the table gave Adam a friendly look and said, 'Message from home, Ted. Wish I was so lucky.'

Adam was grateful. This was the first person who didn't seem to think he was crazy.

Uncle Ted scraped back his chair and got up.

'I'll be right back,' he said, and led the way outdoors. 'Well, then, kid, what is it?'

Now that he was actually face to face with his uncle, Adam wasn't sure what to say. The memory of the argument they'd had about his finding a job at the paper mill tied his tongue.

But he had to try.

'I wanted to ask you to ... to think what would happen to Aunt Lenore and the others if you got hurt or killed.'

'You ... *what?*'

Adam was silent. He'd said what was on his mind, and he had no answer to his uncle's scorn.

'This is war, Adam. We're fighting for what we believe in.' Uncle Ted pushed out his chest.

For Adam, that wasn't the important thing.

'What about Aunt Lenore and the kids?'

'They'll survive.' Uncle Ted turned to go indoors. 'And you get the hell out of here.'

Well, he'd said his piece. Maybe, in a war, you shouldn't try to make a fighting man see sense. But it *was* sensible. It was Uncle Ted who was being wrong-headed, not Adam.

Joe was still there, leaning against the hitching rail, chewing tobacco, holding Princess's reins. Both horse and man drooped, heads hanging, paying no attention to anything.

'What happens now?' Adam asked Joe.

'Eh?'

'*What happens now?*' he snapped. He was tense about the futile and irritating talk with Uncle Ted, uneasy about the whole risky expedition, and that made him impatient.

Joe shrugged, so Adam took the reins from his limp hand and mounted. It felt safer to be on Princess's back, high up so that he could see. He hadn't liked the guards' talk about holding him until Mr Mackenzie returned.

The melancholy man seemed to have no idea what to do. Adam pointed Princess southwards, in the direction of

Toronto, and nudged her into motion. Joe took hold of the bridle and walked mindlessly along beside her.

They had gone only a few yards when Adam heard, above the hubbub around him, a rumbling noise. Others noticed it too, and grew quiet to hear better. When Adam looked in the direction of the rumbling, he saw a stagecoach heading their way from the city. Around it were several dozen men on foot and two or three on horseback, including Mr Mackenzie.

There was an outburst of shouting, through which Mr Mackenzie's strident voice was heard saying that they had taken the western mail – the stagecoach heading for the western parts of the province.

The uproar brought other people running. Suddenly there was a large crowd in the open space near the tavern. Adam had just spotted Gavin McPhee when Cornelia de Grassi appeared from behind a building. She was on horseback, her pony's bridle held by a man with a gun.

She surveyed the scene. Her glance flicked over Adam, moved on, then shifted back. She raised her eyebrows and gave a little smile but then again turned her attention to the crowd and to Mr Mackenzie, who was still shouting something about the mail. He held up a fistful of letters and, with the other hand, pulled off his hat and waved it.

Because Cornelia and her guard had joined the crowd late, they were on the outside of the milling mass. When Adam looked her way again, he saw her jerk the pony's bridle out of the guard's hand, touch the animal with her crop and spur, and set it galloping helter-skelter down Yonge Street. Several of the armed men shot their muskets at her but she kept going.

Adam, without conscious thought, copied her. Joe shouted but no one interpreted the shout quickly enough to stop him. Princess, who had revived from her droopiness when Adam mounted, was happy to follow Cornelia's horse.

Shots were fired but none struck him. Cornelia looked

back over her shoulder. She saw Adam and apparently realized that he was fleeing too, rather than chasing her, because she lifted one hand in a hurried wave and rode on, hunched low in the saddle.

The rebel picket – the men who had stopped Adam earlier – had also been distracted by the stagecoach. The leader shot at Cornelia but missed. The others just stared.

A little way beyond that, Cornelia was fired at again, a single shot from an armed man standing by a farm gate. She rode on.

Before long, the road curved and dipped into a ravine. Cornelia slowed her horse to a walk, and when she was a few yards down the slope, below the rim of the ravine, she stopped.

By the time Adam drew up alongside her, she had taken off her gloves and was stroking her horse. At first he thought she was calming the animal, but then he realized that she had shed her gloves so that she could feel for injuries.

'Are you all right?' he asked, panting.

She disregarded that. 'Were you followed?'

'No. I don't know why not, if they thought we were spies.'

'They had no horses at hand. Mr Mackenzie and that other mounted man by the coach were the only ones ready to follow, and *they* didn't know about me.'

'There were horses in the field behind the tavern.'

'They'd have to be caught and bridled first, and by that time I'd be halfway to Toronto.'

Adam looked over his shoulder to where the rim of the ravine hid the road to Montgomery's Tavern. 'Don't you think they might be doing that right now? If they thought you were spying, wouldn't they want to stop you from reporting what you saw?'

All this time she had been paying more attention to her horse than to the conversation. Now she looked straight at Adam, head up under the perky hat and the flying wisp of veil.

'No leadership!' she declared scornfully, every inch a soldier's daughter. 'That's not an army, it's just a bunch of farmers. I was in that camp for an hour, and I kept my eyes and ears open. Both Mr Mackenzie *and* his second-in-command Mr Lount were away to intercept the mail-coach, and no one was left in charge at the camp. They even let several prisoners escape.'

'You and I were stopped, though. They were very suspicious of me.'

'A few of the men may have been using their wits, but there was no one in charge. Even when he's *there*, Mackenzie doesn't seem to know what to do. I heard them talking about it. Little Mac, they call him, and they say he's acting very strange, that he's nearly crazy with excitement and nerves.'

Suddenly, on the last word, her face changed. While she talked, her fingers had still been exploring for injuries. Now Adam could tell by her face that she had found something alarming. She twisted around so that she could look at the right side of the saddle, almost behind her.

'What is it?' he asked.

'A hole in the saddle. Could be a bullet. Hope it didn't go through.'

Adam rode around to the other side of Cornelia and her horse so that he could see.

'There's no blood,' he said. 'If your horse was wounded, there'd be blood running down from under the saddle.' Then he noticed something else. 'But a bullet must have hit *you* – or was that rip in your clothes there before?'

'Where?'

He pointed to the skirt over her right hip.

She explored it with her fingers, then twisted around to look. When she straightened up, she and Adam locked eyes for a frightened moment.

'No, that's new. They *hit* me – well, nearly hit me.'

'That bullet *did* hit you.'

'Only my clothes. Actually, I remember feeling a sort of bump. It must have just grazed me. There's no blood. But still …. That's scary, Adam.'

He could only nod.

'Come on,' she said in a muted voice. 'We'd better hurry. We've got news about the capture of the western mail as well as about the number of rebels.'

The road sloped down to a small river where there was a sawmill. Like the paper mill, it was not operating.

'Whitmore's,' Cornelia said briefly, her mind on other things.

Adam marvelled at how much she knew about the area. He thought of her as English, because in some ways she was a typical young English gentlewoman, but she'd lived here for six years, nearly half her life.

The road crossed the stream by means of the dam built to provide water power for the sawmill, then curved up the ravine wall beyond to reach level land again.

Cornelia looked at Adam.

'What were *you* doing there, in the rebel camp?'

He explained about the paper Mr Mackenzie had ordered, and about seeing his uncle.

'I tried to find him yesterday, after I talked to you in town,' he said, 'but I got no farther than the place where that fight happened. I expect you heard about it ….'

She nodded. 'The one near the Sharpes' house. Everyone in town was talking about it this morning.' She looked at him, frowning, concerned. 'You were *there?* You saw it?'

He was seeing it again right at this very minute, the fire and smoke, the noise and fear and death, exploding the quiet December evening.

He didn't want to talk about it.

'After the fight, there was no point looking for my uncle. But just now I talked to him for a moment.'

'You weren't spying?'

'No, but they thought I was, because of you. "Another kid," they said. You *were* spying, weren't you? They said you'd come to see someone about a sleigh.'

'That was just an excuse. I went to the wheelwright near the tavern to ask the price of a sleigh. Well, it's December, isn't it?' She was silent, thinking something over, then turned to look at him squarely. Her face was pale, he noticed, and her hair untidy. But her eyes were sharp. 'Adam, if your uncle is with the rebels ... which side are *you* on? *We're* all on the loyalist side, of course, our whole family and practically everyone we know, and I thought you were too. If you aren't ....' She looked at him, her head cocked, her dark eyebrows raised.

He considered her question. 'I'm not on either side, really. I haven't been here long enough to understand it all. But it looks to me as though both sides have good reasons for feeling the way they do.'

'But they're *rebels!*'

'They're human beings with worries and grudges and ... and fears. Just like the loyalists.'

'They're rebelling against their lawful government,' she said. It was obviously something she'd heard grown-ups say. In her voice was a note of puzzlement, however, as though for the first time she realized that there might be something to be said on the other side.

'They want more share in running this province.'

'That's what the Assembly is for. There are elections every few years, and ....'

'They say the Assembly has no power. The ordinary people feel that they're being treated like children, not given any real responsibility, and they don't like it. I don't like being treated like a child. Do you?' Then he remembered how Cornelia and her sister had overruled their parents on the question of riding into town with their father on Monday night. Obviously these two young ladies had more say in their lives than most kids did.

'Of course not,' she said decidedly. 'Who would?'

'Well, then ....'

He left the sentence hanging, afraid that he had already said too much, afraid that if this became a real argument it would spoil the friendship.

Cornelia rode in silence for a little while but Adam didn't feel that she was angry. She was staring straight ahead, her lips pursed as though she was thinking.

*

Soon the road passed a few substantial houses and then dipped again, dropping down through a notch carved in a steep embankment. Horizontally over the notch, high enough above the road so that it was well over the riders' heads, lay a large tree-trunk.

Adam looked up at it as they rode underneath.

'Did that tree fall like that naturally? Or did someone put it there?'

'I don't know. This is Gallows Hill; it was just back there that the rebels were yesterday when I came to see how many there were.'

'Why is it called Gallows Hill?'

'Because of that tree, they say.'

A few minutes after that, they reached a tollgate.

'Yorkville,' Cornelia said. She pointed to the left. 'Over there is Dr Horne's house, that was burned down yesterday.' On their right was a cemetery, and close to the tollgate an inn called the Red Lion.

Around the tollgate stood about a dozen men armed with muskets.

As Adam was reaching into his pocket for a penny, one of the guards greeted Cornelia. When she explained that she was on her way to give the governor important information about the rebel army, he waved her and Adam through without charging toll.

At Elliot's Tavern, Cornelia pointed towards the road going east. 'If you're going back to the Mills, that's the shortest way. Lot Street. It will take you to the bridge.'

'I'm not going home yet. I still have to deliver a note to Mr Helliwell, in the Market Square.'

She raised her eyebrows. 'Doing errands to *both* camps?'

'I know. It seemed dangerous, but Mr Skinner said ....'

'It *would* be dangerous if these were real armies,' she said with the same scorn she'd shown earlier. Then her face grew grave. 'Even so ....'

'We *were* shot at,' he reminded her.

She looked at him gravely. Then she brightened. 'Well, if you're going into town, we'll ride together. I'm going to the governor's headquarters in the market building.'

The town was even busier than it had been on the previous day. Men were everywhere, on foot, on horseback, carrying muskets. A brewer's dray was unloading beer at a tavern on King Street, and another wagon brought hay to a livery stable. The taverns and livery stables, and their suppliers, must be making good money; not everyone suffered during a war.

Adam rode with Cornelia as far as the main entrance to the market building. 'I won't wait for you,' he said. 'I have to see Mr Helliwell.'

'That's all right. Charlotte will be somewhere around, and I expect my father is too, though I haven't seen him today.'

'Goodbye, then.'

''Bye, Adam.'

As she was dismounting with the help of one of the guards clustered around, an officer came out of the nearest door and hurried towards a horse being held by a groom. When he saw Cornelia, he stopped in mid-stride.

'Miss Cornelia!'

'Good day, Colonel FitzGibbon. Is His Excellency here?'

'Yes, miss. Don't tell me that you've been inspecting the

enemy again?' There was something joking and patronizing in his manner that offended Adam – something that belittled Cornelia, almost made fun of her.

Cornelia herself paid no attention. 'I've just come from Montgomery's Tavern.'

That caused a change in Colonel FitzGibbon's manner. Suddenly he was serious.

'Not here, miss. We'll go upstairs to His Excellency.'

He opened the door again and escorted her in. She held up the skirt of her riding habit and preceded him, very much the lady.

Adam, for all his haste, had lingered to hear this, and before he got Princess in motion again – she was tired and reluctant to move – another horse cantered towards them. At first Adam barely heeded it, but then he noticed that the rider was Charlotte.

No one seemed surprised to see her.

She nodded a greeting to Adam and then gave her attention to a man who came to take the reins and to another who helped her dismount. When she was on the ground and had gathered up her skirt, she looked at Adam.

'I took a message to our guards who are on the Kingston Road, beyond the bridge. The captain of the guard out there gave me some information to pass on to His Excellency and Colonel Fitzgibbon.' She turned to the officer on duty. 'May I see His Excellency, please?'

'Certainly, miss. Colonel Fitzgibbon is with him now – and so is your sister.'

He himself held open the door for her.

When she had disappeared up the stairs, Adam looked at the officer. He was searching for a tactful way to ask who had sent Charlotte on such an errand – while remembering that, the day before, Dr Horne had considered it quite in order to ask Cornelia to act as spy. Maybe this was how things were done in Canada.

The officer must have read the question in Adam's face, because he said, 'We needed a mounted messenger, and it was someone's idea to send her. We're short of messengers.'

'Is it safe . . . for a girl?'

The officer shrugged and grinned. 'I know. I wouldn't like *my* daughter to do it. But these girls are independent young ladies, and excellent riders. Besides, no one would suspect them of being actively engaged.'

'The rebels up at Montgomery's Tavern suspected Cornelia. They held her for an hour, and she was shot at when she rode off.'

The officer looked startled. '*Shot at?* Are you sure?'

'Oh, yes. One bullet went into the saddle, and another tore her clothes.'

'Good heavens! What an unmannerly mob! Shooting at a young girl – and one of good family, definitely a young lady.'

Another of the men snorted and laughed. 'She don't behave like a young lady! Riding about the country at all hours, spying on the enemy . . . .'

The officer frowned at him, but he couldn't disagree. 'Spirited girls, those two,' he admitted uncomfortably. 'Not how I'd want my daughter to act.'

Chapter Seventeen

WHEN ADAM reached the Helliwell house, which faced one side of the market building, he rode into the yard behind. At the door of a small stable, the kind that many city houses had, a groom was shovelling manure into a wheelbarrow.

Had Adam been gentry, the groom would have come forward to take his horse. Instead, while nodding a civil greeting, the man kept right on working.

Adam dismounted and led Princess across to him. 'I've come from the Don Mills – from Mr Skinner – with a message for Mr Helliwell. Could you please give my horse some water and hay? She's tired.'

That was a reasonable request. All horses, whoever their riders were, got fed and watered. 'Sure, lad, leave her to me.'

The kitchen door was opened by a maidservant with floury hands.

'I'm Adam Wheeler, from the York Paper Mill, with a note for Mr Helliwell.'

'I remember you. You was here once before. I'll take the note.'

'I was told to see Mr Helliwell in person if he was in.'

'He just got in a minute ago. I'll see if he .... Come in, lad.'

While he stood inside the kitchen door, the smell of food making him hungry and reminding him that he'd had no dinner although it was well on in the afternoon, she went to the front of the house, wiping her hands on her apron and straightening her cap as she went. In a moment she reappeared.

'Through here, boy.'

She showed him into a room between the kitchen and the

front part of the house, a small chamber dominated by a desk and bookshelves.

Mr Helliwell was standing by the desk reading a newspaper.

'Hello, boy. From the Don Mills, are you?'

'Yes, sir. I have a note for you from Mr Skinner.' As he pulled it out of his sleeve, he remembered that he still had Mr Mackenzie's note in his pocket. He'd forgotten all about it. Just as well that the government guards at the Yorkville tollgate hadn't searched him.

Mr Helliwell raised his eyebrows when he saw where Adam had hidden the note, and at its crumpled condition, but he said nothing. When he had read it, however, he glared at Adam. 'This note was written this morning, hours ago.'

'Mr Skinner ....'

'Did Mr Skinner send you off with it right away? What've you been doing since then, boy?'

It was natural that Mr Helliwell should be suspicious, but all the same Adam had to defend himself. He couldn't afford the reputation of being an unreliable messenger.

'I had another errand besides this one, sir. Also for Mr Skinner. Delivering paper.'

'An errand that took half the day?' Mr Helliwell frowned.

Not that it was any of his business, Adam thought. But Thomas Helliwell looked like a stern, rigid man who would have opinions about things which didn't concern him. His face was narrow and furrowed, with bushy eyebrows and a permanent crease between them.

His glance fell on the newspaper he had been reading, and from there he looked sharply up at Adam. 'I hope it wasn't to that scoundrel Mackenzie that you delivered paper. They say he has a printing press up there where he is, and I know that Eastwood and Skinner are his regular suppliers.'

Adam was silent, but probably his face gave the answer.

Mr Helliwell frowned even more severely, but then he

became thoughtful rather than angry.

'Never mind, lad, you were just doing your job. But if you've been to Montgomery's Tavern .... Did you actually see Mackenzie?'

'Not to talk to. He wasn't there when I arrived, and I left the paper with someone else. Mr Mackenzie returned just before I left.'

'What's happening there?' He sat down in the desk chair and gestured to Adam to take the visitors' chair. 'I'm interested.'

Adam described what he had seen, and Mr Helliwell listened carefully. In addition to handling the administration of the Helliwell brewery and distillery, he was a director of the Bank of Upper Canada. He needed to know what was going on.

When Adam reported that Mr Mackenzie had captured the western mail, he scowled.

'Damn it. There were letters of mine on that coach. You say that Mackenzie was waving some letters?'

'Yes – I guess to show that he'd taken the actual *mail*, not only the coach. He had them clutched, sort of crumpled.'

'No respect for private correspondence,' Mr Helliwell muttered. 'And then what happened? I'm surprised they let you go.'

'They didn't exactly *let* me go.' He described his and Cornelia's escape from Mackenzie's camp.

'I heard someone mention that this girl brought useful information yesterday. It was her report that led Sir Francis to change his mind about negotiating with the rebels. Plucky young lady.'

'And Charlotte, her sister, carried a message to the picket out on the Kingston Road today.'

'Did she, now?'

He reflected for a few minutes, then looked up at Adam again.

'You'll be reporting all this to Mr Skinner, of course.'

'Yes, sir.'

'You can pass on a few things from here. Tell him that this afternoon I saw Mr William Allan ....'

'The gentleman who lives at Moss Park?'

'That's the one. Good for you, lad. Mr Allan is also a bank director, like me, and moves in the very highest circles. He's been summoned to a meeting at Archdeacon Strachan's house this evening. All the leading men on our side are to be there, and Mr Allan hinted that they were going to plan an attack on the rebels. There's a good many loyal militia here in town now – more than a thousand, they say – and the information Miss Cornelia de Grassi brought yesterday suggests that Mackenzie has fewer men than that. Certainly ours will be better armed. Though how anyone will turn this mob of unorganized militia into an army, and how long it will take, I don't know.

'You can also tell Mr Skinner that Sir Francis Bond Head, the lieutenant governor, will be moving his headquarters from the market back to the Parliament Buildings. He transferred to the market because it would be easier to defend in the event of an attack on the city, but I presume he no longer fears such a thing. However, Lady Head and several of the other ladies and their children remain on the ship in the harbour where they were taken yesterday.'

He abruptly turned to face his desk and reached for his pen and a slip of paper. 'I'll write down the main points as a reminder to you.'

Adam was about to say that he could remember, but he kept silent. Just as well if Mr Helliwell wrote it down. Suppose he forgot something? Messages like this were important and you had to get them right because other people used the information to make decisions.

When Mr Helliwell handed over the note, Adam asked, 'So there is to be a battle soon, sir?'

'As soon as possible. They talk of tomorrow. There's a good deal of urgency. The town is running out of food and drink and fodder, and all these men are starting to cause trouble. If they aren't put to fighting soon, they want to go home. And the situation has to be resolved, damn it. We can't have rebels hanging about forever, threatening to burn the city. They've got to be squashed. Everyone here is of that opinion, so the sooner the better.'

*

By the time Adam set off for the Don Mills, darkness was falling. It had been a long day and he would be glad to reach home. He could have urged Princess into a trot but she was tired too, plodding along with her head low, and he hadn't the heart to force her to go faster.

Tired and hungry though he was, however, his mind wouldn't stop working. He remembered Cornelia's question about which side he was on. He really wasn't on any side. Mr Mackenzie said that the ordinary people ought to have more voice in how the province was run, that the upper class in Toronto and the smaller towns ought not to keep all the important jobs – sheriff, magistrate, and so on – for themselves. There were other problems too, things to do with land and money that he didn't understand. The harvest this autumn had been the second bad one in a row. Bad harvests here, just like back home, scared people, raised prices and emptied purses which were already none too full.

But the other side – the government side, people like the Helliwells and the de Grassis – were also scared. Mr Mackenzie talked about war and about burning Toronto. If he won the war, he said, he'd take the land now owned by the rich and give it to his followers. He'd separate Upper Canada from England and maybe join it to the United States. This alarmed the gentry, many of whom belonged to families that had left the American states so they could remain British. Therefore

they were up in arms and talked about attacking Mr Mackenzie before he attacked them again. If the army from
Montgomery's Tavern hadn't been stopped on Tuesday evening, if they'd been allowed to reach the city ....

But they're not ferocious monsters, a voice in him protested; they're not even fighters. It's just Uncle Ted and some
others, armed with a few guns and some sticks.

And on the opposite side were men like Captain de Grassi,
also angry and frightened. The more you owned, the more
easily you got scared, the more you needed to bluster and
march and shout. The less you owned, the less you had to
lose, but you still had to march and shout. It was just like in
the Swing riots in England, though most of those 'rebels' had
been much poorer and more wretched than these followers of
Mr Mackenzie's, with much less to hope for. In Canada, if
you didn't already own land you could work and earn money
to buy it, something a poor man could never do in England.

Deep down, it was all about power. Mrs Wright had said
something about that, and now he suddenly saw how it
worked. If you didn't have power, you wanted it. But there
was only so much to go around, and those who had none
themselves had to gather in groups to show what they could
do.

And some people, like Uncle Ted, were just rebels by
nature. It was easier and more fun. You could pride yourself
on having high ideals while not doing your duty by the people
near you.

If Uncle Ted were killed, it would be bad, but think what
would happen if he were only wounded. If he were dead,
Aunt Lenore could remarry. There was bound to be someone
who'd be glad to have her. But if he were wounded – hurt
badly enough so that he could do no work for a while, or perhaps even for the rest of his life – if that happened, Aunt
Lenore wouldn't be able to remarry, would be tied to Uncle
Ted and would have to support the family herself. Harry was

old enough to work but Adam suspected that he wouldn't be much use. Adam would do what he could, but it'd be hard to support a whole family on nothing but the wages of a woman and a boy.

He reached the river. It was nearly dark now, and inside the bridge it was silent until Princess's hooves struck the first planks with the customary thunder – customary but somehow scarier than usual. Away from the noise and activity of town, things were very still, as though earth and sky held their breath to see what was going to happen.

At the tollgate, there was a man on duty. 'What's goin' on in town, young feller?' he asked as he took Adam's penny.

'The important men are meeting at the archdeacon's tonight. Battle tomorrow, maybe.'

The man grunted and opened the gate.

There were lights in the buildings near the far end of the bridge, but no one was around except an old man hobbling from one house to another. The tavern's windows were lit up, and the sound of excited voices seeped out.

After that it was quiet again until, about halfway up the Mill Road, Adam heard a cracking sound. Then, ten yards ahead, there was a movement in the shadows and five men stepped out of the woods. Two of them had guns, the others pikes. One had a dark lantern, which he opened and shone on Adam.

'Stop!'

Adam pulled at Princess's reins. The five men had spread across the road, their weapons pointing at him.

'It's just a kid,' one of them said, scornful rather than kindly.

'Who are you?' Adam demanded. He suspected, from the fact that only two of the men carried guns, that they were Mackenzie's followers.

'Who are *you*, boy?' the leader asked.

'Adam Wheeler. I work at the paper mill. Eastwood and Skinner's.'

'We need your horse, lad.'

'It isn't mine. It belongs to Mr Skinner.' He thought quickly. 'Mr Skinner's a reformer. You wouldn't take the horse of someone who's on the same side as you.'

'Skinner's not a fighting reformer so he don't count,' one of the other men said. 'He ain't one of *us*.'

The leader stepped forward, reaching for the bridle. That made a gap in the barrier of weapons. Adam kicked Princess's flanks and pointed her at the gap. She sprang through and galloped up the road. Adam bent low and hung on for dear life. A bullet whizzed past his head. Then there was another, farther off, and a shout or two. When he glanced distractedly over his shoulder, he saw the men disappearing into the bush again.

He slowed down. He would have liked to gallop past whatever other dangers lurked, but the road was a mass of potholes and frozen ruts. Princess, going at such a pace, could fall or hurt herself.

*

The Mills area was quiet. Adam took Princess into the stable and unsaddled her. Then, remembering Cornelia and her horse Nipper, he led her outdoors again. By feel as much as sight, he began checking her over for injuries from the bullets.

As he inspected her, she gave a soft little nicker and craned her head around to nuzzle his shoulder. The affectionate gesture overwhelmed him, and he put an arm across her and leaned his head against the hollow under her ears. Relief and exhaustion washed over him. Safe, thank God.

'We made it, Princess,' he said. 'We got home all right.'

She blew air through her nostrils.

'You're a good girl.'

He went on with the checking – legs, chest, belly – stroking the smooth coat, feeling patches of sweat and occasionally a twitch or tremor in her skin.

'No injuries,' he reported out loud, and led her back into her stall. Bucket of water from the well, pitchfork-load of hay, and then he went to the house.

There, in Nelly's kitchen, sitting at the table eating, were Aunt Lenore, Harry, and Ruth. Ella lay on the settle, covered by an old quilt.

'Aunt Lenore!' For a moment, coming in from the dark night, he thought he was seeing things. Then he went to hug her. 'What are you doing here?'

'Oh, Adam!' she said, her thin face grey and tense. 'We came to look for Ted. We lost the house and have nowhere to live, so we came here. I couldn't think what else to do. And Ella's worse – she's too sick to walk. Do you know where Ted is?'

Adam felt as though a weight crashed down on him. He stood in front of Aunt Lenore, not knowing what to say.

It was Nelly who helped him. 'Sit down, Adam, and I'll get you a cup o' tea, and you and your aunt can figure things out. Had any supper?'

'No.'

She poured his tea and spooned stew into a bowl. 'There, you eat and drink that while you talk to your aunt.'

'Thanks, Nelly,' he said, knowing that this was her way of showing sympathy. He sat down across from Aunt Lenore. 'So you lost your job and the house?'

'Mr Manley hired people to replace Ted and me, and they got the shanty.'

She was trying to be fair, but she was tired and very worried. Harry was sullenly eating stew, while Ruth picked at her food and cuddled the cat on her lap. Ella appeared to be asleep.

'How did you travel, Aunt Lenore?'

'We were given lifts a few times, and for the rest we walked. Ella .... Mostly I carried her. And, oh, Adam, along the way we heard that Mr Mackenzie's side had won a battle but now Nelly says it's not true.' She looked unhappy, as though that was another personal problem. In a way, it was; Uncle Ted would be in a bad mood if the reformers lost.

'There's been only one small fight, which nobody won.'

'The talk along the road was that Mr Mackenzie's men had taken the city.'

'Really? They certainly haven't. I've just come from there.'

'Do you know where Ted is?'

'With Mr Mackenzie. I saw him today.'

From the corner of his eye, Adam caught Nelly's startled look, and he realized that maybe he shouldn't have told anyone where he'd been. Probably Mr Skinner, worried about being too closely linked with Mr Mackenzie's side, had told no one what Adam's errand was, and Adam had accidentally let the cat out of the bag. Well, it couldn't be helped.

'I asked Uncle Ted ... well, sort of reminded him that if there was a battle, and anything happened to him, you and the kids would ....'

'What did he say?'

'Nothing much,' Adam said. No need for Aunt Lenore to know that Uncle Ted had said, carelessly and thoughtlessly, 'They'll survive.'

'He didn't come away with you, or say that he'd come?'

'No.'

'And I suppose he hasn't found work or a place to live.'

'I don't think so.'

'I'd hoped to see him tonight,' she said, glancing at the window against which the black night pressed, and at Ella.

'Too far, Aunt Lenore. It's more important to find you a place to sleep.' He thought about the attic space upstairs and looked at Nelly, who was standing behind Aunt Lenore. He glanced upward and then back at her in a mute question. Nelly shook her head and mouthed, 'Mrs Skinner says "no".'

He turned to his aunt again. 'There's a woman in the village who rents a room or two. Mrs Murphy. Uncle Ted stayed there. We'll go and see whether she can take you tonight – go now, if you've finished eating. You must be awfully tired, and the girls have to be in bed.'

He had spoken automatically, thinking aloud, figuring out what needed to be done. Now he heard his own words echoing in his head. He had sounded just like an adult. With a grim sense of hopelessness, he felt as though from now on he'd always be responsible for this family, as though he'd become the head of a household before he was even grown up.

His heart felt like lead. He had suddenly run out of – what had Mrs Wright called it? – Christian charity. He was drained dry. He couldn't care about anybody any more, not Ella, or Aunt Lenore, not even Nelly, even though she had been sympathetic. He was desperately weary.

But he couldn't quit yet.

He stood up. 'Come along, let's go see Mrs Murphy.'

Harry and Ruth picked up the little chest and the cloth bundles which held the family's belongings, and Aunt Lenore lifted Ella, holding her while Nelly tucked the quilt around her. The girl was a heavy weight for Aunt Lenore, who was not strong herself, and Adam stood ready to help, but his aunt stopped him with a shake of her head. 'It's all right, Adam. I can manage.' She turned to Nelly. 'Thank you for the dinner, for taking us in.' A look of anguish crossed her face.

Once outside, Adam helped Harry with the wooden chest, each of them holding one of the rope handles. They trudged slowly up the hill.

Mrs Murphy had no rooms left – the militia filled the town and its outskirts – but, happy to earn money, she gave up her own bed to Lenore and the girls and told Harry that he could sleep in the barn.

*

Outdoors again, Adam paused for a moment. It was a clear

night, cold but still, and in the sky was a half moon and a thick sprinkling of stars – so peaceful that it was hard to believe that, earlier this evening, he'd been shot at.

He turned towards home.

As he did so, he became aware of the sound of a horse's hooves, thudding on the frozen ground. He looked down the Mill Road and saw Charlotte de Grassi approaching at a trot.

Remembering the troop of men he'd encountered, he stepped out into the road.

'Hello, Charlotte!'

'Oh, it's you! Hello!'

'On your way home? Where's Cornelia?'

'In town still.'

'I just wanted to tell you – there's a group of rebels in the woods. They stopped me earlier – maybe an hour ago.' He pointed down the Mill Road, to where it had happened. 'Better watch out.'

'You were actually stopped?'

'Yes. They wanted my horse – well, Mr Skinner's horse. I galloped away and they shot at me.'

'Were you hurt?'

'No. You know that Cornelia was fired on earlier today?'

'Yes, I saw her.'

'Any news from town?'

'There'll probably be a battle tomorrow.'

'I heard that the leaders were meeting tonight.'

'Yes, at Archdeacon Strachan's. The meeting was still going on, the last I heard.'

They were silent for a moment; then Charlotte's horse shook its head, reminding them that it was late.

'I'd better get home,' Charlotte said. 'Good night, Adam, and thanks for the warning.'

'Good night. Be careful.'

He watched her ride on, neat and plump and self-contained, until she rounded a bend and disappeared.

He crossed the road and wearily, hands in trouser pockets, began trudging down the familiar slope to the Mills. As he did so, the quiet of the night exploded with a burst of musket fire.

Adam jolted to a stop. At first he was not even sure where the sound had come from, but then there was another single shot.

It came from the place where Charlotte must be by now. Adam raced up the road and around the bend towards the Forks. He was just in time to see a dozen or more men running at Charlotte – a larger group than the one that had stopped him earlier, and with more guns. Charlotte's pony was rearing and trampling around in a confused way but she hung on, and then it bolted, jumped a fence, and galloped off across a field, with Charlotte hunched as low as the sidesaddle would permit. There was another, more distant sound of muskets firing.

Should he go after her? No sense – he was on foot, and she was galloping for home and would be safe there.

As he once again started down the hill, he suddenly felt such a surge of anger and protest that he didn't know how to contain it. Damn them all! Mr Skinner for sending him on that tricky errand with the paper, the de Grassi girls, his aunt and uncle!

He kicked a loose stone so fiercely that it went bouncing down the rutted road. 'Damn it!' he said out loud.

In his head he heard Mrs Wright's voice: *Adam, your language!*

'Well, what would *you* say,' he snapped, 'if you were in this fix? Damn it, damn it, damn it! I don't care what happens to the whole bloody lot of them!'

Chapter Eighteen

WHEN ADAM entered the kitchen, Nelly said, 'I told Mr Skinner you were back. He wants to see you in the parlour.'

'Oh, *hell!*' he exclaimed. Would they *never* give him *any* peace?

Nelly looked at him sharply. 'Adam!' she exclaimed, in surprise as much as reproach.

'I'm sorry, Nelly. It's just ....'

'You've had a bad day.'

She didn't know the half of it, he thought.

'He ain't mad at you, I don't think,' she said. But she didn't sound very sure. Maybe it was just her squinting eye, but something about the way she looked at him wasn't reassuring.

Adam drew a deep breath, ran his hand over his hair to tidy it, and went to the front of the house. He hesitated for a moment before knocking at the parlour door; from inside the room came Mr Skinner's voice, reading aloud. Adam would probably interrupt something, but he'd been asked to report, so he knocked.

'Come in!'

Mr and Mrs Skinner were both there, sitting by the table in the centre of the room. She was knitting a stocking. Mr Skinner closed the book from which he had been reading but kept his finger in the place. They looked at him in a kindly way.

Adam, as he paused in the doorway, blinked and then again felt the anger surge up inside him. Here he was, just come in from the December night, from seeing Charlotte shot at and being fired on himself, from coping with his aunt's problems, from a world full of danger and worry and fear – and here

were these two comfortable, middle-aged people reading and knitting in this blissfully tranquil room, warm and quiet, smelling of the wood fire and a dozen other nice things that Adam couldn't identify.

So safe! So protected!

The fury choked him.

Why should these two people be so bloody safe and comfortable? It was Mr Skinner who had sent him on today's awful errand to Montgomery's Tavern, Mrs Skinner who had refused to take Aunt Lenore and her kids in for the night. And here they sat ....

Instead of pleading with Uncle Ted, he should have *joined* him!

The poor against the rich, Mrs Wright had said. *Those who have nothing rising up against those more fortunate.*

'Come in, lad,' Mr Skinner said. 'Come and sit down. Tell us how you made out today.'

The turmoil inside him almost drowned the words.

Mrs Skinner put down her knitting and came over to him. 'Sit down, Adam. We're not going to eat you.' She took him gently by the arm and led him to the third chair at the table. 'There. You just sit quietly while I get you something to eat. You look plain done in.' To her husband, she said, 'Don't ask him any questions until I get back.'

Adam felt rather than heard the words. Mutely he stared at the fire until the door opened again and Mrs Skinner came back into the room with a mug of beer, which she set down in front of him.

'Nelly says you've had your supper but we thought this might hit the spot.'

'Thank you, ma'am.'

While she settled herself into her chair again and resumed her knitting, he took a sip, and then another. It was 'small beer', weaker than the regular brew, or maybe the regular brew diluted, but it was a comfort. He rubbed his hand over his face, and twitched his shoulders to relax them.

He was in fact calming down, and at the same time his resentment was fading a bit. These were not malicious, selfish people. They probably didn't even know what was going on, though the worried looks on their faces as they waited for his report suggested that they did not expect good news.

He was also comforted by the realization that he was being treated like a boy again, after that scary experience of being an adult. Treated like a boy – but treated well, like a person who mattered, even though he was young.

He drew a deep breath. 'I rode to Montgomery's Tavern like you said, sir.'

'Were you stopped?'

'Yes, by guards near the tavern. I explained about the paper. They nearly didn't let me through because they thought I was a spy.'

'A spy!' Mrs Skinner exclaimed.

'Well, there was a girl, Cornelia de Grassi .... Oh!' he exclaimed, remembering, 'you know the de Grassis. Well, Cornelia was there, and they were holding her because they thought she was spying. She had told them some story about wanting to see a sleigh at the wheelwright's shop near the tavern, and they thought my errand with the paper was also ... sort of an excuse.' He turned to Mr Skinner. 'I had to show them the order from Mr Mackenzie, sir, before they'd let me through.'

'That's why I gave it to you, lad.'

'Cornelia was *there?* In the *camp?*' Mrs Skinner demanded. 'Did you see her?'

'Yes, we broke away and rode off together. They shot at us.'

'*Shot at you!*' Mr and Mrs Skinner burst out, both at the same time.

'Were you hurt?' Mrs Skinner asked anxiously. She had stopped knitting. 'I mean, either of you?'

[214]

'No, ma'am, but bullets went into Cornelia's saddle and through her clothes.'

'Dear God!'

The danger came into this safe room like a cold draft.

'It's all right, ma'am. We got to town safe.'

All the same, he was not sorry about the cold draft. That was *reality,* out there. That was what was going on.

'You *did* manage to deliver the paper to Mr Mackenzie?' Mr Skinner demanded.

'I left it with Mr Linfoot, the innkeeper. Mr Mackenzie was away when I arrived, though he came back while I was there. He'd captured the western mail. Mr Helliwell – Mr Thomas, who I saw in town – was very annoyed when I told him, because he had sent letters by that mail.'

'How do you mean, he captured the mail?' Mrs Skinner asked.

'I guess he stopped the stagecoach. When he came back to the tavern, he had the coach and driver with him, and he was waving a handful of letters. In the confusion about that, Cornelia and I got away.'

By now both Mr and Mrs Skinner were looking very worried. Mrs Skinner was frowning, even though her hands had resumed their automatic knitting.

'So you did reach my brother-in-law safely?' Mr Skinner asked.

'Yes, sir, and gave him your letter. There's no answer.'

'There wasn't one needed. Did he say anything else – about the situation in town, for instance?'

'Yes, sir.' Adam pulled out the note from Mr Helliwell, and also Mr Mackenzie's order for paper, and the penny that he had not needed at the Yorkville tollgate. He laid them on the table in front of him and opened Thomas Helliwell's note.

'He wrote down the main points so that I'd remember. There's a meeting tonight at the archdeacon's to decide whether to offer battle to the rebels. If there is a battle, it may be tomorrow. The town's running out of food. The governor is moving his headquarters back to the Parliament Buildings, but Lady Head and some other ladies are still on a ship in the harbour.'

Then he remembered one more thing. 'The meeting at the archdeacon's is still going on. I saw Charlotte de Grassi just now....'

'*Charlotte?*' exclaimed Mrs Skinner. 'Those girls! You don't mean to say that she was also out?'

'Yes. She was shot at too. Just now, just a couple of minutes ago. There are rebels in the woods up here.' He gestured towards Todmorden at the top of the hill. 'I was stopped by them – a different group, I think – on the way from town this evening. They wanted Princess but I got away by getting her to gallop. They shot after me but didn't hit me. Nor Princess either. I checked.'

'My God! Shooting at kids!' Mr Skinner said, thumping the book against the table.

Adam, watching him, saw a thought pass over his face, saw him glance at his wife and then at Adam and then at the lamp. 'I'm glad to see you safe, lad. If I'd known it would be this dangerous ... shooting at kids ... well ....'

It was a sort of apology, and Adam accepted it. He himself hadn't expected to be shot at. Maybe Mr Skinner should have foreseen the risk, but Adam was coming to realize that adults didn't know or control everything.

'That's all right, sir. I got home safe.'

Mrs Skinner was looking at Adam. 'Dear boy, what a day you've had! And now this about your aunt.'

'We'll go into that in a moment, Mary, but first I want to know ... Adam, how did the rebel army look? Were there lots of men there, lad, at Montgomery's Tavern?'

'It's hard to say, sir. There were people in and around the buildings, but I'm sure there were more I didn't see. When Mr Mackenzie rode up with the stagecoach, dozens came out to see, and they were still coming when I took off.'

'And how did things look in the city? How many men there?'

'Mr Helliwell said it was more than a thousand. He said that the leaders wanted to attack the rebels soon because something had to be done with all those militia, who were getting restless.'

Mr and Mrs Skinner exchanged glances. 'We'll hope for the best,' she said. Then she looked at Adam again. 'Your aunt, Adam. Tell us about her. Nelly says she turned up here with a sick child in her arms, and two other children, looking for you. I didn't see her, but it sounds .... What led to this?'

He told them briefly about coming to Canada with Aunt Lenore and Uncle Ted, and about their separating when he found work here at the mill and they went to Dundas, and about Uncle Ted joining Mr Mackenzie's forces.

'I saw him – Uncle Ted, I mean – today. I wanted to ask him to think what would become of Aunt Lenore and the kids if he were hurt in the fighting. He just said, "They'll survive." He didn't seem concerned, but someone has to be.'

He remembered again that Mrs Skinner had refused to take Aunt Lenore and the kids in. A meal, yes, but not shelter for the night. Obviously Mrs Skinner didn't feel that *she* had to be really concerned.

Grimly and wearily, he sorted through the things on the table in front of him.

'Here's Mr Helliwell's note, sir,' he said, handing it to Mr Skinner. 'And here's the one from Mr Mackenzie. And your penny back – I didn't need to pay anything at the Yorkville tollgate because one of the guards knew Cornelia and, when she said she had information for the governor, he let us through free.'

Mr Skinner pushed the penny back to Adam and added another from his trouser pocket. 'That's for you, lad. You did well – very well indeed.'

[217]

'Thank you, sir.' Adam put the two pennies into his own pocket. 'Will that be all?'

'For tonight, yes. We'll see what tomorrow brings.'

'Adam, about your aunt ...,' Mrs Skinner said hesitantly.

'Yes, ma'am?'

'Where is she now?'

'At Mrs Murphy's,' he said flatly. 'Mrs Murphy gave up her own bed for my aunt and the girls, and Harry is sleeping in the barn.' Then he was afraid that that had sounded too much like criticism. But he couldn't take it back – and after all it was plain fact.

Mrs Skinner was silent for a moment, then said, 'Let me know how things go with her.'

The angry words crowded into his throat, but he choked them back – and then he realized that Mrs Skinner too was almost apologizing. Her eyes were on her knitting. When she wanted to she could knit without watching what she was doing, but now she used the busy needles as an excuse for not meeting his eyes.

And then abruptly she did look up. 'You *will* let me know, won't you?'

He was silent for a moment, wondering whether to accept the apology. But there was no point in being difficult. Mrs Skinner was his boss's wife, and it would be wrong for Adam to argue.

And after all, she had apparently come round. Goodness knows why she had earlier turned Aunt Lenore away, had not even seen her. Goodness knows why she was having second thoughts now. Maybe she had suddenly realized that Adam and his family were human beings – the rich sometimes had trouble grasping that about the poor. Or perhaps it was the news he had brought, the cold draft from the world outside. Whatever it was, she appeared to have changed her mind. If she wanted to, she could still do something for Aunt Lenore, so Adam had better accept the apology.

'Thank you, ma'am. I will.'

'We'll hope for the best,' she said again, but her face was grim. 'Good night, Adam.'

*

When he was in bed, he shivered. The room was cold after the warmth of the parlour. His body clenched itself against the icy sheets. *Another* thing to put up with.

He reflected on the evening. Never before in his life had he been so angry. Everything seemed to be dumped on him ....

But no, he must not exaggerate. True enough, it was he who had been sent to take the paper to Mr Mackenzie, but he was a servant and it was reasonable for his employer to give him such a task. Nothing unusual in that. The only other thing was Aunt Lenore's coming here, but that was because she had no other way of finding Uncle Ted. She hadn't expected Adam to provide her with food and shelter. If Adam worried about her and the family – and about the de Grassi girls – it was because he was that kind of person.

He was sorry about having been angry at Mrs Wright – yet he understood why he'd been angry. She'd taught him to be a good boy. *Think of other people*, she'd say. *Remember your place* – meaning that he should keep in mind that he was only a working man's son. *Don't lose your temper.* That was all very well, but she hadn't prepared him for being in a strange country, for being in a war, for having to make so many difficult decisions. How *could* she have?

That didn't mean he had to turn his back on her completely. She had taught him a lot. But for the rest, he'd just have to do what he could, figuring things out for himself.

And he was, wasn't he? Mr Skinner said he'd done well, and Mrs Skinner had fetched him a mug of beer – brought it herself, not told Nelly to do it. Mrs Higham wouldn't have done such a thing for her servants. Nor would Mrs Higham have apologized.

Adam wouldn't have been in Mrs Higham's parlour in the first place.

That was what Upper Canada was like. There were rich and poor, all right, just like back home, but the differences weren't quite so great.

Cornelia and Charlotte were friendly too. Although not at all 'democratic', they were friendlier than the rich children he'd sometimes seen in England. Even Mr Higham's three boys, who were nothing more than the sons of a rich tenant farmer, had treated Adam as though he was invisible, or as though he was a ... a gatepost. Cornelia and Charlotte actually regarded him as a person.

That brought the memory of the day's events flooding over him again, the shooting, the tension and danger, the looming battle, Aunt Lenore and her sick child.

'Oh, hell,' he muttered into his pillow. What was going to happen? Was there anything he could do for Aunt Lenore? He remembered her struggling up the hill carrying Ella. At this very moment she was probably watching over the child and worrying.

And tomorrow there was going to be a battle – a battle in which Uncle Ted was almost sure to take part, unless he deserted. Was he really brave enough to fight? Argue, yes, talk hot-headed, yes, but actually risk his skin?

If he deserted, where would he go? Perhaps to Dundas, thinking that Aunt Lenore was still there. But Adam suspected that he'd come here first.

He sighed and turned over.

Battle tomorrow. What were they thinking and feeling, all those men who might be facing death? And what did the leaders think? Did they ever give a thought to their men as people having families and work and *lives?*

Men ... soldiers. An army was made up of soldiers, but it was impossible to think of someone like Uncle Ted as one. Even Adam's own father, who had actually been a soldier in his youth, in the war against Napoleon, was hard to picture in uniform. Sergeant Phillips, on the ship, had described the uniforms, the guns.

'What about armour?' Adam had asked, thinking of knights.

Sergeant Phillips had stared, then laughed. 'Soldiers don't wear armour any more, kid.'

'Not even when they're fighting?'

'Armour isn't much good against guns.'

Neither were uniforms. Adam winced at the idea of tender human flesh with nothing but some cloth between it and a bullet – like Cornelia's, so nearly wounded today that the cloth of her skirt was torn. The thought of her soft body, which might by now have been hurt and bleeding, made him bury his face in the pillow for a moment.

The two armies fighting tomorrow wouldn't even have uniforms – except maybe a few like Captain de Grassi wearing uniforms from other wars. They would be ordinary men in their everyday clothes. No armour, no prancing steeds. Just ordinary folk, two lots of them, walking towards each other on an ordinary Thursday, risking their lives, and some of them not coming back.

Chapter Nineteen

BEFORE DAWN THE NEXT morning, Adam was awakened by pounding hooves. A little later there was an urgent rapping at the back door. Nelly, who had already begun her day's work, answered it and then came plodding up the stairs to the Skinners' bedroom. A minute or two later, Adam heard Mr Skinner going downstairs in his stocking feet.

At breakfast, he heard what it was all about.

'Battle today,' Nelly said. 'Someone came to tell Mr Helliwell. He's in the militia. He's gone to fight, but first he came here to have a few words with Mr Skinner – in case anything happens to him.' She set Adam's porridge down.

So the real fighting was to take place today – or at least start today. It wasn't just rumour and guesswork any more.

He had barely finished eating when Mr Skinner came into the kitchen. He gave Adam a glimmer of a friendly look that recalled yesterday evening, but his mind was on business.

He had instructions for Adam. 'I know there's talk of a battle today,' he said, 'but there's also things to be done. I'm putting Mrs McDonald and Mrs O'Neill to work cutting rags because it does no harm to be beforehand with that. I want you to untie the bale that's lying beside the counter where McPhee left it, and help the women with the sorting. You can also carry firewood to the mill and sweep the floor and wipe the equipment.'

'Yes, sir.' These were some of his regular jobs. The paper-making machinery, and the inside of the building, had to be kept clean to avoid unnecessary dirt soiling the paper. It was bad enough, Mr Morris grumbled, cleaning and bleaching filthy rags so that they'd produce white paper without having dirt from the building itself making matters worse.

Mr Skinner was about to say something further when there came a knock at the back door. Upon Nelly's opening it, Aunt Lenore hurried in, her thin face full of trouble.

Adam got to his feet. 'Aunt Lenore, what ...? Oh, Mr Skinner, this is my aunt, Mrs Wheeler.'

'Good morning, Mrs Wheeler,' he said. 'How is your little girl today? Better, I hope.'

'Oh, sir, I think she's ... I think she's not going to get better. That she's ... dying.' Aunt Lenore, though she had started in a rush, barely whispered the last word. 'Mrs Murphy thinks so too, though she won't come right out and say it.'

'I'm sorry to hear that,' he said, seriously but in a detached kind of way. 'You may need a doctor. We always send for ....'

'I can't afford a doctor, sir. Mrs Murphy's doing all she can.' Aunt Lenore pulled herself up, as though preparing for action, not merely endurance. 'But I want to go to my husband. He's with Mr Mackenzie – Adam talked to him yesterday. I'd like Adam to come with me, to fetch ....'

'Nothing doing, ma'am. There's going to be a battle today, and a battlefield's no place for women and kids.'

'But ....'

'In any case, there's nothing your husband can do. Nelly, you're good with sick folks. Will you go and see Mrs Wheeler's little girl? Take whatever you need from here.'

At that moment Mrs Skinner came into the kitchen. She'd heard her husband's last words and grasped the situation at once.

'You must be Mrs Wheeler,' she said to Aunt Lenore.

'Yes, ma'am. I was asking whether Adam could come with me to find my husband. But Mr Skinner thinks ....'

Mr Skinner himself interrupted. 'Of course they can't go anywhere near the battlefield,' he said firmly. 'I've told Nelly to do what she can for the sick little girl.'

'Quite right,' Mrs Skinner said. 'You can call on me too.'

She gave Adam a quick glance, and he felt that it was partly for his sake that she was offering to help, that she was making up for having refused Aunt Lenore shelter last night. 'Besides, I'm sure you'd rather stay with your child. It could take you most of the morning to fetch your husband.'

Aunt Lenore turned her troubled face towards Adam. He could see how torn she was, but he thought the Skinners were probably right.

He went to her and touched her arm in a sign of sympathy. 'When I finish my morning's work, I'll come to Mrs Murphy's to see how you are,' he said. It was all he could think of.

Aunt Lenore nodded. She seemed on the verge of crying.

'All right, lad,' Mr Skinner said briskly. 'Off you go to the mill. Mrs Skinner and Nelly will help your aunt.'

*

Adam trudged down to the paper mill, still fretting but also relieved to be away from the atmosphere of worry and crisis that he could do nothing about.

But he found that he could not stop thinking. As he split kindling, carried firewood in, swept the floor, untied a bale of rags, his mind was on Aunt Lenore, a stranger here, far from her friends, with a dying child, a husband who might, in the next few hours, be wounded or killed ....

A bit of yesterday's anger returned, not at specific people but at the whole frightening mess.

He had finished the cleaning and was helping to cut rags, chafing each one up and down against a knife-blade fixed in the work-counter to loosen the fibres from each other, and listening with half an ear to a story Mrs McDonald was telling about a young man who had courted her back in Glasgow, when there came a sound of running feet. A dark form filled the open doorway. It was Aunt Lenore.

'Adam ... Ella's dead. She just ... died!'

Her voice was as taut as stretched wire. On the last word it snagged and faltered, so she repeated it fiercely. 'She's *died!* I have to reach Ted and tell him. I want you to come with me.'

He and the two women stared.

'Oh, Aunt Lenore!'

He put down the rag he was holding and went to her.

He'd meant to hug her, but comforting was not what she needed. When he came within reach, she snatched his arm. She was angry; he could feel how angry by the way her fingers dug into the fabric of his coat and shirt.

'Come with me to the Skinners. At once, Adam. Ruth and Harry are already there. I've left Ella with Mrs Murphy.'

Still clutching him by the arm, she marched him to the Skinners' house, in by the back door, past Ruth and Harry sitting in shocked silence at the kitchen table. Seeing that no one else was in the kitchen, she strode on until, in the dining room, they found Mr and Mrs Skinner and Nelly, standing in a little group.

Lenore looked at each of them in turn, fiercely determined. 'I'm going to that place where Mr Mackenzie's men are, and I'm taking Adam along to show the way. I must get to my husband.'

Adam had never seen her like this.

'You *can't*, Mrs Wheeler,' Mr Skinner said, exasperated. 'There's a battle being fought today, maybe this very minute.'

'You don't understand. *My child is dead.*'

'Women and children don't belong anywhere near a battle. Mackenzie's men won't let you cross their lines.'

Lenore's face twisted in anguish, but she remained immovable.

'I *must* go, sir. I must see Ted. He brought us here, and now ... Mrs Skinner, please help me. We have to go *now*, this minute. There's no time to lose.'

Mrs Skinner looked at Adam. 'You were there yesterday, Adam. What do you think? Are there "lines", like my husband says?'

'I don't know about "lines", ma'am. I was stopped by a guard asking what I was doing there. But it's not what you'd call an army. It's ... they're not real soldiers, I guess. No one's in charge, except Mr Mackenzie, and he ....'

Lenore interrupted. 'I don't care about safety, or lines. Don't any of you understand? I have to reach Ted! *Please*, Mrs Skinner, I'm in a hurry. I must find my husband. He's got to *do* something for once. You can't stop *me*, Mr Skinner, but I guess you have the right to decide about Adam coming with me. I need him to show me the way. And we have to hurry.'

'I can't see that a few hours will make so much difference in telling him about your child's death,' Mr Skinner grumbled. 'You'll see him after the battle ....'

'He thinks I'm still in Dundas. When the battle is over, *if* he's not hurt or taken prisoner, he'll go there. It would take *days* before he got back here to us. If he *ever* did. Meanwhile I'm left here with no money, no work, no roof over our heads, a dead child needing burial. I can't ....' Her control was cracking again.

'It *is* hard for Mrs Wheeler,' Mrs Skinner said to her husband.

'I sympathize,' he said agitatedly. 'I just don't see what's to be gained by her going to Montgomery's Tavern and maybe finding herself in the middle of a battle. It's no place for a woman.'

'There isn't any sense talking like that, Colin,' Mrs Skinner said. 'Mrs Wheeler is desperate. Her child is dead and she must find her husband – before the battle, if possible, and before he sets off for Dundas. Adam has to go with her, to show the way and be company for her. It would be even *worse* if she went alone.'

Mr Skinner frowned and, turning on his heel, walked to the window. Adam could see his shoulders twitching in irritation, hear the faint rasping sound as he rubbed his hand over his face.

He doesn't like making hard decisions, Adam thought, remembering his look yesterday, worried and smiling at the same time.

Adam, recalling his own decision to make a life of his own, his feeling that both choices were wrong, sympathized. Did anyone enjoy making difficult decisions?

Mrs Skinner took matters into her own hands. 'You said it wasn't really a camp with lines, Adam. If your aunt goes there and tells the guard that she wants to see her husband because their little girl has died ...?'

At first Adam thought that Mrs Skinner was doing what her husband had done yesterday – asking Adam to decide. But this was different. Aunt Lenore was determined, and nothing would stop her. The only question was whether Adam would be allowed to go too. Adam, looking at Aunt Lenore's thin, white face with the staring eyes, at her hands fidgeting impatiently at the fringe of her shawl, decided that he had to go with her. She was the person who mattered most to him right now. He could not let her undertake such a journey alone.

But Mr Skinner *didn't* want to let him. He thought it was not safe.

Yesterday, however, he'd actually *sent* him on a similar errand. Why was that different from this? Was it that Mr Skinner was fearful of Adam running such risks again – risks he hadn't foreseen yesterday? Was it because a battle was almost certain to take place today? Was it that Adam was supposed to be working? Or was it that errands for his employer were all right but personal ones were not?

There was no way of knowing.

Adam remembered Mrs Skinner's question.

'They'll probably let her through,' he said. 'They're just ordinary men with wives and children of their own.' He looked again at Mr Skinner's back. 'With your permission, sir ... I don't think my aunt should go alone. I would like to go with her.'

Mr Skinner turned around. He was a dark shape against the window, so Adam couldn't make out every detail of his face, but he could see the shoulders relax.

Mrs Skinner glanced at her husband, frowning and about to ask him a question. Then, without asking it, she turned back to Adam.

'Be careful, Adam. I know you will be.'

'Yes, ma'am.'

Mr Skinner rubbed his hand over his face again. 'Go the way you went yesterday, Adam, along that ravine.'

'I was planning to, sir. But I wanted to ask – isn't there a better place to cross the river, a shallower place? Yesterday, on horseback, I kept dry, but the water was at least two feet deep. I was wondering ....'

'There's a ford further upstream but that will take you out of your way. Hold on – someone mentioned that there were Indians camping along here ....'

'I saw some yesterday.'

'They'll probably paddle you across in their canoe. Otherwise you may have to wade.'

'We can wade,' Aunt Lenore said impatiently. 'Come on, Adam.' Then she remembered her manners. 'Thank you, sir, for letting Adam go with me.' The way she spoke showed that she was aware that it was Adam who had decided, not Mr Skinner. But she'd won her point, and that was all she cared about.

She managed a tense little smile for Mrs Skinner. 'Thank you, ma'am.'

Then she turned to Nelly. 'May I leave Harry and Ruth here? I'll tell them not to be a nuisance.' Her face clenched with renewed anguish. 'I'm sorry to be such a bother, but I don't know what else to do. I've no one but Adam and Ted.'

'It's all right, Mrs Wheeler,' Nelly said. 'I'll keep an eye on them. Just you go ahead.'

*

For the first few minutes, going down the hill to the river, Aunt Lenore was nearly running. At the bottom she waited for Adam to catch up.

'Oh, Adam ...!' she said, her lips trembling.

'It's awful about Ella. I'm *so* sorry. I don't know what to say.'

'You do understand why I have to reach Ted.'

'Of course.'

That seemed to satisfy Aunt Lenore. She marched on along the trail, staring ahead of her. Some of her anger seemed to be fading now that she was actually doing something.

Adam wondered what would happen when they reached Uncle Ted. Was there any point reminding him again that he had a duty to his family? Would even his daughter's death do that?

They followed the track along the flats past the dam and for a short distance further, until they reached the Indian camp, located on one of the small hillocks close to the edge of the ravine, presumably to be out of the way of floods. There were two tents of bent poles covered with canvas and brush, and between them a fire with an iron cooking pot hung over it. An elderly woman in a dress, a man's coat, and high moccasins was putting more wood on the fire, and playing children could be heard but not seen.

Adam was about to go up the little hill and ask her whether there was anybody to take them across the river, when he noticed an Indian man in a canoe coming downstream towards them.

'Have you any money, Aunt Lenore?

'A bit. Mrs Manley paid me for the work I did after Ted left.' She patted the side of her skirt where, underneath, in a pocket tied round her waist with tape, she carried what money she had.

Like the old woman by the fire, the man in the canoe wore a mixture of native and European clothes – cloth trousers, shirt, and coat, all ornamented with fringes and beads, and high moccasins. He had evidently been tending his trap-lines; in the bottom of the canoe, as Adam could see when they came close, was a furry pile with a couple of rabbits on top.

The Indian had noticed them and, when they began walking in his direction, paddled towards them.

'Would you please be so kind as to take us across the river?' Adam asked. He gestured at the canoe and at the far bank.

The Indian surveyed them at leisure, then nodded. He moved the canoe near to the bank and they got in. It took only a few paddle strokes to cross. He helped Aunt Lenore out, accepted the penny she offered him, then made a sign of thanks and farewell.

To reach the ravine Adam had followed yesterday, they had to go downstream a short distance, picking their way through weeds and scrubby growth. Once they reached the trail, Aunt Lenore began walking faster again. They hardly talked; there was nothing more to say about Ella's death, and it was impossible to chat about other things. Adam's mind was filled with worrying pictures about what they'd find at Montgomery's Tavern, or wherever they caught up with Uncle Ted. Would they be in time? Would the battle be over? Would Uncle Ted even be there still?

He was also watching the woods for armed men like those who had stopped him yesterday evening. True enough, he had no horse now, and there was no other obvious reason for anyone to stop him, but Aunt Lenore was a woman, and in wartime ....

To his relief they saw no one. There were no men felling trees at the edge of the big clearing. It was eerily silent. Even the wildlife seemed to know that something was brewing.

When they reached Yonge Street and had begun walking

north they heard, very far in the distance behind them, an unusual sound. It was so faint that at first they were not sure what it was. They looked at each other, puzzled.

'Is that ... *music?*' Adam asked.

'That's what I thought it was.' Then Aunt Lenore's hand flew to her face in alarm. 'Oh, my lord! Could that be the army coming – I mean the government army? With a band? Oh, Adam, we have to hurry!'

They ran.

On this side of Montgomery's Tavern, standing in the road and staring, were a few men with pikes and muskets, the same sort of picket as the one that had stopped Adam yesterday. At first Adam thought they were looking at him and he felt his shoulders hunch in sudden fear. Some of these men might be the very ones who had shot at him yesterday. They might recognize him – and then what?

But then he realized that they too had heard the music and were paying no attention to them. Adam glanced over his shoulder but nothing was visible. There was only the faint pounding of band music far away.

Men were gathered around the tavern, much like yesterday, though there seemed to be more tension in the air. Some groups were talking heatedly, gesturing with hands and sticks and pikes. Others stood smoking in gloomy silence, or drinking from whisky jugs. A drunken voice was singing, and someone was hammering metal on an anvil. There was enough noise to cover the sound of the band.

'How are we going to find him among all these people?' Aunt Lenore asked Adam, her voice taut with urgency.

They asked several men if they knew Ted Wheeler. The third one directed them to the wheelwright's shop, where they found him watching another man attach a pike-head to a staff which had the twigs lopped off but the bark still on. This was the hammering they had heard.

'Ted, Ella's ...!' Aunt Lenore began, her voice angry.

'Lenore! What are you doing here?'

'Ella's dead. I want you to come with me.'

Uncle Ted frowned and looked back and forth from her to Adam.

'Ella?' He said the name as though he'd never heard it before.

'Oh, Ted, I need your help. She's lying there at Mrs Murphy's, in the back kitchen because we couldn't leave her in Mrs Murphy's bed, and there's no one to watch with her, and we'll have to have a funeral. You've *got* to come, Ted.'

She went towards him, looking for comfort.

Adam had been watching Uncle Ted's face – the annoyed surprise changing to a moment of genuine shock and alarm which turned into a look of noble sorrow. When Aunt Lenore went to him, he held out his arms and enfolded her in an embrace.

'Oh, my dear wife,' he said. 'What a grief for you … what a grief for us both.'

It sounded as though he was putting on an act, but Adam remembered the moment when his face showed real shock, and again that hint of fear in his eyes. What *was* it that Uncle Ted was afraid of?

There was no time to work it out now. Someone ran past the shop shouting, 'The army's coming! For real, this time! No false alarm! Get your weapons, men!'

The man making the pike finished the job with two or three more blows of the hammer and hurried out to join the noisy crowd outside. Other running feet pounded past. A horse neighed and then galloped off.

In the shop there was silence. Aunt Lenore had pulled back a little and, still loosely embraced, was wiping her eyes. Uncle Ted was staring past her with an unbelieving look.

A man put his head in at the door. 'Come on, there, we've got to muster. Enemy's in sight.'

Uncle Ted raised one hand to his forehead. 'I will not be

taking part. I have just been told of the death of one of my children.'

The face in the doorway gave a scoffing grunt, then vanished.

Aunt Lenore looked up as though wanting her eyes to confirm what her ears had heard.

'You're coming with me, Ted? Oh, I'm so glad. We'd better leave right away.' She turned to Adam. 'What's safest – the trail we came by?'

'With the government army coming up Yonge Street, we'll have to cut across the fields.'

Several horses were heard galloping away. Uncle Ted, taking his wife's arm, went out. Adam followed.

In the open space in front of the tavern, there was by now a sizeable gathering. But not everyone was mustering. As Adam watched, two men furtively slipped away from the edge of the crowd, ran across Yonge Street, and disappeared into a patch of woods to the northeast. Another man followed, hurrying as though to catch up with them.

Uncle Ted, in spite of his words about not taking part in the battle, lingered, watching what was going on. He seemed to have forgotten Aunt Lenore's presence until she grabbed his sleeve and shook it.

'Come on, Ted. We have to get away from here before the battle starts.'

He looked down at her, then lifted his head and, like everyone else, stared south towards the sound of band music. At that instant, Adam felt as though he could see into his mind. Uncle Ted had two different pictures of himself. One was of the heroic fighter, taking up arms for what he believed in; the other was of the suffering husband and father supporting his bereaved family. And he had to choose between them.

'Come *on*, Ted! *Please!* We've got to get back to Ella and the kids. This isn't your fight. You haven't even got a weapon!'

Adam watched several more men melt away from the crowd.

Just then two riders galloped up, Mr Mackenzie and a much older person. In spite of the mild, sunny weather, the little newspaperman appeared to be wearing several coats, one over the other.

'Men! Patriotic Canadians!' Mr Mackenzie shouted, bouncing up and down in the saddle and waving his hat. 'The enemy are coming – we've seen them with our own eyes, Colonel Van Egmond and I. It's a large army but we shall triumph. If you hold them off for an hour or two, our reinforcements will arrive and our victory will be assured!'

'Reinforcements?' Adam asked a man standing next to him.

The man shrugged. 'He's been talking about reinforcements all morning. No details. But he sent Matthews off with some of our best men to burn the Don bridge and stop the eastern mail – men we could have used now.'

Mr Mackenzie was still yelling and was now waving his red wig as well as his hat, one in each hand. 'Well, men, are you ready to fight for your freedom?'

The crowd shouted but to Adam's ears there was not much eagerness in the sound.

'Colonel Van Egmond,' Mr Mackenzie said, turning with a self-important air to the rider beside him, 'will you arrange the disposition of our troops?'

Colonel Van Egmond, speaking in a strong accent that Adam didn't recognize, summoned to the front the men who had muskets, and some of those with pikes, and divided them into two parties. He told both to go south about half a mile and conceal themselves to either side of the road. He pointed: the larger group would hide in the woods to the west of the road and the smaller among the stumps of a roughly cleared field opposite. The men set off at a run.

'The rest of you remain here,' he said. 'Defend the

building. Your pikes ....'

He left the sentence hanging. There was nothing encouraging to say. Some of those assigned to defend the tavern did not even have pikes or pitchforks, only sticks. A few, like Uncle Ted, carried no weapon at all.

Several men went into the building. Adam stayed with those remaining outside, staring towards the south where, in the distance, sunlight glinted on bright metal.

He felt a tug on his arm. It was Aunt Lenore. Past her he spotted Uncle Ted hurrying across Yonge Street and clambering over the zig-zag rail fence at the far side.

Adam and his aunt followed. They found Uncle Ted crouched behind the fence, watching what was going on. Even Aunt Lenore, for all her sense of urgency, seemed prepared to linger for a few minutes to see what would happen.

The two groups which had been sent southwards were in hiding by the time the government army reached that spot and halted. They had two cannon with them; as Adam watched, they unhitched the horses that had been pulling them.

Adam saw smoke near the woods where Mackenzie's men were concealed and then, a few moments later, heard the stutter of musket fire.

Then came the smoke and the deep-throated blast of the cannons' firing, and the crash of large branches falling in the woods. The smoke hung in the air.

There was another rattle of musket fire from among the trees, and one from the government army. Then the cannon, reloaded, bellowed again. The next round of firing from the woods was definitely weaker. There was a shout and some sort of commotion.

A few moments later came further cannon fire, aimed at men fleeing northwards across a cleared field. Then the horses were again hitched up, and the big guns began once more moving up the road.

'They're going to attack the tavern!' Uncle Ted exclaimed. Adam, glancing at him, saw on his face a look of blank surprise, as though he had never realized that such a thing might actually happen.

Some of the watchers outside the building ducked indoors, but most ran off.

Looking at the oncoming army, thinking of the few dozen unarmed men in the tavern, Adam said, 'Your side has lost, Uncle Ted. We'd better get away from here.'

'Where can we go?'

Aunt Lenore answered. 'Back to Todmorden.'

Adam remembered something Sergeant Phillips had told him about the war in Spain.

'They'll chase those who ran away. Come on, we'd better hurry.'

'I didn't ...!' Uncle Ted began, then fell silent.

Adam, exasperated, nearly burst out, 'You *did!* Look at you now, crouching behind a fence, *watching* the battle instead of fighting!'

But he stopped himself. No one would ever know whether Uncle Ted, left to himself, would have stayed and fought. The fact that he hadn't was largely Adam's doing and Aunt Lenore's. They had pressed him hard not to fight. Adam suddenly felt weighed down by responsibility, bothered, overburdened. He had thought it was merely silly to try to persuade Uncle Ted not to fight – but could it actually have been *wrong?*

He shook himself. No time for that now.

'All right, we persuaded you,' he said to Uncle Ted.

Their glances met briefly, and again there was that glint of fear in Uncle Ted's eyes. Adam, remembering the dead man two days ago, and his own despairing desire on the way home that evening to lie down by the road and give up, thought that perhaps he understood one of the reasons for that fear. Life was ....

He felt a touch of protectiveness – or maybe it was the Christian charity that Mrs Wright had urged on him. With it came quite a lot of exasperation.

'Uncle Ted,' he said, 'you joined a rebel army and stayed with it long enough to be linked with it in people's minds.'

'I didn't fight!'

'That's right,' he said, trying to be patient, feeling that Uncle Ted had to see at least this one thing clearly. 'You left just before the battle. One side will call you a rebel, the other side a deserter. Come on, we've got to get away from here.'

Chapter Twenty

HE THREE OF THEM set off for Todmorden. On the way they met a man who had been with the Matthews troop, sent by Mr Mackenzie to burn the Don bridge. He said they'd had a fight with a government force.

'Who won?' Uncle Ted asked.

The man growled something. Obviously the rebels hadn't, or he would have boasted.

'Did you burn the bridge?' Adam asked, thinking how much the people living east of the river depended on it.

'We tried, but the fire was put out. We ... they ... burned some buildings nearby.' The man pointed to smoke visible above the southern rim of the ravine.

When Adam told him about the defeat of Mackenzie's force at Montgomery's Tavern, the man, instead of continuing in that direction, began scrambling up the slope to the north, his feet slipping among the fallen leaves.

As the Wheelers hurried on, Adam asked, 'Uncle Ted, what are you going to do now?'

He was wondering whether Uncle Ted would want to see Ella. How important was paying your respects to the dead when your own life was in danger? And what about the funeral, which would have to be held tomorrow or the next day?

Adam himself would go to the funeral, of course, if Mr Skinner gave him leave. He'd brought with him from England the mourning they had given him when his mother died: a black armband, and a bit of black cloth to tie around his cap.

Uncle Ted was not thinking about funerals.

'I'll stay out of sight until I see what happens. There'll be

somewhere in those mills of yours where I can hide.' He spoke casually, offhandedly.

Adam was alarmed. 'You can't hide on strangers' property! If Mr Mackenzie's followers are searched out and punished, that would get them into trouble!' And me too, he thought.

'Oh, they needn't know about it. You can find me a place and bring food. They won't punish a boy ....'

Aunt Lenore interrupted. 'No, Ted, you can't put those mill people in danger. Nor Adam either, after all he's done. When the funeral's over, you and I and the kids will go away again.'

She stopped, but Adam could almost hear the voice inside her head. Go where? Could Uncle Ted ever be persuaded to keep a job? Would his having been among Mackenzie's followers count against him in the search for work?

If the government was really thorough and aggressive in hunting down rebels, would he even be free to search for work? He might be arrested and tried and perhaps convicted.

They had been in this country for little more than two months, intending to make a new life, and this was what they had come to: no work, no home, no money, a dead child, perhaps imprisonment and execution.

No wonder Aunt Lenore looked grim.

But the first thing was to find a safe place for Uncle Ted. Aunt Lenore and the children might be able to stay on at Mrs Murphy's, but he would have to hide somewhere.

Outdoors? But this was December, the trees were bare and offered little shelter or cover, the nights were long and cold.

Aunt Lenore's mind had been running along the same track. 'For tonight maybe you can hide in Mrs Murphy's barn – I mean, once it's dark. We don't want to get Mrs Murphy into trouble either. Then you can see Ella – I'll let you into the back kitchen after everyone's in bed.' Her voice failed, but in a moment she went on. 'This afternoon I'll go and arrange about the funeral.'

'What'll I do until dark?'

'Hide in the woods, I suppose. Anything else would be too dangerous. Come to Mrs Murphy's barn tonight and I'll bring some food and tell you about the funeral.'

'It'll be cold in the woods.' The angle of the sun showed that Uncle Ted would have several hours of hiding outdoors before it was dark enough for him to come safely to the barn.

'Ted, you're an outlaw now. If you'd come away from Montgomery's Tavern yesterday ....'

'Well, we might have won. Then we wouldn't be outlaws. We'd be the new government of this place, taking over the land and the big houses ....'

He fell silent. Even Uncle Ted was beginning to realize that the future would not look like that.

'When you come with the food,' he said grimly, 'bring a lantern.'

'Too dangerous,' Adam said promptly. 'If anyone sees a light in a place where there usually isn't one ....'

'All right, all right. No lantern.'

When they reached the river, there was the problem of getting across. The helpful Indian was not in sight; Adam could see his canoe up at the camp but no doubt he and his family, having heard of the battle, were keeping out of the way.

So the Wheelers walked along the bank looking for a place to wade across and eventually found a likely-looking spot where, as it turned out, the water was barely above their knees. They had taken off their shoes and pulled up their garments, and at the far side Uncle Ted demanded the use of Aunt Lenore's shawl to dry his legs before putting his shoes on again. 'Bad enough being in the woods till dark but I ain't going to do it with wet feet,' he grumbled.

Then they parted company. Uncle Ted went off into the hilly and broken country along the valley, and Adam and Aunt Lenore followed the trail on the flats back to the Don Mills. Aunt Lenore collected Harry and Ruth, thanked Nelly for having given them their dinner, and set off for Toronto to arrange for Ella's funeral.

*

Adam, left alone, suddenly felt desperately forlorn and depressed. In spite of all that had happened, it was only mid-afternoon – the Skinners' hall clock had struck three while Aunt Lenore was talking to Nelly. Three o'clock on a Thursday afternoon was still working hours, so he wandered down to the mill to see if the women were cutting rags. The building was closed and empty.

He should have offered to go with Aunt Lenore, as he'd done that morning. But she hadn't asked him. He'd be no help anyway in arranging a funeral – that was something she knew much more about than he did. Four of her children had died earlier, and it was she who had seen to his mother's funeral . . . .

While going with Aunt Lenore to Montgomery's Tavern, and discussing afterwards where Uncle Ted could hide, he'd had the sense that he was growing up. Now he was just a kid again, no use to anybody.

But last night he'd hated being grown up, hated being loaded down with adult problems.

Oh, hell. It was too complicated.

He hunched his shoulders in wretchedness and shoved his hands into his pockets.

Maybe Nelly would have a cup of tea for him. He'd had nothing since breakfast. Miserably, he trudged home.

Nelly was taking freshly baked loaves of bread out of the oven. 'Hello, Adam,' she said.

He plunked himself down on the settle. 'Smells good.' His heart wasn't in it, but Nelly was proud of her bread and liked a compliment.

'I'll bet you haven't had any dinner,' she said. 'Again.'

'Bad habit.'

'We'll give this bread a coupla minutes and then I'll cut you a heel. It'll be too fresh to eat, really, but the old's all gone and I ain't got nothin' else to give you. Meantime, help yerself to tea.'

He fetched a cup and saucer from the shelf.

'Pour some for me too, there's a love,' Nelly said, 'and add some of that there boiling water to the pot.' She was busy setting the loaves out on racks to cool. When she'd done that, she sat down in her rocking chair, heaved a great sigh, and looked at him.

For a few moments they were silent. The only sound was the fire hissing.

'Well, lad,' Nelly said at last, speaking more softly and gently than usual, 'you're looking down in the mouth and no wonder, with your little cousin gone and all this worry about your uncle and aunt, and ....'

The sympathy loosened something in him that had been clenched tight. He set down his cup and put his hands over his face.

'Oh, Adam, love.'

In a moment, Nelly was sitting on the settle beside him, her arms around him. 'There now, there now. And I'll bet you're missing your mom, too.'

He could only cry and cling to her, desperately in need of comforting.

Nelly talked on, hugging and rocking him. 'Mr Skinner's real pleased with you, Adam. He was saying so this morning. He says you did real well yesterday. He felt bad about sending you to Montgomery's Tavern with that paper, and then all the way into town, and about your being shot at, but you did everything right. And he was pleased that you looked after Princess when you got back. "Some kids would just've left her, after all that," he said.'

Her words at first only intensified his sobbing, but gradually he calmed down. When he could, he moved away from

Nelly and blew his nose. She handed him his cup of tea; he took it and drank.

'Well, then,' she said more briskly. 'Let's see how that bread looks.' A moment later she handed him a plate bearing two slices liberally covered with jam. He ate them gratefully, while she watched from her chair.

When he had finished, he felt better. He put the plate down and gave her as much of a smile as he could manage. 'Thanks, Nelly.'

'D'you want to tell me more about what happened at Montgomery's Tavern?'

Aunt Lenore had already, in a few hurried words, described the battle and its outcome.

'There *is* nothing more.' He was silent for a moment. 'I wonder how many men got killed or hurt, how many people there are like Uncle Ted, outlaws, needing to hide.'

'People hurt and killed … we'll hear about them soon enough. Outlaws … that depends on what the government does, how hard they try to round up the rebels, how hard they punish them. Like you say, there could be quite a few outlaws around.'

There had been outlaws in England too after the Swing riots, men living in the woods, pilfering food or a laundered shirt left to dry on a bush overnight, making occasional stealthy contact with their families. But he thought too about the other side – not the outlaws themselves, but the world they'd fled. There'd be gaps in families and in all the small villages dotted across the country, a shopkeeper missing, a blacksmith gone, a woman left to run a farm on her own.

Such a lot of misery and upset, Adam thought.

But if Mr Mackenzie had won there would have been as much, perhaps more.

Besides causing unhappiness and muddle, would the rebellion do any good?

All he could do – all anyone could do – was wait and see.

*

Shortly before supper-time, Adam and Nelly heard what had happened in town that day. Mr William Helliwell, the one who lived at the Mills, had been stationed at the Parliament Buildings, and when he returned about dusk he came to have a word with Mr Skinner. The two men stood in the entrance hallway of the house, and Adam and Nelly overheard Mr Helliwell say, 'No, thank you, Colin, I won't sit down. I want to go home and pull off my boots.'

Then, in reply to a rumbled question from Mr Skinner, he reported that the government army had won. There had been some men wounded in both battles, the one at Montgomery's Tavern and the one at the Don bridge. 'On the way here I met some poor fellows being taken to the hospital in carts. Hurt in the fight at the bridge, I guess. The bridge has a guard of militia on it, by the way – wouldn't let me pass.'

'Don't see why not,' Mr Skinner said. 'You're militia too, on the loyalist side, same as them.'

'They weren't letting anyone by, not even kids. There was a girl on a pony who was also turned back.'

One girl? Adam wondered. Which one? And where was the other?

'How did you cross the river?' Mr Skinner asked.

'Walked up the bush road along the far side to just opposite here and then hollered for one of my men to ride a horse over and ferry me across on horseback.'

'All quiet in town when you left?'

'Not *quiet* – too much going on. Taverns all full, lots of cheering and rampaging around. But no more danger.'

*

Adam had just finished dinner when his cousin Harry came looking for him.

'Mother wants you,' he said in a surly way. 'Up there

behind Mrs Murphy's house. Dad's come in from the woods. Mother's in a taking about something.'

'About what?'

Harry shrugged, as though it didn't concern him.

While they trudged up the hill, Adam asked how their trip to town that afternoon had gone. 'I heard the bridge was guarded and no one allowed to cross.'

'Yeah.'

'They let you through? Other people were stopped from passing.'

'Mother told them it was about a funeral and they let us by.'

'When's the funeral to be?'

'Tomorrow. We had to go all the way to the palace to arrange the damn thing.'

'The *palace?*' Adam demanded, thinking of kings and queens.

'That's what it's called, the house where this guy lives. The rector.'

'You mean to say that the rector here lives in a *palace?*'

'He's not an ordinary rector, like we had at home. He's a big-wig. With a title or something. Name of Strachan.'

'Oh, you mean Archdeacon Strachan.' Adam knew that the archdeacon was an important person in both the church and the government – that in fact it was at his house that last night's meeting had taken place. Maybe he was important enough for his residence to be called a palace.

All the same, Adam was impressed and interested.

'Are you saying that Aunt Lenore had to see Mr Strachan *himself* to arrange the funeral?'

'Seems so. We went to the church first but some old guy there sent us to the palace. Hell of a long way – right at the other end of town, near that fort where you and me went.'

When they reached Mrs Murphy's house, Adam asked, 'Aunt Lenore's somewhere out back, did you say?'

'Yeah.' Harry waved towards the darkness of the yard. 'She said she'd be watching for you. I gotta work.' He twitched his head towards a lean-to against the back kitchen, where a lantern hung from a nail. 'They've got me to split firewood – and Ruth's washing dishes. Help pay for our keep, mother and Mrs Murphy said.'

Adam crossed the yard. 'Aunt Lenore!' he called softly.

It was an evening for caution and furtiveness; as he and Harry walked through Todmorden, he had seen several dark figures sliding out of sight. The coming weeks would be a troubled time. Some people would help to conceal rebels, others would be ready and eager to hand them over to the authorities. Everyone would be watchful or suspicious or nosy or afraid.

Aunt Lenore appeared from behind the barn and hurried towards him.

'Thank heavens you've come, Adam.'

He heard panic in her voice, and his heart sank. 'What now, aunt?'

'Ted's got a new bee in his bonnet. He's been down to the Kingston Road to see a friend of his and learned that a lot of Mackenzie's men are fleeing to the American states. He wants to go too.' She turned and spoke towards the darkness. 'Ted, it's okay. I'm talking to Adam.'

Uncle Ted came forward. He had his back to the half moon which, with the stars, gave what light there was. Adam couldn't read his face, but he could see the big frame hunched, hands deep in pockets.

'The United States, Uncle Ted?'

'It's the only thing to do. If I stay here I may be caught. Killed.' He reared his head and shoulders, as though remembering something. 'I've got to save myself. What use will I be to you all if I'm dead?'

'Will you take the family along?'

'Certainly not. I'll be living a footloose life – picking up a bit of work here and there. We may be raiding across the border, keeping up the pressure. There won't be room for women and children. For now,' he added hastily, with a glance at his wife.

'How will they get along here by themselves?'

'Lenore'll find work as a servant. Lots of demand. She'll probably be given lodging.'

'Lodging for three people? And if she has to live out and pay rent ...?'

'Ted!' Aunt Lenore protested, 'you make it sound as though we'll manage easily, as though there'll be no difficulty. You can't ....'

'I'll send you money sometimes, when I can,' he said impatiently. 'There!'

Adam was exasperated. The understanding and protectiveness he'd felt that afternoon was gone. This was Uncle Ted at his worst, irresponsible, swaggering, avoiding reality.

'Uncle Ted, this isn't right!'

'I'm an outlaw now, ain't I?' Uncle Ted demanded, with an air of satisfaction. 'I can't live here safely. So I'll be off. We know a man with a boat. We'll cross the lake at first light ....'

'First light *tomorrow?*' Adam burst out. 'What about the funeral?'

He hunched his shoulders again. 'It's dangerous to wait,' he said, half defiant and half sullen.

A sound of hooves came from the road, and then a voice speaking loudly, not furtively. In the silence, Adam could hear almost every word.

' ... proclamation by the governor!' the man announced. 'A price on Mackenzie's head and the other leaders' heads, but easy terms for everyone else.'

'Forgiveness?' asked another voice.

'They're supposed to return to their duty and he'll be easy on them.'

'It's the only thing for the government to do,' said someone

else. 'How can they possibly punish everyone? Only the leaders ....'

Adam ran out to the road. 'Did you say that followers
would be forgiven?'

'If they return to their duty,' the mounted man told him.
'No more armed revolt, lad.'

'*I* didn't revolt!' he muttered as he returned to Uncle Ted
and Aunt Lenore. 'You heard that?' he asked. 'There's no
need to go to the United States, Uncle Ted.'

Uncle Ted was, so far as Adam could tell in the dim light,
looking glum rather than relieved. When Aunt Lenore said,
'Oh, Ted, isn't that good news!' his only reply was a grunt.

'How do I know whether I can trust it? It could be a trap.'

'No, the man's right. They can't punish everyone.'

'I've got to follow my principles.'

'I think you should look after your family, Ted. You
brought us here and you can't just leave us ....'

Adam moved away, but not far enough to be out of earshot.
He stood in the windy dark, with here and there a light showing. The nearest was the one in the shed where Harry was
working – if it could be called work, Adam thought, hearing
how few and far between the axe blows were.

'You can at least stay for the funeral tomorrow, Ted. I'm
sure Mrs Murphy would let you sleep in the barn, where
Harry is. It gives us a couple of days to see about work, and if
you still can't find any ....'

'Well ....'

'It means you don't have to leave *tonight*. There's less
hurry.'

Adam thought that it was precisely the idea of leaving
tonight that had appealed to Uncle Ted – an emergency, something dramatic. Now that there was no hurry, he lost interest.

'We've got to see whether this ... this forgiving everybody
is real or only a trick,' Uncle Ted muttered. 'You don't want
me to end up in jail, or dead.'

'Of course not. We'll know by tomorrow or Saturday, and then, if you have to, you can still go to the United States and find work and send for us.'

That was not the way Uncle Ted had pictured it. Adam didn't know how his version and Aunt Lenore's would ever be made to fit together.

There was a pause. The axe hit a chunk of wood and split it with a tearing crack. Along with the noise of the two pieces falling off the chopping block, there was a distant sound of another horse galloping. A dog barked. A man's voice whooped, perhaps at the news of the governor's proclamation.

'All right,' Uncle Ted said. 'I'll stay until Saturday. I can see that I *have* to be at the funeral, to support you. And I want to be there. Poor Ella, such a lovely child ... my dear daughter .... Let's go in and see her, if it really is safe.'

He and Aunt Lenore came towards Adam and the three of them went into the back kitchen.

Ella was wrapped in a white sheet and lying in a simple coffin – the wood only roughly planed, not varnished or painted – set across a couple of trestles. A lantern, its candle nearly used up but still burning, stood near the head.

Aunt Lenore folded back the sheet to reveal Ella's face, very white and still and empty.

Uncle Ted removed his hat, and Adam quickly pulled off his cap.

The sight of Ella reminded Adam of his mother, and again the tears stung his eyes. But he was not going to let them show. He fiercely blocked them, blocked all thinking, just stood there until Uncle Ted looked up, put on his hat, and turned away.

'Where'd you get the coffin, Lenore?' he asked.

'A friend of Mrs Murphy's made it – as a favour to her. And he's driving us to the church tomorrow. I don't know what we can do to thank him.'

[251]

'What time's the service?'

'Half past ten o'clock. The service'll be at the church, but Mr Strachan, the rector, explained that the cemetery is quite a distance away, somewhere up Yonge Street near a tollgate. He said he'd find someone with a wagon to take us there.'

'All that'll cost a hell of a lot.'

'Mr Strachan said he'd charge us nothing for the funeral or the use of the pall, or for the wagon from the church to the cemetery. "A funeral is important," he told me. "God makes no difference between a poor person dying and a rich one. I'll make sure that it's done properly for you," he said. He's a kind man.'

Kind! Adam was startled. Archdeacon Strachan was one of the leaders of the Family Compact, the small group of men that governed Upper Canada and that Mr Mackenzie and the rebels hated so violently. From Gavin McPhee, Adam had heard a lot about the archdeacon's arrogance and greed for political power. Aunt Lenore seemed to have seen a different side of the man.

She was still talking. 'He'll take the service himself, not leave it to his assistant. He treated us real well, a lot better than those militia soldiers guarding his palace who didn't want to let us through at first. They weren't even polite.'

'What do you expect? They're just ordinary fellers who never learned any manners.'

'Anyway, the rector was a real gentleman. And Mrs Murphy is coming to the funeral with us, so there'll be someone other than the family.'

'What time do we leave, Aunt Lenore?' Adam asked. 'If the funeral's at half past ten ....'

'Mrs Murphy says we'd better start at nine o'clock.'

'Is there anything else you need me for tonight?' he asked. Then he felt that he'd put it badly, made it sound as though he was eager to get away. It was true that he'd be glad to be home, but he didn't want to hurt Aunt Lenore's feelings.

'No, Adam, thanks.' She looked at him, giving him her whole attention. 'You should be in bed.' She gave him a warm hug. 'Thanks for everything, love. See you tomorrow morning.'

*

The funeral party was driven to town by Mrs Murphy's friend Mr Nelson, a gnarled but fit old man. Mrs Murphy sat beside him on the driver's seat and the Wheeler family behind, on the floor of the wagon, with the coffin. It was a cold, windy day with scudding clouds, and Mrs Murphy had lent Aunt Lenore a blanket to wrap around herself and Ruth.

Shortly after they set off, they passed Bert, the Skinners' hired man, walking up the road. At the sight of the pall-covered coffin, he took off his hat and stood still while the wagon passed. Adam was touched; the action made Bert more human than he'd ever seemed before.

No one said much. Besides the fact that the occasion made everyone subdued, Uncle Ted was grumpy about the outcome of yesterday's battle, and Aunt Lenore was worried about how and where they'd live ... tomorrow, and the day after that, and in the weeks and months to come. Ruth was nestled in the crook of her arm, under the blanket, and Harry was tapping a stick against the side of the wagon in rhythm with the horse's plodding tread.

At the church, Uncle Ted and Mr Nelson lifted the coffin out of the wagon and the others lined up behind. A woman sweeping the steps of the church saw them and went indoors, apparently to announce their arrival because a moment later a man in a surplice appeared – Archdeacon Strachan, Adam assumed – and came towards them. He nodded gravely, then turned and led the way to the church. As they walked, he read aloud from his prayer book.

They went into the building and up the aisle to where two trestles were standing ready at the foot of the chancel steps.

When Uncle Ted and Mr Nelson had placed the coffin on them, and Mr Nelson had quietly departed, the rector took up his position on the chancel steps and the others stood around the coffin.

The solemn, dignified words seemed to fill the big church, even though their party – and the coffin itself – were so small.

'Lord, thou hast been our dwelling place ... thou turnest man to destruction ... thou carriest them away as with a flood ... the days of our years are threescore and ten ....'

Threescore and ten meant seventy, Adam remembered Mrs Wright saying. Ella had been six when she died. She hadn't had nearly her full share.

Soon they left the church. The coffin was put on another wagon. This time the Wheelers and Mrs Murphy did not have to ride in the same one because Mr Strachan had also provided a vehicle with seats, two benches behind the one for the driver, so that they could all sit properly. This wagon and Mr Strachan's carriage followed the one bearing the coffin – along King Street and up Yonge Street to just beyond the tollgate in Yorkville, the one where, only two days ago, Cornelia and Adam had been stopped on their ride into the city from Montgomery's Tavern.

Many of the people along the way, noticing the funeral cortège, stopped and waited respectfully while it passed, the men removing their hats, the women standing with bent heads and folded hands, the children staring.

All for Ella, Adam thought.

But not only for Ella, he realized. For death. For the awareness that they themselves would die, that the dead person, though a stranger, was human like themselves.

When they reached the graveyard, a man raking the paths helped Uncle Ted carry the coffin to the grave-side. Another workman laid down his shovel and, while the family and Mrs

Murphy watched, the two men began to lower the coffin into the grave.

Uncle Ted stood with head uncovered and bowed, the wind ruffling his hair. Aunt Lenore had one arm around Ruth and with the other hand wiped her own eyes. Mrs Murphy sniffed into a black-bordered handkerchief.

As the coffin descended, Adam realized with a shock how final it all was. This was the end of a human life. Ella was gone, had stopped existing. At his mother's funeral he had been too stunned and unhappy to grasp it, though the feeling had come to him later as, day by day, he learned to live without her. Now, watching Ella's coffin sink into that hole in the ground, he understood that this was the moment when that final disappearance, that final wiping out, happened.

How pitiful! How unimportant life was, if that was how it could end at any moment! How silly to keep struggling, racking your brains to figure out what was right, making yourself exhausted and miserable, when this was all it came to in the end.

Not just pitiful. Appalling. Terrifying.

He clenched his teeth and throat-muscles and barely breathed, trying not to cry out with the shock of his realization. In horror and panic, he concentrated on what the rector was saying.

'Forasmuch as it hath pleased Almighty God of his great mercy to take unto himself the soul of our dear sister here departed, we therefore commit her body to the ground, earth to earth, ashes to ashes, dust to dust; in sure and certain hope of the Resurrection to eternal life, through our Lord Jesus Christ; who shall change our vile body, that it may be like unto his glorious body ....'

Vile body! Adam thought. Is that what they think of human bodies ... of Ella?

The two workmen picked up shovels and began filling the grave. The sharp, cracking sounds of the first clods of soil hitting the coffin shocked and frightened Adam further. He put his hands over his face. *Vile body!* Was Ella vile? How could she be vile when she was only six years old? And the awful sounds of the soil crashing down on that pathetic little box!

When he looked up again, the coffin was no longer visible.

The dignified words continued.

'I heard a voice from heaven, saying unto me, Write, From henceforth blessed are the dead which die in the Lord: even so saith the Spirit; for they rest from their labours.'

Blessed are the dead.
Rest.
Sleep.

Adam watched the shovelfuls of earth now falling softly on the layer of soil already covering the coffin.

A sweet, trilling whistle distracted him for a moment. He looked up and saw a small bird, speckled black and grey. It gave another single trill of liquid sound, and flew away.

Rest.

Ella was … it was like being put to bed. That was what dying was. And *resurrection to eternal life* – well, he didn't know about that. But he could understand the part about the dead resting from their labours.

The rector said, 'Amen.'

There was a moment's silence except for the gentle thudding of earth on earth. Then Mr Strachan put his prayer book in his pocket and shook hands. The handshake with Uncle Ted was manly and firm, but when he took Aunt Lenore's hand he clasped it in both of his in a gesture of real sympathy.

He returned to his carriage and the coachman drove away, back towards town, the horse's hooves clip-clopping on the frozen ground.

The other two wagons had already left; the Wheelers and Mrs Murphy were expected to look after themselves now.

'What's the best way home from here?' Uncle Ted asked, not speaking to anyone in particular.

It was Mrs Murphy who answered. 'Down Yonge Street and across to the bridge.'

So they trudged back to the Don Mills. They were going to the Skinners' house where Nelly, with the Skinners' permission, would provide the funeral party with a meal.

It was a long walk. After a while Mrs Murphy, who had rheumatism in her hip, had to ask Uncle Ted to give her his arm. They were the only ones who talked at all, commenting on yesterday's battle and wondering what might happen now. Adam listened with half an ear; he still felt numb after the emotions he'd been through and was trying not to think of his mother. *Rest*, he kept saying to himself. *Sleep*. Hold on to that.

*

The warmth of the Skinners' kitchen was very welcome after the long, cold walk. The first thing Nelly did was pour tea for them all, adding a drop of whisky for those who wanted it. Then she served them a meal of ham and cabbage and potatoes, with apple pie for dessert.

Adam drank his tea and ate his meal in silence. The familiar kitchen, the hot food, and Nelly's comfortable presence at the end of the table soothed him and provided a kind of protective layer so that he did not have to think or feel. He'd been forced to do too much thinking and feeling in these last few days. He just ate and drank and let the voices wash over him.

When the meal was finished, Mr and Mrs Skinner came into the kitchen. Adam and the adults at the table got to their feet and so, after a hasty prod, did Harry and Ruth.

Mr Skinner shook hands with Uncle Ted and Aunt Lenore. 'We just came to say how sorry we are about the death of your little girl,' he said.

'We really do sympathize, Mrs Wheeler — and Mr Wheeler,' his wife added. 'It's a sad way for you to begin a new life here.'

'Thank you,' Uncle Ted said to them both. 'It *is* hard, I have to admit. But we'll survive and carry on.' It was spoken in a tone of resolute courage which didn't sound real to Adam. But the other adults seemed to accept it. It was proper for the occasion.

'That's all we can ever do,' Mrs Skinner said, and she smiled at Aunt Lenore.

'Well, now, Mr Wheeler,' Mr Skinner went on in a getting-down-to-business voice, 'I hear you're looking for work.'

'That's so, I'm afraid.'

'There's a fellow called Smith, out on the Kingston Road, who needs a hired hand. Shanty for the family to live in, so I'm told.'

'Right away?' Aunt Lenore demanded. 'I mean, does he want someone *now*, and is the shanty empty?'

'Far's I know, yes, Mrs Wheeler.'

Aunt Lenore and Uncle Ted exchanged glances. There was a moment's silence.

'What kind of work, sir?' Uncle Ted asked.

'You'll have to ask.'

'On the Kingston Road, you said.'

'Maybe half an hour's walk east of the bridge.'

'Thank you, sir. I'll go and talk to him.'

After the Skinners returned to the front part of the house, the others sat down again.

'Tomorrow's Sunday,' Uncle Ted said. 'I'll go see that feller on ....'

Adam knew he was going to say ' ... on Monday.'

Aunt Lenore must have been expecting the same, because she interrupted. 'Why not go this afternoon, Ted? I know you've had a long walk, but .... It's important.'

They all watched his face.

'The sooner we can move to a house of our own, Ted ...,' Aunt Lenore reminded him.

He still hesitated.

'Besides,' Mrs Murphy added, 'if you've got a job people may not be so quick to remember that you was with the rebels.'

'I'm not ashamed ...,' Uncle Ted began, but he stopped. Adam watched the bravado fade from his face. For a moment the fearful look appeared, twitching Uncle Ted's eyebrows. Then he blinked and slowly nodded.

'You could be right,' he said to Mrs Murphy. 'This damn business ain't over yet. I've heard of men being hunted down and arrested .... Best play it safe. And with winter coming ....' He got to his feet. 'I'll be off, then, Lenore. See you later.' He touched her shoulder.

Adam could see how relieved Aunt Lenore was. She got up too, and offered to help Nelly with the dishwashing.

Nelly refused to let her. 'You go and do whatever you have to do, Mrs Wheeler. Adam and I'll attend to this.'

So Aunt Lenore thanked Nelly for the dinner and the hospitality, and all the guests left.

While they tidied the kitchen, Nelly told Adam that Mr Morris and Mr Carver had been in to ask what was happening at the mill, and that Mr Skinner had decided to get it operating again on Monday.

'They're coming tomorrow to prepare,' Nelly said, 'and you're to be there too. Mr Skinner is hoping that the other men show up, or maybe stop by on Sunday to find out when they'll be needed. If you happen to see anyone, you can let them know.'

*

That evening, Aunt Lenore came to the Skinners' house again. She looked exhausted and gladly accepted a cup of tea from Nelly.

When she was sitting on the settle, she told Adam and Nelly that Ted had taken the job and that they were moving to the shanty the next day.

'What sort of work is it, Aunt Lenore?'

'Helping to clear land.'

Clearing land, Adam thought. Precisely the kind of work that he had *not* been able to picture Uncle Ted doing.

He remembered his own realization that Uncle Ted might do better at some other kind of work. He would mention it to Aunt Lenore sometime, but not now. She looked depressed and tired enough already. Adam was glad to see her talking with Nelly. Perhaps they would become friends.

'Will you be working too, Aunt Lenore?'

'Mrs Smith says she can use help with the livestock and in the house.' Aunt Lenore was trying to be hopeful. And indeed, this news made the prospect better than it had been a day or two earlier.

'I'll come and visit you on Sunday,' he said.

Chapter Twenty-one

ADAM, AS HE TRUDGED DOWN TO THE mill the next morning, wondered whether the rebellion was really over. Mr Skinner's reopening of the mill suggested that he thought it was – or *hoped* it was – but Adam kept thinking about those men who, according to Uncle Ted, were crossing the border to the United States, intending to continue their pressure on the government in Upper Canada. And what about the leaders, who had a price on their heads now? And what was happening in other parts of the province, and in Lower Canada?

He, for his part, had had enough of it all. Like Mr Skinner, he hoped things would return to normal.

As for the paper mill, no one knew yet who would show up today. Presumably there would be little real work done, because that required all or most of the employees to be on hand. Certainly no paper would be made unless the fire under the vat had been started at three o'clock.

When Adam reached the mill, that had not happened. Mr Morris had just arrived himself and was tying on his apron, telling Mr Carver, the clerk, that he had spent the rebellion days on duty at the Parliament Buildings. Mr Carver had been on guard at the court house.

Adam looked at their faces as they spoke. He found it hard to picture peaceable men like this turning suddenly into soldiers – and even harder to think of them turning back afterwards into exactly what they had been before. It was only four days since Tuesday morning, when they had all been here together, working as usual. Since then they had been scattered around the city, leading completely different lives than normal. No doubt they had been forced to think about

politics and what they believed in, to face the possibility of killing other men or being killed themselves. They had probably slept rough, with a musket beside them, gone unshaven, eaten what and when they could, mingled with strangers. The gentlemanly Mr Morris, master paper-maker, who was tying his apron on over his waistcoat, was not the same man as the one who had shed that apron on Tuesday.

The two women were the next to arrive. Mrs O'Neill, normally a non-stop talker with a knack for saying disastrously wrong things, was nearly silent. Before the rebellion she had been reform-minded; now that her side had been defeated, she probably felt that it was safer not to talk too much in case she let slip something she shouldn't have said.

Abe had enjoyed the rebellion. He'd been with the government army marching up to Montgomery's Tavern, and on the way had spotted a pretty girl. 'Nothing like a soldier for catching their eye,' he said, 'even if you've got no uniform but only a musket. And it's the music too, see.' He reported that he'd been to visit her the day after the battle and that she liked him even when he wasn't carrying a gun and marching to the sound of a band.

Steven had, for the first time in his life, been really drunk. He had recovered, but the experience left him muttering, 'Never again.' Abe said he'd better join the Methodists and live a sober life, and Steven seemed to be taking the advice more seriously than was intended.

Steven also reported that his cousin Fred was sick but would return to work when he was well again. Mr Morris gave Adam a quick lesson at sorting paper into different grades and counting it into reams so that if Fred were not back on the job by Monday Adam could do at least some of his work.

Bert appeared later in the day, as silent as ever. He said nothing about how he had spent the rebellion days.

Gavin McPhee did not turn up. Remembering how

outspoken he had been for reform, Adam did not expect to see him again.

During the morning, Mr Morris inspected the stuff which had been left in the vats when the mill closed on Tuesday, and checked the rags that Mrs McDonald and Mrs O'Neill had cut during the week. Then he and Mr Carver went up to the Skinner house for a meeting with Mr Skinner and Mr Eastwood.

When they returned, Mr Skinner was with them; he went into his office and summoned Adam.

'Yes, sir?' Adam said, taking off his cap.

'Come in and close the door, lad.'

When Adam had done so, he continued. 'How old're you?'

'Fourteen, sir.'

'When's your birthday?'

'February, sir.'

'So you're nearly fifteen. We got word yesterday that Sam won't be back. His father was with Mackenzie and fled to the States after the battle on Thursday. Sam and his mother are going to join him. We're looking for an apprentice. Normally we'd want someone already fifteen, but you're nearly that.'

'I can't afford the premium, sir.'

'We wouldn't charge you one, lad. Premiums aren't always required. You're the sort of person we want – hard worker, good with other people. We're pleased with what you did these last few days, especially that tricky errand on Wednesday.'

'Thank you, sir.'

'For the next week or two you'll do pretty much what you've been doing. We've got to get the mill back on the go, hire someone to replace Gavin and someone to do your work. But when we can, we'll take you off the firewood and ... by the way, as of Monday you'll start the fires. Up at three o'clock, lad. It's part of learning the trade.'

'How will I wake up in time?' he asked, and then was

embarrassed at having asked such a personal question.

Mr Skinner grinned. 'Nelly says she's a light sleeper and complains about hearing the clock striking all night long. We'll get her to prove it. When it strikes three, she can wake you. Be sure to go to bed early.' He turned to his desk, then looked up at Adam, his head cocked in a question. 'This okay with you, lad – I mean the whole arrangement? You'd like to learn the trade? You'd like to stay here? Maybe we've been taking too much for granted, but it seemed to us ....'

'Oh, yes, sir! It's what I want to do. I like the paper-making business and ... I like it here.'

'Good. We'll attend to the apprenticeship papers when you really start. For now, help us to get the mill going again, there's a good chap.'

As Adam thought it over, those last few words meant as much as the offer of an apprenticeship. 'Help us get the mill going again, there's a good chap,' Mr Skinner had said, making him an important part of the group.

He recalled the other occasion when he had been told that his work mattered. That was when Uncle Ted had implied that his plan of clearing land and starting a farm depended on Adam's taking part. Adam remembered how burdened he had felt. What was different now?

Was it because of the people, that he liked Mr Skinner better than Uncle Ted? Was it because he liked paper-making better than clearing land?

Partly that. But even more, it was the way they treated him. To Uncle Ted he was little more than a tool – and one that had to be bullied into being useful. For Mr Skinner he was part of a group of people working together, a person who'd shown himself reliable and was being asked to do his best.

Well, he would.

*

On Sunday, Adam went to see his family. It had snowed fairly heavily during the night and turned colder. Here and there were sleigh tracks, but for the rest the snow was marked only by birds and animals, like the deer he saw vanishing among the tree-trunks. Except for an occasional cawing crow, the world was silent.

It was a long walk, down to the Kingston Road and then eastwards, away from the bridge. By the time he reached the Smith farm, having asked directions, Adam reckoned that he had been walking for a couple of hours.

The part of the Smith farm nearest the road had been cleared completely, so far as you could tell with the snow, but behind that was an area still full of stumps.

The present farmhouse was a substantial building containing several rooms. The shanty Mr Skinner had mentioned as lodging for the hired man and his family was off to one side. Out of the chimney came a curl of smoke, light-coloured against the dark woods behind. The shanty had a two-paned window – small, but better than nothing. The floor, as Adam discovered when he entered, was of earth, strewn now with fresh-smelling evergreen boughs against the worst of the chill and damp. The bed was a mere shelf against the wall. The only other furnishings were a few backless stools, a table, and the little wooden chest which had been the Wheelers' main piece of luggage.

It was a cramped and comfortless place. The only cheering things were the fire, and the smell of dinner cooking in the black pot hung over it.

'Oh, Adam, how good to see you!' Aunt Lenore said, hugging him.

'Hello, Aunt Lenore.'

Adam looked around for the others, but only Ruth was there, unpicking a pair of man's trousers so that the cloth could be used for making something else.

'Ted and Harry are out getting firewood,' Aunt Lenore said.

'In the bush? With all this snow?'

'The Smiths will let us have some dry wood but only enough to keep the wet wood burning. We have to supply the rest ourselves. There's plenty in the forest, of course, but now, with the snow, it's harder to find. We were lucky to arrive here yesterday and be able to gather these boughs for the floor while they were still dry.'

Aunt Lenore didn't look happy, but that was understandable. He wondered whether the good news of his apprenticeship would cheer her; he could hardly contain it but wanted to announce it, with a bit of ceremony, over dinner.

As though she also felt the need to brighten things up, she said, 'But at least I have my treasures out again. Come and look, Adam.'

There, on a shelf against the wall, were objects he had not seen since leaving England – a small crockery jug with a flower design on it, two vases, two small bowls, a pair of silver sugar tongs which was the only thing Aunt Lenore had from her mother. There too was the family Bible with its record of marriages, births, and deaths.

They, along with the iron cooking pot now hanging over the fire, and the barest supply of plates and cups, cutlery and linen, had been packed in the wooden chest.

When they were sitting on stools near the fire, Adam asked Aunt Lenore how she liked the Smiths.

'I've hardly seen *him*, but she seems kind. She gave us food for our first few days ....' She gestured at the pot hanging over the fire. 'And those trousers that Ruth is unpicking are her husband's, which she gave me to make over for Harry. Unfortunately her husband is shorter than Ted, so none of the clothes will fit him. Not that Ted likes wearing other people's old clothes, of course.'

Soon Uncle Ted and Harry appeared outside the window, dragging branches across the snow and roughly piling them near the shanty, to be broken or cut into fireplace lengths later. When they came in, their boots and clothes were snowy and the cold bulk of them chilled the small dwelling and filled it almost to suffocation.

Of course they were both grumpy about the weather, the hard work, the demands made by Mr Smith.

During dinner, Adam told them his news. Uncle Ted said, 'Well, I guess that means that I can't count on you *at all* for helping to clear my land.'

'Adam's getting ahead in his own way, Ted,' Aunt Lenore said. 'We should be happy for him. *I* am.' She smiled at Adam.

Harry spoke up. 'Do you really *want* to clear land, dad? That work we did for Smith yesterday ....' He made a disgusted face.

Adam, watching Uncle Ted, saw something shift behind his eyes. It was gone in an instant. 'To be landowners, we gotta buy land and clear it.'

Adam and his aunt both looked at him. This was a change from the old assertion that Uncle Ted was definitely going to buy and clear land.

'There's other things to do in this country, other ways to live,' Aunt Lenore said thoughtfully. 'Other *good* ways to live.'

'Mother, can I have a kitten?' Ruth demanded. 'Mrs Smith says I can have one of hers if you say it's okay.'

'We'll see. Ask me again later.'

The talk about the family's future was finished for the moment, but Adam was sure the subject would be raised again.

*

Adam's route home along the Kingston Road took him past a side road which his informant that morning had said led to the Forks of the Don. On impulse, he turned into it. He could reach Todmorden from there, and it was probably not much farther.

He didn't know whether it was proper to arrive uninvited at the de Grassi house, but he had not seen any of the family since his encounter with Charlotte on Wednesday evening, when she was shot at, and had never found out why, on Thursday, one of the girls – it was almost certainly one of them – had been returning alone from town.

Besides, he wanted to remain friends with them. Most of their meetings so far had been accidental, caused by the unusual events of this past week. He hoped that, when things settled down, he'd still see them sometimes.

A sleigh in front of the house, its horse blanketed against the cold, suggested the presence of visitors, so Adam went to the back. The servant answered his knock. Past her, he could see Charlotte sitting in a rocking chair by the stove, her right wrist bandaged. Cornelia stood at the table, arranging cookies and cake on a platter.

'Oh, Adam,' she said, 'how good to see you! Go and sit with Charlotte. I'll just take these in and then come and talk.'

He swept the snow from his boots, took off his coat and cap, and went to sit on the settle near Charlotte, glad of the fire and the smells of baking and cooking, appreciating the comfort here after the wretchedness of the shanty where his relatives were living.

'Hello,' he said.

'Hello. Didn't I see black bands on your cap and coat? Why are you wearing mourning?'

'A cousin of mine died.'

'Oh, I'm sorry.'

He shrugged. It was nice of her to ask, but he'd rather talk about other things. 'How did you hurt your arm?'

'Remember Wednesday evening in Todmorden? You warned me about a rebel band being in the woods near there. They shot me.'

'They actually *hit* you? I heard the firing – I ran to see, but you were riding away and I didn't think you were hurt.' He looked at her bandaged wrist. Bullets and soft flesh, he thought again, his own body cringing at the thought.

'Several shot at me from the side, but one came round and fired in my face. Well, not right in my face, I guess, but that's what it seemed like.'

'I thought of coming after you, but with you galloping away there was no sense.'

While he was talking, Cornelia came back and sat down beside him on the settle. 'So you saw it all!'

'I didn't know Charlotte was hurt. Is it bad?'

'No, only a graze,' Charlotte said. 'Mother kept me home on Thursday. I could perfectly well have gone with Cornelia.'

Adam looked at Cornelia. 'I suppose that it was you that Mr Helliwell saw at the bridge on Thursday evening, trying to get across?'

'Yes, and I saw him too. The militia barred us from passing. I rode back into the city and left my pony with friends of ours and walked home. By then there was someone on duty at the bridge who knew me and let me through.'

'She saw the battle,' Charlotte said.

Adam was about to say 'So did I,' but caught himself in time. If he mentioned it, he would have to explain that he had seen it from the rebels' side, and even with the governor's pardon it might not be safe to link himself with them.

As for Cornelia's being there ... well, nothing these girls did would surprise him any more.

She explained. 'When I was in town that morning, I saw Chief Justice Robinson. He asked me to ride up Yonge Street behind the army and then come back and tell him what happened. So I did that.'

The maidservant, busying herself about the kitchen, was standing where Adam could see her. She shook her head in severe but resigned disapproval of such goings-on.

Adam thought it better not to comment. Instead, he asked, 'What does your father think will happen now?'

'He says there's no knowing. Many men have been arrested, in spite of the governor's proclamation that everyone but the leaders and the worst trouble-makers would be pardoned if they returned to their duty. But Mackenzie hasn't been found so there could be further unrest.'

'Is there any word about the numbers of dead and wounded?'

Charlotte answered. 'Father's been collecting reports. Five men are known to be dead, and several in the hospital. But of course there must be some injured men being nursed at home by their families.'

'And then there are those who've gone to the States,' Adam added. 'One of Mr Helliwell's men sent word that he wouldn't be back. He's left a wife, who's pregnant, and five children. And debts.'

He nearly told them that Sam's departure had led to his own promotion – but again he stopped himself. No need to draw attention to his being only a working man. It might be a big step for him, but it still wouldn't bring him anywhere close to them. They were treating him as a friend now; better leave well enough alone.

They drank tea and ate cookies like the ones Cornelia had taken to the parlour. Then, as the afternoon was darkening, Adam took his leave and went out again into the snowy December Sunday.

Thinking things over as he walked along, he realized that a new phase of his life was beginning. He too, like his fellow workers in the mill, was not the same person that he'd been on Tuesday. He had taken part in important events – events which had stirred up people's normal lives. Just as Mr Morris had slept rough and gone unshaven, so Adam had become friends with the de Grassi girls – something which would probably not have happened otherwise – and become better acquainted with the Skinners. He had quarrelled with Uncle Ted but made some sort of peace with him, and he had formed stronger links with Aunt Lenore.

He had a better sense of who he was. He liked his work and the people around him. He had a place among them, a young man who earned his own living and had a future. Being an apprentice was just a start – no knowing where he'd be in ten years.

Not too bad, he thought, tramping home, for someone who, only a few months ago, had been nothing more than a parcel.

THE END

The de Grassi Family: Detailed Note

The involvement of Charlotte and Cornelia de Grassi in the events of December 1837 was known to their contemporaries but forgotten later. Only now are historians rediscovering it.

Captain Philip de Grassi and his family came to Upper Canada in 1831; before that, he had had a military career in Europe and the West Indies, and had spent sixteen years teaching languages in Chichester, England. Upon arriving in Canada, the family took up land and built a house at the Forks of the Don River, near Toronto (then still called York).

Captain de Grassi, in his own 'Narrative' – an unpublished autobiographical sketch – says that he and his wife brought seven children with them to Canada, but no names or ages are given. A son is mentioned in connection with the building of their house during the winter of 1831-32, and at least one more child was born in Canada. I have been unable to find much information about the other children; Charles Sauriol, in *Pioneers of the Don*, mentions several but does not give their precise ages, and I was therefore unable to reconstruct the whole family as it was in the autumn of 1837. Charlotte and Cornelia were apparently the only ones, other than Captain de Grassi himself, who took part in the events of the Rebellion of 1837, and are therefore the only children I mention.

There are only a few sources for the story. So far as I have been able to discover, there are three contemporary ones: the unpublished 'Narrative' of Captain de Grassi himself (mentioned above); an article published on 6 October 1838 – less than a year after the Rebellion – in the *New York Albion* and reprinted in a paper entitled 'The Story of Charlotte and Cornelia de Grassi' presented by W. Stewart Wallace to the Royal Society of Canada in 1941; and a pamphlet published by William Lyon Mackenzie in 1853 entitled *Head's Flag of Truce*.

In modern times, the story has been researched and told by Charles Sauriol, W. Stewart Wallace (in the paper referred to above), and Ann Guthrie. Cornelia de Grassi's expedition to Montgomery's Tavern is mentioned by Colin Read and Ronald J. Stagg in their Champlain Society book, *The Rebellion of 1837 in Upper Canada*, published in 1985, and by Carl Benn in *Historic Fort York*, published in 1993.

In order to make Captain de Grassi and his daughters into real characters, I fleshed out the bare historical scenes and facts with several scenes which, though imaginary, are based on the historical material, both that which directly concerns these characters and that which describes conditions, events, and the life of that time. The historical scenes are the following:

• The journey of Captain de Grassi and his daughters to Toronto on the night of Monday, 4 December 1837, and Charlotte's encounter with the group of rebels.
• The spying expedition by one of the de Grassi girls (the sources do not say which one it was) to Gallows Hill on Tuesday, 5 December.
• Cornelia's spying expedition to Montgomery's Tavern on Wednesday, 6 December, and her ride back to Toronto, during which she was shot at and nearly injured.
• Charlotte's being sent with a message to the picket on the Kingston Road on Wednesday, 6 December.
• Charlotte's being shot at and wounded on her way home alone that evening.
• Cornelia's riding up Yonge Street with the militia on Thursday, 7 December, commissioned by the chief justice (who was John Beverley Robinson, though the *Albion* article does not name him) to collect intelligence for him.

[276]

- Cornelia's being prevented (on Thursday evening, 7 December) from returning home mounted because of the bridge being blocked, and finally reaching home on foot.

These incidents are fictional:

- Adam's encounter with Captain de Grassi and his daughters near the bridge (in chapter 7).
- Adam's encounter with Cornelia and her father on the path near the river (in chapter 8).
- Adam's visits to the de Grassi house (in chapters 9, 12, and 21).
- Adam's encounter with the de Grassi girls at the post office (in chapter 10) and their ride home.
- Adam's encounter with the girls near the City Hall (in chapter 14). The meeting is invented, but the *Albion* article says that the girls were in town on that day.
- Adam's encounter with Cornelia at Montgomery's Tavern and his accompanying her back to Toronto (in chapter 16). Her presence there is well documented, but Adam's is invented.

As is often the case with historical records, different accounts of the same incident can disagree, and any of the accounts may contain mistakes. Here are the major omissions, errors, and discrepancies, and what I have done about them.

1 The contemporary sources do not say explicitly which of the girls was the elder, but they gave the information needed to work it out. Captain de Grassi says that it was 'one of [his] daughters about 13 years of age' who went to Montgomery's Tavern, and the *Albion* article identifies her as Cornelia. The *Albion* article also refers to 'his [Captain de Grassi's] daughters, the elder of whom had not completed her fifteenth year', which means that she was fourteen. In December of 1837, therefore, Cornelia was thirteen and Charlotte fourteen.

2 The *Albion* article states that there was moonlight on Monday night, 4 December 1837, both when Captain de Grassi and his daughters set off for Toronto and during part of the girls' journey home. In fact, according to almanacs of the time, and information I obtained from the McLaughlin Planetarium, on that night the moon set at about 11:00 p.m., which (according to the *Albion* article) was the time when Captain de Grassi and his daughters left home for Toronto. There was, therefore, no moonlight during their journey or during the girls' return home.

3 Both the *Albion* article and Captain de Grassi's 'Narrative' mention the incident, which took place during the journey to Toronto, in which Charlotte distracted the Matthews troop so that her father and sister could pass unobserved, but neither source gives much detail. I have reconstructed it in a way that seems reasonable and probable.

4 The *Albion* article and Captain de Grassi's 'Narrative' differ about what the girls did later that night. Their father writes that he sent them home before he reached Toronto. The article says that all three of them went to Toronto, and the chronology makes that the more likely alternative. According to the *Albion* article, it took them about two hours (11:00 p.m. to 1:00 a.m.) to ride to Toronto, and the girls did not reach home again until 4:00 a.m. If Captain de Grassi sent his daughters back before they all reached the city, why did it take the girls so much longer to reach home than it had taken to travel in the other direction?

5 Modern historians such as Carl Benn, Colin Read, and Ronald Stagg refer to Cornelia de Grassi's spying expedition to Montgomery's Tavern on Wednesday, 6 December 1837. Stewart Wallace and Charles Sauriol, in supporting the authenticity of this incident, cite William Lyon Mackenzie's

booklet, *Head's Flag of Truce*, as evidence. In it, Mackenzie himself writes: 'Dr Horne had employed a woman as spy [De Grassi, I *think* he called her] whom we let pass'.

But Mackenzie was referring unmistakably to an incident which occurred on Tuesday, 5 December, in the interval between the two 'flag of truce' missions sent out by the lieutenant governor, and which took place at Gallows Hill, some distance south of Montgomery's Tavern. Therefore we have Mackenzie's own evidence for the fact that one of the girls (he does not give her first name but does say that Dr Horne sent her) came to spy on his forces on Tuesday, when he and his men were at Gallows Hill.

The *Albion* article, however, speaks of Cornelia making a spying expedition on the following day, Wednesday, to Montgomery's Tavern. Captain de Grassi says that one of his daughters (the one who was thirteen years old) went to Montgomery's Tavern but does not give the day. He does say, however, that while she was there Mackenzie returned to the camp with the captured western mail coach, and we know from other sources that that incident occurred on Wednesday.

There were, therefore, two spying expeditions.

Mackenzie does not say which of the de Grassi girls went to the rebel camp at Gallows Hill on Tuesday, nor does Captain de Grassi indicate which of his daughters rode to Montgomery's Tavern, nor on which day this was. The *Albion* article says that it was Cornelia who made the expedition on Wednesday. I have conjectured that it was also Cornelia who went to Gallows Hill on Tuesday – that it was, in fact, her safe completion of the Tuesday expedition (when, as Mackenzie himself says, the rebels noticed her but permitted her to pass) that led her to undertake the second spying venture on Wednesday. Her Tuesday expedition apparently took the rebels by surprise (which is why they let her pass) but on Wednesday they were not fooled again and, according to the

Albion article and her father's account, held her for nearly an hour until she escaped. Perhaps it was Dr Horne's sending her out on Tuesday that put the possibility of spying into her mind and led to her venturing out again on Wednesday.

Both expeditions are, therefore, historical. It is conjecture on my part that it was Cornelia who undertook the Tuesday expedition mentioned by Mackenzie, because she was also the one to ride to Montgomery's Tavern on Wednesday.

Mackenzie's few words in *Head's Flag of Truce*, and information from other historical sources about the events of those few hours on Tuesday, make it clear that Sir Francis Bond Head *did* receive and make use of information about the strength of the rebel force gathered at Gallows Hill. On Tuesday morning, in a state of panic because rumour reported that the rebel force numbered in the thousands, Head sent Dr John Rolph and Robert Baldwin to the rebels with a flag of truce and an offer to negotiate. Mackenzie sent the envoys back to the city demanding that the terms be put in writing. By the time Rolph and Baldwin returned to government headquarters, Head had received more accurate information about the size of the rebel force and was confident that his militia could defeat it. Therefore he sent Rolph and Baldwin back to Gallows Hill to say that after all no truce would be offered. It was on this second occasion that Mackenzie, according to his own account, was taken aside by Dr Rolph and told that it was the de Grassi woman's information that had led Governor Head to change his mind.

6 There is disagreement among the sources as to whose idea it was that Cornelia go to Montgomery's Tavern on the Wednesday to spy out the strength of the rebel force.

Captain de Grassi, in his 'Narrative', writes: 'I sent [said] that I would endeavour to ascertain the number of rebels on Yonge Street. One of my daughters about 13 years of age, accordingly who was a capital rider rode out under pretence of wishing to know the price of a sleigh ....'

The *Albion* article, on the other hand, says that Cornelia had ridden up to 'the advance post, at the turnpike in Yonge Street' – which was almost certainly the tollgate at Yorkville – in search of her father. Not finding him there (he was on duty at the Parliament Buildings) and 'perceiving the general horror on every countenance, in consequence of the report that the rebels were 5000 strong, she resolved to proceed alone to Montgomery's Tavern, their headquarters, and ascertain the truth or falsity of the rumour.'

7 The *Albion* article is the only contemporary source that deals with Cornelia's return home on Thursday evening and the difficulties she encountered because the bridge over the Don River had been set on fire by the Matthews troop. It reports that she returned to Toronto and gave the alarm.

The bridge was indeed set on fire but, according to other sources, the reporting of it to the authorities did not depend on Cornelia. Government troops had been stationed at the bridge before the rebel attack, and there was a sharp skirmish between them and the Matthews men. The fire was put out before much damage was done, though several nearby buildings were burned down. However, a guard of government militia was left at the bridge that evening, after the skirmish and the fire. It prevented William Helliwell from crossing (as he reports in his diary) and, according to the *Albion* article, barred Cornelia de Grassi as well. The article says that she returned to town, left her pony with friends, and walked home. The article does not indicate how, on that second occasion, she did manage to cross the bridge; I have conjectured that, though stopped on the first attempt, she was later allowed to pass because one of the guards recognized her.

When I came across the first bits of the story of the de Grassi girls' involvement in the 1837 rebellion, I realized that this piece of Canadian history ought to be more widely known than it is. It was to achieve this aim – as well as others – that I gave my book the shape which it now has, and to describe in detail, in these notes, the sources of the de Grassi girls' story and explain the ways in which I used the material.

Other Notes

The de Grassi family are not the only historical characters in
this book. Besides people well known to history, such as Sir
Francis Bond Head and William Lyon Mackenzie, there are
the Helliwell, Eastwood, and Skinner families. Here, too, I
have had to invent scenes and characteristics in addition to
those which appear in the historical record, but all of them
are based on known facts about these families, the settlement
at Todmorden and the Don Mills, and the life and circumstances of the time.

I have done my best, with the help of the staff of Todmorden Mills Heritage Museum and Arts Centre, to reconstruct
what the village of Todmorden and the settlement below it,
on the flats beside the Don River, looked like in 1837. Some of
this is, again, guesswork but any such guesses are based on
what is known to have been the case. Initially it was guesswork that led me to assume that there was an alehouse in Todmorden at that time; later, I came across a reference in the
Don Valley Conservation Report to the existence of such an
alehouse in the 1830s. The name 'Todmorden' does not
appear in the records until a few years later, but such records
usually incorporate names which have already been in common use for some time. It is not certain which house was
occupied by the Skinner family in 1837; according to the
present occupants of the former Skinner property, it was the
brick house along the road leading from Todmorden village
down to the mills by the river. It is not known whether the
Skinners offered accommodation to any of the paper-mill
workers, but the Helliwells did lodge some of their employees
in their attic.

I have also had to make some conjectures about the process

by which paper was made in the York Paper Mill. It is known that the mill had progressed from hand-made to machine-made paper in the early 1830s, but no information is available on which of several different technologies was used. I researched all this extensively and, in the book, described what seemed to me – and to Gerard Brender à Brandis, illustrator of this book and an amateur paper-maker – to be the most probable.

About the Author

Marianne Brandis is the author of the much-loved 'Emma' trilogy – *The Tinderbox*, *The Quarter-Pie Window* and *The Sign of the Scales*, each of which won a 'Choice' selection from the Canadian Children's Book Centre. Her most recent young-adult historical novel, *Fire Ship*, won a commendation from the Toronto Historical Board in 1993.

Marianne Brandis has also written a two-volume fictional biography, *Elizabeth, Duchess of Somerset*, as well as a short novel, *Special Nests*.